CROSS KILLER

L. E. WILLETTS

Matador
9 Priory Business Park,
Wistow Road, Kibworth Beauchamp,
Leicestershire. LE8 0RX
Tel: 0116 279 2299
Email: books@troubador.co.uk
Web: www.troubador.co.uk/matador
Twitter: @matadorbooks

ISBN 978 1785891 748

British Library Cataloguing in Publication Data.
A catalogue record for this book is available from the British Library.

Printed and bound by CPI Group (UK) Ltd, Croydon, CR0 4YY
Typeset in 11pt Aldine401 BT by Troubador Publishing Ltd, Leicester, UK

Matador is an imprint of Troubador Publishing Ltd

MIX
Paper from
responsible sources
FSC
www.fsc.org
FSC® C013604

For Mum and Dad

Mum: I'm really glad that you think I deserve an OBE for this book
Dad: I'm really glad that you enjoyed the bit about the dog

CLIFFBOROUGH CROSS
A NEW YEAR: A FRESH START

In due time their feet will slip.
Their day of disaster will arrive
and their destiny will overtake them.

(Deuteronomy 32:35)

PROLOGUE

H ad EJ Mahoney's killer stopped to ask her what she wanted for Christmas, her request almost certainly wouldn't have included being strangled with the elastic of her own knickers. Nor would she have chosen to be laid out like Mother Teresa in the layby that adjoined the A38 where, under normal circumstances, police would loiter discreetly to catch drunken drivers during the festive period. Had the men in white suits not been so preoccupied on the morning in question with camouflaging her remains from prying eyes and securing and protecting the scene from contamination, they might have noticed the otherwise nondescript Volvo, which had passed by the scene of the crime in both directions an unnecessary amount of times during the course of the past couple of hours.

Despite the lack of care taken to disguise her corpse, thanks to the treacherous weather conditions the previous evening it hadn't taken long for the freezing rain to render the road impassable to vehicles and so it was almost twelve bitterly cold hours before a dog walker had discovered it – or to be more precise, before the dog had discovered it. Not that it mattered personally to EJ, since her mind had switched off and her body closed down hours before she had even been brought here and dumped by the side of the road. Nor was it of any consequence to her now that the thin smattering of frost that covered her and the arctic temperatures of the previous evening had probably helped to preserve her body and slow down any natural decomposition that may have otherwise occurred.

Had things been different, EJ could have saved the police and the pathologist a lot of unnecessary time and trouble. For not only did she know how she had died, but also the identity of her killer and why they had taken it upon themselves to bring her short life to an even shorter conclusion. But as she now lay on a slab on the mortuary table, with no signs of a struggle and no obvious cause of death since strangulation had almost certainly taken place post mortem, it was looking like they were going to have to figure that one out for themselves.

1

It had started with the same old argument they'd been having for years: Malcolm asked for sex and Eileen told him to get stuffed. But then the fireworks signalling the beginning of the New Year had started and an equally explosive argument that Malcolm was never going to win had followed about whether the dog should or shouldn't be allowed to sleep on the bed with them.

'Have you any idea what it's like for him?' Eileen scowled defiantly at her husband, as though daring him to challenge the matter further. He didn't.

'It's torture, that's what it is,' she continued. 'Buddy can literally hear a pin drop, can't you, Buddy?'

Malcolm stared at them both huddled up under the duvet together. Eileen glaring at him menacingly and Buddy giving him the benefit of those big brown eyes of his as though butter wouldn't melt.

'Can't warn us not to stand on it though, can he? I don't know why you don't just marry the dog and be done with it.' Malcolm knew it was a childish jibe, but when push came to shove, he couldn't seem to help himself.

The quarrel had gone on for quite some time until they had both worn themselves out and they now lay in bed, side by side in relative silence. Malcolm with his back to Eileen, her favourite position by all accounts, as he wrestled for his fair share of the duvet that the dog had firmly wedged in the wrong place, and Eileen on her back, fists clenched into tiny little balls of rage as she stared at an invisible mark on the ceiling. And Buddy, their canine contraceptive, sprawled between them, paws forcefully shoving at Malcolm's back as though his mere presence in the bed were a complete inconvenience.

Malcolm stared into the darkness for what felt like hours, the only sound, Buddy's snoring, which seemed to get louder and more exaggerated with every breath that he took. Well aware that it was only a matter of time before the dog would wake Eileen, he gently nudged him, but blissfully unaware of the problems he was creating, Buddy didn't even stir. And then the sharp point of Eileen's elbow connected with Malcolm's ribs and he winced.

'Ow!' He sat up and glared at her in the darkness.

'Snoring,' she mumbled tersely.

'It's not me, it's Buddy.' Malcolm knew he was wasting his breath, but all the same, why should he be expected to just lie there and take the blame for something he hadn't even done?

'It's you alright, now sssh!' So typical of his wife – always had to have the last word did Eileen, couldn't just leave it.

'You can't snore when you're awake,' he snapped back in retaliation.

'Well, do us all a favour and stop breathing then.' *Oh yes,* he thought to himself, *she'd just love that, wouldn't she?* Whatever he did was wrong and it was pointless trying to convince her otherwise, and so careful not to disturb the dog or else he'd never hear the end of it, Malcolm turned on to his side once more and at some point, he finally fell asleep.

★★★

The Chase was on ITV, only this time Malcolm knew one of the contestants. Staring back at him was a younger version of himself and he was instantly struck by how relaxed, how at ease with himself and his surroundings he was – so much so, he barely recognised the vision of his former self eyeballing him from within the screen. It was a stark reminder that once, many years ago, he had been happy. He was the only remaining contestant in the final round of what was surely the most nerve-wracking version of the quiz show to ever be aired and with less than thirty seconds left on the clock, the live audience watched on with baited breath. The excitement was real, the air thick with the scent of it. As the Chaser lunged forward and threatened to catch him literally seconds before the clock struck zero, Malcolm had no idea whether he had been caught or walked with the money as Eileen's angry face suddenly filled the screen and glared back at him from inside the otherwise empty box.

He leaned closer towards the TV to get a better look at his wife who was now smiling, and appeared to be sharing a little joke with someone he couldn't yet see. Dressed in a low-cut blouse, tight short skirt and killer heels, she looked every inch as elegant as she did sophisticated – barely recognisable from the uptight cow that glowered back at him over the breakfast table of a morning.

Eileen was sitting on a couch opposite an interviewer he didn't recognise and his anger and resentment about her recent neglect soon evaporated. It was hard to remain angry at something so beautiful and as the opening credits rolled, he watched, mesmerised as the camera moved slowly to the other end of the couch… where Buddy came into view.

You have to be kidding me? Malcolm shook his head in disbelief as he stared at the dog who, dressed in a tuxedo with hat and bow-tie, was sitting upright on the sofa staring out of the set to the world with that supercilious grin of his that only one dog owner to another could possibly understand. Malcolm hadn't smoked a cigarette for almost ten years now, an achievement he was immensely proud of since not a day would pass without him craving the instant hit that only nicotine (and probably more hard-core drugs that he'd never dared try) could give. But right then, in that bizarre dream which felt more real than anything he'd felt in years, he reached for a cigarette, lit it and took several deep drags in rapid succession. He instantly felt dizzy and light headed. There was a nagging voice in the back of his head, one that was warning him that Eileen would go ballistic if she caught him smoking indoors, but he couldn't have cared less if he tried. Eileen wasn't there to complain, was she? Eileen was far too busy by all accounts taking part in some freaky daytime television interview with the dog. He leaned back in his chair and took the weight off his feet by resting them on the coffee table in front of him – another pet peeve of Eileen's, but if he was honest with himself, he was secretly starting to enjoy rebelling against all of these rules and regulations that she seemed to have secretly snuck into his life over the years.

'Good morning and welcome to *Hellarity*,' the interviewer (who appeared to have turned into Lady Gaga) announced. 'Today, we'll be talking about relationships and our first guest is Eileen and her dog Buddy, whom she describes as the love of her life… Eileen, hi. You and Buddy have been companions now for…?'

'Five years.' Malcolm reached across the table for the remote, careful not to take his eyes from the screen for a single second in case he missed something, and increased the volume to max.

'But you're married though aren't you, Eileen? Just so our viewers can get to know you a little better.'

'I was married yes, but I'm afraid he had to go.'

'Go?'

'Well, yes. Three was becoming a bit of a crowd you see and he made me choose. Naturally, I chose Buddy.' Malcolm watched, transfixed as his wife leaned forward and took a hold of one of the dog's paws and gently squeezed it as though it were a human hand. He couldn't believe his eyes – or ears.

Was married? 'WE STILL ARE, YOU STUPID COW,' he yelled at the screen, even though he knew she wouldn't be able to hear him. Had she completely taken leave of her senses? But then he remembered the ultimatum – except that it was so stupid, just a silly little squabble really that had resulted in both of them saying things they hadn't really meant. He couldn't even remember verbatim what he'd said. *'It's me or the dog.'* Something like that, wasn't it? But really? She'd actually picked the dog over him? She couldn't be serious! She wouldn't. She couldn't. Could she?

It was the interviewer's turn to speak. 'Fifty percent of married women with dogs claim that they get more emotional support from their pets than they do their husbands. Is this a sentiment that you would agree with, Eileen?'

'Oh good God, yes,' she gushed. 'There's absolutely no doubt in my mind. When was the last time your husband jumped off the sofa in excitement to greet you when you came in from the shops?'

The interviewer smiled knowingly, but said nothing and Malcolm found himself fighting the urge to punch the screen. *You've gone and done it now,* he thought. *Give her an inch and she's sure to take the proverbial mile.* As much as he wanted her to shut her face and stop being so ridiculous, he also couldn't wait to hear what was going to come out of her mouth next. Finally he was getting to the truth. Finally he was discovering how she really felt about him and even though it hurt, it was also extremely enlightening. It didn't take long, the interviewer's silence seemingly all the encouragement she needed to proceed.

'I rest my case. You see,' she gently caressed Buddy's chest as she spoke, 'dogs are always happy to see you... men, not so much. Dogs don't get embarrassed or offended by you regardless of what you say or do. Do you know, I once gained two stone in as many weeks, but you didn't mind did you, Buddy?' Malcolm shook his head in complete disbelief. *Disloyal little git,* he thought as Buddy sprawled back on the couch and spread his legs for his belly to be rubbed, thumping his tail aggressively as inch by inch, she stroked each and every one of his erogenous zones.

'Okay, Eileen, just so the audience understands. Presumably there are pitfalls? I mean it's not like Buddy can clean up after himself, can he? And talk about facial hair!' The interviewer turned to Buddy then. 'No offence, Buddy.'

For one second, despite the fact that the interviewer now appeared to have turned into Maggie Thatcher, Malcolm found himself warming to her. But then she had to open her big mouth and go and spoil everything and it occurred to him that she had set the whole situation up deliberately. *Man-hater. Probably a lesbian.*

'The thought of all those hairs in the bathtub sends shivers down my spine. And he must surely have appalling table manners?'

Eileen tittered. 'Of course… I forget you've not met my ex-husband.'

'Would you quit with all this ex shit, Eileen? Enough is enough!' Malcolm snapped, glaring furiously at the screen. And where was his invite to the show, his opportunity to tell his side of the story? It was all so typical of her, not even giving him the chance to defend himself.

Eileen leaned in to the camera then as though she was going to confide a deep, dark secret. 'I'll tell you something else. Malcolm has a tendency to sulk. Holds grudges for weeks sometimes. But you don't have to tolerate that kind of nonsense with a dog. Buddy's always available to listen to my problems, aren't you, Buddy?' She was talking in that babyish voice again that he'd had to warn her about previously – the one that went straight through him like nails on a blackboard and reminded him that his appointment with the dentist for his annual scrape and polish was overdue.

Malcolm was almost glad when the interviewer brought it to a close. Almost, but not quite. There was a small part of him, this tiny, weird, sick, depraved piece of him, that wanted it to go on forever – wanted yet further insight into his marriage and the wife that he clearly didn't know or understand at all.

'And that's just about all we have time for today, Ladies and Gentlemen,' she announced. 'Let us put our hands together and give a round of applause to Eileen and Buddy. Eileen… you may now kiss the dog.'

And she bloody well did. Disgusted, Malcolm watched in disbelief as Eileen leant forward towards Buddy, puckering her lips and gazing adoringly into his soulful brown eyes as he set to business with his tongue. This was exactly the kind of behaviour he had been on about and a little bit of sick erupted unexpectedly in his mouth. She wouldn't kiss him, but she'd happily slobber over the dog all day long.

What kind of a programme was this anyway? They were barking, bloody mad – all of them. Even the producers for agreeing to air such preposterous codswallop in the first place! Malcolm had seen more than enough and reached for the remote, just as the interviewer signed off and suggested to the viewers that if they could perhaps try to love their husbands or wives as much as the dog did, that they in turn might love them like they loved their dogs.

Of course there was one fundamental problem with this. Eileen wasn't like normal people. Eileen clearly really was more in love with the dog than she could ever be with him and the idea that she might one day be remotely pleased to see him was laughable. Or was it?

The dream shifted then. Buddy and Eileen were still the

focus of the screen, but they now appeared to be locked in the garage. Malcolm had no idea how they came to be there, but Buddy looked bored as he lay on the cold, hard floor, seemingly resigned to his fate, whilst Eileen screamed blue murder and chucked her weight back and forth against the heavy metal doors.

What to do? His wife really was most unpleasant when she was angry and so leaving her in the garage seemed like a good alternative. But presumably he would have to let her out eventually? And surely, the longer she was left there, the angrier she was likely to become until she was quite possibly beyond redemption?

But what if, on the other hand, he were to heroically rush to her aid and rescue her from her unfortunate predicament? How could she possibly justify being anything other than grateful if he proved himself to be her knight in shining armour during her hour of need? Eileen would forever be in his debt and he trembled with excitement as the possibilities of how she could repay him played out in his head.

The wind whipped against his cheeks and stung at his skin as he stepped out into the bitterly cold night and Malcolm pulled his jumper up over his mouth and as much of his face as possible. Still he choked as the ice-cold air swelled uncomfortably in his chest, burning his lungs and making it almost impossible to breathe. Standing still a moment, he tried to catch his breath, but Eileen's desperate cries for help spurred him on. As he released the shutters, the roller doors clattered loudly and reverberated around the otherwise silent street, and he glanced up at the surrounding windows, terrified he might have disturbed the neighbours. Eileen would kill him if he had.

No sooner were the doors released, she was on top of him, thrusting her full weight directly at him, and he staggered backwards, taking several steps before he was able to correct his balance. Arms firmly clasped around his neck, she clung on to him with all her might and even though he knew it wasn't really appropriate, Malcolm started to feel quite excited at the prospect of her breasts pressed up so tightly against him and he squeezed her back firmly, determined to savour the moment. But then the tightness in his chest returned and he moaned softly.

'Eileen… honey, you need to let me go.' The last thing he wanted to do was push her away. Not now when he finally had her where he wanted her, but what choice did he have? He couldn't breathe and was trying his hardest not to panic.

Maybe if he could get her to release her grip a bit? Persuade her to hug him slightly less vigorously? Perhaps then he would be able to catch a few deep breaths and everything would be okay? Malcolm pushed at his wife with the palms of his hands, gently at first and then a little firmer, until in desperation, he shoved as hard as he could with every last bit of strength he could muster, but still, she refused to release her grasp on him.

Malcolm didn't want to die. Not now. Not when Eileen finally seemed ready to behave like a proper wife again.

At least allow me that, God. God? Are you there? Five years. No sex. Five… lonely… celibate… years. You wouldn't deny me this last pleasure would you? Please God, air. I… need… air. It didn't take long for him to give up asking God for help; he obviously wasn't listening at any rate.

At some point the dream merged with reality, although Malcolm had no idea what had woken him in the first place, or at what point he had even realised he was no longer asleep and that it had all just been a horrible, weird nightmare. Except that it hadn't just been a horrible, weird nightmare because…

He still couldn't breathe. *Help!* He gulped desperately for air, but still there was nothing – just an empty, breathless void. His chest felt heavy, so heavy. Like someone had laid a lump of tarmac on it, but then he realised it wasn't tarmac. It was

Eileen. His wife was straddled on top of him on the bed.

Stay with it, Malcolm. Eileen is sat astride you, finally behaving like a proper wife should. So why did it all feel so wrong? He tried to reach out, to get into the swing of it and enjoy the moment for what it was, but his arms were clamped viciously to his sides with her thighs and refused to co-operate as she pressed the pillow down firmly against his face.

Oh dear God. I'm going to die. My wife is trying to kill me and I'm going to die...

2

Tod awoke with a start, the racket coming from EJ's flat across the hall seeming to get louder with every second that passed. *What is she doing in there?* This time last week, he would have got up and had a look, made sure everything was okay, but not now. Not after the way she had spoken to him. She could rot in hell for all he cared.

Treating him like a child and talking to him like he was as bad as what she had managed to step on in the street and get caked across the bottom of her brand new D&Gs. It was the shoes that really riled him. She was happy to spend a small fortune on them even though she must have hundreds already, but lend a few quid to save him from eviction? Oh no. Apparently, he was too big a risk and couldn't be trusted to repay the debt.

Tod sat up and assessed the four walls of the scabby bedsit that surrounded him. The dated woodchip walls were thick with magnolia paint that had turned a dirty yellow from nicotine, and a large worn rug that disguised the shit-brown carpet littered with fag burns beneath it covered the majority of the floor. With no proper heating to speak of, a solitary electric fire fuelled by a coin-operated meter that he was certain the landlord had fiddled for his own benefit hung from the nearest wall, and at the far end of the room, a partitioned box served as his kitchen. The tiny worktop was camouflaged by unopened packets of food and a mini stove crusted in ancient food stains

– yet one of the many legacies his thoughtless predecessor had left him to inherit. With the exception of the grubby old stainless steel sink that currently contained EJ's shoes, there was little room for anything else in the ridiculously cramped space.

He shouldn't have lost his temper, he knew that now, but he'd panicked. EJ had been his last option and when she had so needlessly turned him down, not even seeming to care that he was about to face the New Year living out of a cardboard box, he'd just flipped. It happened sometimes, the burning hatred appearing out of nowhere and exploding from inside him before he had the time to stop it. He reached across the bed to the small makeshift box that doubled as a bedside table and picked up his mobile phone, awaking the screen and reading the last message he had sent her one more time.

YOU'RE DEAD TO ME BITCH.
BETTER WATCH YOUR BACK!

Tod's eyes moved inadvertently once more to the shoes in the sink. He wasn't sure what he had hoped to achieve by stealing them from the mat where she had discarded them last night. He had just wanted to spite her, like she seemed to want to spite him. He just wanted to talk, to make her see sense, but she'd refused to answer her door, instead just turning her music up a notch and pretending she couldn't even hear him knocking. *Stupid cow.* She was more like his mother than he'd given her credit for.

Tod leaned back into the pillows and closed his eyes again as though the mere action alone could permanently remove the vulgar sight that had become his life. His mother had warned him all those years ago that survival wouldn't be easy. *Didn't exactly beg me to stay either though did you, Mummy dearest?* To the contrary she had stood, still in her nightdress on the stone steps that rose from the gravelled drive and led to the front door, all smiles as, bingo wings flapping in the wind, she waved him off like a demented scarecrow for the final time. It had dawned on him then that he was, and always had been, nothing but a mere inconvenience in Gloria Black's otherwise *perfect* existence.

Sent away to boarding school at the age of five, everyone knew that this had nothing to do with providing Tod with a better education and everything to do with getting the kid from under her feet. What with her ladies' luncheons and afternoon tea parties, it was little wonder she had time for the shopping excursions and extra tennis tuition at the local club that she attended several days a week, let alone the disruption of a child hovering in the background and cramping her style.

But it was okay for her. Tod didn't suppose she'd ever get the opportunity, but would be willing to bet nonetheless that his mother could wade through a pool of crap and still come out the other end smelling of roses. Having spent his whole childhood flitting from relationship to relationship, sucking every last ounce like the greedy, gluttonous leech that she was from each and every man who had the misfortune to take them in, Gloria had finally stuck her claws into Roger Black. Roger, a retired millionaire banker, had made it clear from day one that Tod wasn't, and never would be, part of the package. *Once a banker, always a wanker,* he thought to himself bitterly.

Tod returned his attention to the shoes. Maybe he could sell them once he'd had the chance to clean them up? Must be worth a few bob. Not enough to cover all the rent arrears, granted, but a fair whack towards it surely? And then another thought occurred to him. What if he were to add to his collection from work? People were always forfeiting the lockers in preference of leaving their stuff lying around in the changing rooms as though money were no object. Nobody would suspect him.

The voices outside in the hallway grew louder and a stab of jealousy twisted his intestines as though a fist had reached inside him and squeezed with all its might. *Has she got visitors? Who?* This wasn't part of the deal. She belonged to him and one day, not so far from now, she was going to realise what had been staring her in the face all the time. One day, not so far from now, their friendship was going to progress to a new level.

He held his breath as he strained to hear, but he still couldn't make out what was being said. Pushing the duvet away from his body, he swung his legs over the side of the bed and levered himself up from the mattress with the tips of his fingers. Padding barefoot to the door, he pressed an ear up against the wood, but it was no use. *Bulletproof, never mind soundproof,* he thought to himself as he withdrew from the thick timber fire door and picked up his wash bag. Clicking the latch open as quietly as he could, he began his pretence of going down the hall to join the queue for the grotty, mould-ridden shower room that he shared with three other occupants so he could better see what was going on.

At first it didn't register that there was any kind of problem. EJ's door was propped wide open and he could just about make out two men in the distance, wrapped from head to toe in…*forensic gear?* As his eyes slowly digested the ribbon of tape secured from one end of the hallway to the other to create a barrier across her entrance, the sight was so surreal it seemed almost natural.

Tod couldn't be sure of anything right then. Only that his imminent eviction was going to be the least of his problems.

3

When Eileen awoke there was definitely something amiss, but groggy from a lack of sleep the previous night thanks to the outrageous racket that Malcolm had been making, it took a moment for her brain to engage in the present. As she lay in bed in relative silence, the only sound the hushed whisper of next door's willow tree as it whistled in the breeze, realisation dawned. There was no other sound, not so much as a single grunt from the pot-bellied pig that usually wallowed in his pit beside her. Despite needing no confirmation, she opened her eyes anyway and checked her husband's side of the bed. Empty.

Deep down, she knew she should probably be worried. Malcolm never rose before her, but the peace and quiet was too welcome to concern herself with his whereabouts now. Closing her eyes once more, she tried to relax and make the most of it. After all, it would only be a matter of time before he returned to the room and spoiled it – just like he seemed intent upon spoiling everything these days.

How had it all gone so wrong? When had the man who was every inch as charming and charismatic as he was handsome, who had stood next to her at the altar on their wedding day started to resemble a rather unpleasant, highly contagious skin condition? These days, disgusting things seemed to delight Malcolm, such as lifting his cheek to break wind at the dinner table, or picking his nose and wiping it underneath – or worse still, on her – all the while giggling like an overgrown schoolboy.

Behaving like a child had, of course, only been the start of it and his recent need to also be treated like one was frankly nothing short of alarming. At first, when Malcolm had suggested spicing up their sex life by dressing up and taking part in what he described as a little bit of role-play, images of her dressed as a prostitute, or a schoolgirl with pigtails in her hair, had come to mind. Not for one second had she imagined the disturbing truth. Malcolm hadn't wanted her to dress up at all. Malcolm didn't care two hoots what she wore as it turned out… just so long as he could dress up and behave like a baby. And as if that wasn't bad enough, the filthy little sod even wanted to soil his nappy so that she could change it. And for her to breastfeed him!

Her mind wandered back to the day that they had met as, weighed down with shopping, she had struggled to board the tube. Malcolm had swooped out of nowhere to carry her bags, the thought that he might run off with them not for one second crossing her mind. Full of small, yet tasteful gestures such as opening doors and standing back to let her enter a room first, Malcolm was what her mother had once described as a dying breed. The true definition of a gentleman if ever she saw one, she'd said.

The same certainly couldn't be said for him today and the change was so drastic it was as though he had stood back, taken a good hard look at himself and deliberately clicked the self-destruct button because he didn't like what he saw. Eileen wondered if her husband was having one of those mid-life crises you heard so much about, but every time she tried to discuss it with him, she was met with the same old brick wall of defunct emotion.

'It's all up here,' he'd say, tapping his temple with his forefinger when she questioned him.

Perhaps she was to blame? Eileen couldn't deny that over the years, a suffocating boredom had started to creep in and threaten to smother her soul. She missed her job. She missed having a purpose and a reason to get up in the morning. Of course, all those years ago the promise of the pitter and patter of tiny feet rushing through the house, and childish giggles and squeals ringing out from the garden, had been more than enough to convince her that she was doing the right thing. But as it turned out, Mother Nature had chosen to be most cruel. Mother Nature had denied her the right to children and decided to punish her because Malcolm would have been an unfit father.

She reached down to ruffle Buddy's fur – the closest thing either of them would ever get to a child – but to her alarm he wasn't there either and she leapt up and scanned the room for him. *He'll be with Malcolm.* Of course he would. She instantly calmed herself. Malcolm often took him for his morning walk and the fact that he would still be sulking about the pillow thing would explain his disappearance at such an ungodly hour.

Eileen sank back against the comfort of the pillows and allowed herself a smile as little snippets of last night's dream played out in her mind…

★★★

They were in a boat. That's right, they were in a boat, which was strange since neither of them had travelled by boat throughout their marriage. Neither of them could even swim, which was what had made this dream so exciting because in this particular dream, Eileen could actually swim (and Malcolm only had himself to blame for the fact that he couldn't). She had tried to persuade him to learn during the early years of their marriage, of course she had, even suggesting classes at the local pool, but

Malcolm had apparently known better and arrogantly assured her that there was no reason he could think of why he would need to learn.

'I've managed twenty-five years without, so I'm quite sure I can manage another twenty-five, thank you very much,' he'd declared smugly.

The boat was only small, like a rowing boat, except this one had an outboard motor attached to the rear – a dory, or at least that's what she thought it was called, not that it really mattered in the grand scheme of things. They were in a boat and the sea was rough, which made it rock uncontrollably as the waves crashed over the edge and soaked them both in ice-cold seawater.

Malcolm's words had echoed in her ears. *I've managed twenty-five years without... I'm sure I can manage another twenty-five. Twenty-five years without... another twenty-five.* And then it had hit her. Twenty-five years old when she had first suggested lessons, plus twenty-five years of purgatory thereafter, equalled fifty. Malcolm was fifty. The night he had gagged and tied up the local district councillor in the cellar until he agreed to approve the planning application for their new conservatory, Malcolm had turned fifty.

I'm sure I can manage another twenty-five... Eileen had barely been able to contain her excitement at the prospect of finding out. *Twenty-five years.* His words got louder and louder as they pulsated in her ears and reverberated around her brain. Even the rippling swell of the ocean seemed to find a new energy as the waves crashed relentlessly against the small boat and shoved it further out to sea, and she chuckled with pleasure at the memory of him struggling against the force of the waves that washed over him.

The feelings of guilt started to creep in then, but she reminded herself that none of it was real – just a little dream – and she tried to relax once more and indulge her imagination.

Was it really so wrong to fantasise about the demise of your husband? Eileen didn't think so. In fact, she felt confident that every woman alive must do so from time to time. To imagine getting rid of your husband once and for all was absolutely fine. Perfectly normal. Harmless fun. Just so long as she didn't make it a reality.

In the dream, the dark clouds had loomed overhead then and the energy and strength behind the south easterly winds had forced the waves to catapult the small boat across the water. The two bright orange life jackets aboard the boat reflected out of the corner of her eye and she had known instantly what she must do. Buddy was thankfully an extremely strong swimmer, but even the most powerful of swimmers would quickly tire in such conditions and so as quickly as possible, she had fitted the first jacket to the dog as best as she could, before shrugging herself into the other.

'The dog? You'd save the dog over me?' Malcolm's horrified voice, a mixture of fury and panic, had risen in tone with every word he spluttered as he clung to the side of the boat as though his life depended on it. Which of course it probably did and Eileen allowed herself a little snigger as she pictured the predicament he found himself in.

Another huge wave had crashed into him then and as Malcolm gagged and choked as he tried to speak, Eileen had waited a moment out of respect. He was as entitled as the next man to have his final words heard before he died. She could do that one last thing for him. Just so long as he didn't take too long.

'Come on, come on.' She had looked angrily at her watch. 'Spit it out, Malcolm, we haven't got all day.' But still, he didn't speak. Selfish to the bitter end, not for one minute taking the time to consider that his dawdling could mean the difference between life and death for her and Buddy.

It hadn't taken long for her to lose patience and slipping one arm between the dog's shoulders, she slid the other around his belly and jumped straight into the ocean without so much as a backward glance at her husband. Kicking frantically at the water below, she had finally broken the surface and treading water to stay above it, she'd gulped greedily at the delicious fresh air. The wind and rain had stopped, replaced with a hot sun burning down on the ocean and the sound of waves breaking softly on a beach in the distance.

As she and Buddy had swum towards the shore, seagulls screamed above their heads and the sea gently lapped rhythmically around them, but the scene behind them had been quite different. The freak waves continued to lash against the sides of the small boat and tossed it around effortlessly in the air like a discarded Styrofoam container caught in the wind. Malcolm's small cries for help could only just be heard above the roaring of the ocean until finally, the boat had capsized and floated out to sea.

Raising her upper body on her elbows, she had settled back against the warm sand to watch. Her eyesight wasn't what it was, but she had just been able to make him out, arms flailing in the air as his head bobbed up above the water level and then down again as the force of the current pulled him beneath the surface once more. As his body had been submerged again, she had known deep down that the next time it emerged it would be lifeless. As calm and still as the sun that beat down on the beach and the water that surrounded the rest of the ocean except him.

Eileen had held her breath in excited anticipation of what she felt sure was coming next…

But then she had jerked in bed. Instantly awake, she had never felt so cheated in all her life. She hadn't asked for much. Just five more minutes so she could witness her husband die. Silently fuming, she had tried to finish the dream in her subconscious, but Malcolm's mere presence and the fact that he was still alive, not to mention the atrocious din he was making, had all been far too distracting.

As he had let out another God Almighty grunt, she didn't know what had come over her. It was most out of character, but in that split second the only thing that had mattered was shutting him up once and for all. She hadn't meant him any harm, not really. After all, who would look after Buddy if she got herself banged up in jail? Not Malcolm that was for sure, since presumably, he would be dead.

Grabbing the pillow from beneath his head, she had pressed it down firmly, but gently against his face as though she was afraid to wake him. But rather than silence him, he had let out a further snuffle, louder this time, and so she had pressed down a little harder. And then a little harder again until suddenly, before she was even aware of what was happening, she had been sat astride him, pressing the pillow down on his face with every last ounce of strength that she could muster.

4

DI Lucas Elliott allowed his eyes to settle on the man sat in front of him, the only clues that he was remotely uncomfortable with the situation, the unmistakeable repetitive twitch of his eyelid and the way that his leg jigged awkwardly of its own volition under the table.

Malcolm Muldoon had been accused of all sorts over the years, but had never been formally arrested for anything. Over the past year alone, he had been accused of the attempted murder of a minor, attacking a practising Jew who he believed to be a suicide bomber on a return flight from JFK International Airport, and locking a local district councillor in the basement of his three-storey Victorian house until he agreed to approve the planning application for his new conservatory. The man either had an uncanny knack of being in the wrong place at the wrong time, or he was extremely clever at evading punishment for his crimes.

'You knew the victim, is that right?' Lucas studied Malcolm as he stared vacantly at the plate of untouched biscuits that sat on the table between them. Following his gaze, Lucas' nose inadvertently wrinkled in disgust at the thin layer of skin that had visibly formed on the top of Malcolm's mug of tea. Hardly surprising, he supposed, since even the strongest of stomachs would struggle with the events that Malcolm had been exposed to that very morning. Lucas could still recall the first time that he had seen a dead body as though it were yesterday, the vision of a pair of glazed eyes staring unseeingly back at you being something that travelled with you for life.

'Where's Buddy?' At least the man was finally talking, Lucas thought to himself.

'He's with Derek,' Lucas jabbed his thumb backwards over his shoulder as he continued. 'Taken him for a run in the scrubland behind the station.'

'What?' Malcolm fidgeted uncomfortably in his seat. 'Eileen doesn't like him to be off the lead. She'll kill me if anything happens.' Lucas cocked his head to one side and looked at the man curiously. Whilst it wasn't uncommon in his experience for the woman to wear the pants in the household, Malcolm seemed genuinely terrified of his wife. He decided to get the conversation back on track. Malcolm wasn't under arrest and was free to leave at any time, but Lucas was determined to get some answers before he did.

'It says here that EJ cleans for you.'

'Emily – EJ,' Malcolm corrected himself, '*used* to clean for us.' He rubbed his hand over his follicly challenged head and Lucas found himself wondering if this was a habit that he had developed before his hair had deserted him. He cleared his throat.

'Well, yes, I guess she can't anymore.' Distinctly uncomfortable, Lucas was determined that the man wasn't leaving until he had given him something, and he glanced surreptitiously at his watch for the tenth time in as many minutes while he waited for him to continue. After what seemed like an eternity, Malcolm finally spoke.

'We had to let her go.'

Pleased that he was finally prepared to communicate, Lucas didn't miss a beat for fear he would clam up once more and that silence would once again envelope them in its embrace.

'She was dismissed?' Lucas asked, scribbling a note on his pad lest he should forget although he somehow doubted it. Nonetheless, he was well aware of the backchat from his colleagues at the station, each and every one of them claiming that he had only raced through the ranks because of his father. Robert Elliott had held one of the most senior positions at Cliffborough Cross for in excess of twenty years until he was killed in the line of duty when he had heroically stepped in and taken a stray bullet intended for a colleague. The man was considered by everyone to be a hero, his son a fraud, who at just thirty-one years of age hadn't earned his right to hold such a senior post. Lucas was determined to correct the conjecture – for both his and his now deceased father's sakes.

'She was a thief!' Malcolm's angry outburst surprised him. If only to himself, Lucas had to admit that up until this point, he had been feeling slightly disappointed, the image of Malcolm Muldoon hardly befitting the reputation that preceded him. When Malcolm's name had been disclosed only a few hours ago as the dog-walker who had discovered EJ's corpse, a frenzy of excitement had overwhelmed the incident room. Suddenly, everyone in the room had wanted to be the one to attend this very interview and meet the infamous face behind the name.

'Do you have any evidence to substantiate that claim, Malcolm?' It wasn't overly relevant, since EJ was no longer in a position to be held accountable for her actions let alone defend herself, but it could explain his lack of empathy at the woman's plight when he had discovered the body. It could also confirm whether or not they had any valid reason to consider him a suspect.

'Thought we were born yesterday, she did. As though we wouldn't notice the designer gear she suddenly started wearing to work. Like she could afford that kind of clobber on the salary we paid her,' he scoffed. 'Couldn't prove it of course. Eileen could clothe a whole third world country from her dressing room, but we knew. Didn't stop there either. Anything and everything that wasn't glued down was at risk. So that's when I had the idea about the piggies,' he continued.

'Piggies?' Lucas shook his head in confusion, hoping the man wasn't having a derogatory pop at the police.

'She was clever, I'll give her that. Didn't totally empty them, but I was weighing them so I knew.'

'You planted piggy banks full of money to test her integrity?' Whilst admittedly a little childish, Lucas couldn't deny that the idea was also ingenious.

Malcolm nodded. 'Of course, she totally denied it when I challenged her. Said I couldn't prove it – which of course I couldn't. Even threatened to sue me for unfair dismissal if I didn't let her stay, but I stood my ground.'

The irony of this latest revelation wasn't lost on Lucas. EJ Mahoney: fired for the theft of clothing and money from her employer, and then brutally murdered during a period when tradition dictated employers distributed money and clothing to their employees.

'So you argued?' Lucas couldn't see Malcolm admitting to any kind of fracas, but he also couldn't see such a petty squabble resulting in EJ's murder, let alone the dumping and subsequent discovery of her body.

'Sort of.'

'Sort of?' Lucas pricked his ears and sent a silent plea to the heavens that Malcolm was about to give him what he needed to prove to his colleagues that he was more than worthy of his ranking.

'Jabbed her finger – nail extension and all – right in my face, she did, and threatened me. Told me I'd be sorry before storming off without so much as a backward glance.'

As the pieces of the jigsaw finally slotted awkwardly into place, Lucas nodded solemnly at the man before him. Whilst Malcolm had undoubtedly been the first on the scene, and whilst his involvement couldn't totally be ruled out at this stage, an anonymous tip-off by phone had meant that officers from Cliffborough Cross weren't far behind. When they had arrived and approached EJ's corpse, Malcolm had distinctly been heard singing the song 'Who's sorry now?' as he rocked back and forth on the soles of his feet and stared vacantly at her dead body.

5

'You tried to kill me,' Malcolm stated matter-of-factly
between mouthfuls of Coco Pops. By the time the police
had finished questioning him about the discovery of EJ's
corpse, and by the time Eileen had then finished interrogating
him as to his whereabouts, lunchtime had been and gone, but
Malcolm had never been able to function properly without a
proper breakfast inside him.

It was only now that he had enough energy to tackle her
about her recent behaviour, but if he had been hoping for any
signs of remorse, he was clearly barking up the wrong tree.
Any discussion that he hoped to have with his wife about her
antics was clearly going to be brief.

'Oh don't be so melodramatic, Malcolm. Sleeping with
you is like settling down for the night on a building site. It was
just time to silence the pneumatics, that's all.' Eileen glanced
at him as she spoke, but quickly looked away and turned
her attention back to Buddy who was begging underneath
the table. It was curious how something as harmless as an
innocent little fantasy could rapidly turn into the kind of guilt
that rendered you unable to clap eyes on the very person you
had otherwise shared every waking thought with for the past
twenty-five years.

'By suffocating me to death with a pillow?' He couldn't
believe she could try to just shrug it off and refuse to
acknowledge that what she had done was wrong on any level.

'You're still here, aren't you?' *More's the pity.* Did she just mutter that under her breath? Malcolm couldn't be certain, but he felt sure that she did. He was struggling to look at her in the same light after the dream, or Buddy come to that, and if he was entirely honest with himself, he'd have gone right off the idea of snuggling up with either of them after lights out, even if he hadn't caught her trying to smother him to death.

Malcolm didn't see why he should have to, but needs must and so he suggested sleeping on the sofa until further notice, an idea that Eileen grabbed with both hands, even taking the time and trouble to make up a temporary bed on his behalf. It looked far from comfortable and he wished now more than ever that he had cracked on and converted the garage into an annexe like she had been nagging him to do for the past God knows how long.

'The sooner you see the doctor the better,' she patronised as she plumped up the cushions that would serve as his pillows until such a time that he deemed it safe to return to the marital bed.

'Why? Can he make the fact that my wife wants me dead better?'

'Oh for goodness' sake, now you're being utterly ridiculous!' She sat down on the edge of the couch. 'You're not well, Malcolm, you're doing... bad things.'

Bad things? I'm doing bad things? She's a fine one to talk. 'At least I haven't tried to kill anyone.' *Yet.*

'And when the pushchair mysteriously fell into the swimming pool with the child still strapped inside it in Tenerife?' Eileen crossed her arms and eyebrows raised, gawped at him indignantly. Malcolm might have conveniently forgotten about the whole sorry incident, but she certainly hadn't and a tiny, crawling sensation prickled at the base of her neck and sent little tingles down her spine as she recalled it.

'How many times, Eileen? I did *not* push him!' He couldn't believe she was dragging all that up again.

Eileen studied her husband, particularly the look on his face, the look that warned the recipient that he was capable of anything. She wasn't stupid and she knew what she had seen. Malcolm – her Malcolm – had tried to kill another human being and unless the situation was somehow addressed, his next victim might not be so fortunate. Finally she trusted herself to speak.

'You pulled up a chair and sat down to watch, Malcolm!'

It was regretful, he couldn't pretend otherwise, but what else was he supposed to do? She knew full well that he couldn't swim! And there wasn't a single person around that pool who hadn't been grateful for a moment's peace that day. On and on and on, screeching and howling like an injured animal, the child's parents all the while blissfully unaware that their little darling was, in fact, an irritating little bastard.

'And EJ?' she continued.

'What about her?' Malcolm didn't like the look on her face, not one little bit. As though she knew something nobody else knew.

'You threatened her, Malcolm.'

'Only because she threatened me!' First the police and now Eileen. What was it with everyone today? 'We all say things in the heat of the moment we don't really mean,' he muttered indignantly.

'Did you kill her?' Eileen tried to look her husband in the eye, but afraid of what she might see, she looked away and stared at the dust collecting on the window shelf behind him. *No doubt I'll have to deal with that now,* she thought bitterly to herself as she waited for him to respond.

'I don't have to answer that.' Malcolm glared angrily at his wife. 'I don't have to answer any of your stupid questions!' He slammed his hand down in fury on his thigh before continuing. 'You win. I'll see the doctor, okay? I'll see the doctor.' Using the arm of his seat for leverage, he pulled himself up and shakily made his way to the door. He wouldn't admit it to her, not when she was treating him like a common criminal, but he did have the somewhat delicate little matter of a rather embarrassing lump that he wouldn't mind running past a doctor for advice should the opportunity present itself.

'The experts will know what to do,' she sighed, relieved that he had at least agreed to seek help.

Malcolm wanted to remind her that they were called GPs for a reason and that a person who does a little bit of this and a little bit of that could hardly be classed as an expert. But as his wife droned on and dramatically waved her hand in the air at him as though conducting an orchestra, it was quite apparent he wouldn't get a word in edgeways even if he tried. There was just no talking to some people – particularly when they were the type of person who was always right even when they were wrong.

'I'm going for a lie down.' As Eileen finally came up for air, Malcolm seized the moment and butted in.

'But it's only five o'clock!' she stuttered indignantly, furious that he could even consider sleep at a time like this.

'In case you'd forgotten, it's been a rather long day… and I had little to no sleep last night,' he muttered bitterly as he left the room. He had also promised to take his mother to the shops in the morning – an excursion that would undoubtedly require every last ounce of energy he possessed. Not that he intended to mention the trip to Eileen. She might want to join them if he did, and right now, he needed precious time away from her to think.

★★★

No sooner had Malcolm left the room, Eileen reached for the phone book and scanned the pages for the number of the local swimming baths. New Year's Resolution Number One: Learn to swim. If she had established one thing after last night's escapades, it was that it was high time she confronted her fear of water and mastered the art of swimming once and for all.

6

L ou hated this time of year, and the fact that it was dark when she left for work of a morning and the same when she returned home in the evening only served to aggravate the situation. As she made her way down the high street towards the retail park, rain snaked down her forehead and she brushed it away impatiently with the sleeve of her coat and pulled the collar up as far as it would go to protect herself as much as possible against the driving rain.

The stiletto heels of her new black leather knee-high boots echoed loudly as they clicked and clacked in rhythmic succession on the uneven tarmac and reverberated off the glass shop-fronts that lined the road on either side. High-definition headphones encased her ears and determined to block out the elements and the irritation of being in this predicament, she concentrated on the music and sang along determinedly.

Except that Nancy Sinatra clearly didn't know what she was talking about, she thought angrily to herself. The boots were anything *but* made for walking and she winced as one of the heels snagged in a crack in the tarmac and forced her ankle sideways.

What the hell possessed me, today of all days? An image of Lucas instantly sprang to mind, excitement wrenching at her guts and sending a shockwave of lust straight through her. He was totally into her, she was sure of it. She'd seen him hanging around the hospital watching her. She had even tried to catch his eye a couple of times, but as though sensing her gaze he always looked away a split second too soon, a fierce scarlet rash staining his cheeks as he did so.

On a good day, she was tempted to bite the bullet and ask him out, but then the self-doubts would all come flooding to the surface and she'd chicken out. What if she had misread the signals? What if his interest in her related to what happened all those months ago with his mother? But no. That made no sense. He knew she hadn't meant any harm.

Determined to ignore the stiff leather as it strangled her toes, Lou focused once more on her music and gritted her teeth against the pain as she marched down the hill with renewed vigour at the prospect of seeing him. *Will he even be there today?* He wasn't always, but if she didn't make the effort, she could pretty much guarantee that he would be. Instruments of torture the boots might well be, but everything worthwhile in life came with a price attached, she thought to herself. No pain no gain in this instance, and there was no denying how liberated and empowered she felt every time she thought of Lucas' reaction to her wearing them.

As she rounded the bend at the bottom of the hill in the direction of the car park that served both the retail outlet and the hospital where she worked, Lou stopped dead in her tracks as she observed the midnight-black Mercedes with private plates turning right into the entrance ahead of her.

The parking pig. Up to his usual tricks, no doubt. Six lousy months having to walk everywhere and it was all his fault! Thanks to him hogging the last two available spaces, she had been forced to park on double yellows and they had towed and crushed her beloved Nissan as a result. She held back and watched as he retrieved his ticket from the machine and the barriers slowly lifted and granted him entry.

7

Shoes had always fascinated Rita. They were her guilty secret. The craving she never quite seemed able to satiate. Even as a child she had displayed an unhealthy interest, always remaining far more interested in the shoes her mother's visitors would leave by the front door than the actual people who had left them there.

Hours she would spend online sometimes, checking out image after image of ladies' feet. Fat ankles, slim ankles, mediocre ankles – all the while trying to decide what colour and style would suit her best. But nothing could beat the real thing. Experiencing first hand the feel, the colour, the shape and even the rich aroma of expensive leather so strong she could almost taste it. Which was why she found herself pounding the pavements that particular morning as she desperately searched for her next suitable pair.

Nose pressed up against the window for a better look at the shoes on display at Discount Daphne's, the latest bargain basement store to spring up on the retail park selling everything from contemporary chandeliers and designer handbags and shoes to verruca treatments and adult incontinence pads, the staccato click of approaching heels grew louder behind her and she turned slowly to get a better look.

Loopy Lou. *Interesting*. Rita watched in fascination as Lou, complete with her headphones that everyone knew were attached to nothing, ground to a halt and stood motionless as she glowered angrily at a Mercedes entering the car park. Never in a million years would Rita have ever associated the mad woman who boogied around the parked cars to her very own special music with the elegant specimens on her feet.

Jimmy Choos. Rita prided herself on her ability to detect a quality pair of footwear from so many of those cheap imitations that littered lodgings the world over, and there was no question in her mind that Lou was wearing the real McCoy. The attention to detail, from the finely crafted straps to the minute metal buckles, was absolutely exquisite and she licked her lips in appreciation. Tentatively stepping as close as she dared for a better look, Rita was painfully aware of the trouble she had got into the last time. But it wasn't like she was hurting anyone. She was only looking, after all. Just so long as she didn't touch she'd be fine, and so determined not to draw attention to herself, she kept what she considered to be a safe distance as she carefully studied Lou and those sensational boots of hers.

They really were absolutely breathtaking and Rita felt the familiar desire to try before she decided to buy kick in. The urge to touch them, or better still wear them, was immense, but some people could be so peculiar when she stopped them in the street to ask if they would mind. But what else was she supposed to do? Look at the trouble she had got herself into when she had last decided to dispense with the niceties and just help herself. Hours the police had held her until they finally seemed to accept that it was all just an innocent misunderstanding.

Rita crept a little closer towards Lou as she deliberated what to do, the memories of her ex that she had hoped she'd put to bed once and for all springing to the forefront of her mind once more. Rita had really grown to love her. She'd thought she was different. And she was different. She never nagged. Never pressured her into doing anything she didn't want to do.

'What's mine is yours,' she had declared happily when they had finally moved in together. Wasn't saying that when she borrowed her favourite outfit without asking though was she! Rita felt the all-familiar knot of anger tighten involuntarily in the pit of her stomach. Nobody treated her the way she had done and one day, when she was good and ready, she was going to pay handsomely for that mistake!

8

Working in a shop meant that the last place Malcolm wanted to be when he wasn't working was in a shop, but he had promised his mother a shopping trip and so a shopping trip she would have. Besides which, he needed to extract himself from Eileen's murderous clutches whilst he figured out what the hell he was going to do. Talking to somebody impartial, someone who wouldn't automatically think that he was insane, would really help, but since he didn't actually know anyone like that, he had little choice other than to discuss the matter with his mother instead.

'You know she wants rid of me,' he blurted out as he gently nudged his Mercedes back and forth into the parent and child-parking bay until he was happy he had left enough space between the vehicles on either side so none of the doors could touch his paintwork. Totally preoccupied with what he was doing, he barely even noticed Lou as she inched closer to the car and glared menacingly at him from the other side of the windscreen.

What the hell is wrong with him? Lou thought to herself. *Do the signs and painted lines on the ground not give him the faintest idea what's expected of him?* And there was no child in that car, she'd be willing to bet her next wage packet on it. As she stood and watched him manoeuvre his vehicle as though his life depended upon its ultimate location, the anger that she had worked so hard to control of late threatened to explode in a bubble of rage.

'Well, living with you can't be easy, dear.' Malcolm's mother climbed out of the car, giving the door its usual God Almighty slam, and Malcolm winced. *Does she do it deliberately?* Time and time again he'd told her there was no need and asked her to shut it properly. He held his breath and counted to ten rather than say something he would ultimately regret, before he purposely closed his own door as gently as possible in the hope that he could somehow make the point telepathically instead.

Lou crept around the back of the car for a better look and peered through the rear windscreen. As suspected, there was no child in the vehicle. Arms crossed in defiance, she stepped out directly into the man's path and waited for him to acknowledge her presence and explain himself. He didn't. Instead, to her absolute disgust, he completely blanked her as he sidestepped around her and rushed away from the vehicle towards the entrance of the nearest store. Barely able to breathe for anger, the switch flicked and darkness flooded her mind.

'What's that supposed to mean?' Malcolm asked as he caught up with his mother by the trolley park.

'Well, life's difficult enough when you marry a normal man, Malcolm.'

'I am normal,' he protested vehemently as he fed the trolley with a one-pound coin and extracted it from the embrace of the others.

'Normal?' she scoffed, leaning on the trolley for support. 'I can think of many a word to describe you, but normal wouldn't be one of them. Good grief, Malcolm, nobody liked you, not even back then when you were knee high to a grasshopper. Found you peculiar they did. Your father, God rest his soul, used to wrap sausages round your neck just so the dog would like you.'

Malcolm stood and stared at his mother, waiting for her to take back what she'd said, but it was clear she had no intention of doing any such thing. The comment about the dog really hurt and only served to remind him of his current predicament, but she was right. Making friends had never been his forté, which was why he had taken to Facebook like a duck to water. Over 1000 friends he had now and still counting. If only persuading Eileen and Buddy to like him was as easy.

'Excuse me... excuse me.' The damned boots were crippling her toes and Lou was struggling to catch up, but this was far too important and there was no way she was letting him get away with it again. Malcolm, on the other hand, was so busy contemplating his mother's comment that it didn't even register at first that the woman was talking to him. Not until she grabbed his arm and almost forced it out of its socket as she swung him around to face her.

'You've left your child in the car.' Lou pointed at the vehicle and convinced it was a case of mistaken identity, Malcolm's eyes followed the direction of her pointed finger but sure enough, it was aimed directly at his Mercedes.

He opened his mouth to explain her error – that he was in fact the child, but blinded by the glint of metal from her concealed weapon, panic knocked the wind from his lungs and rendered him speechless. *Not,* the fleeting thought occurred to him, *that I would have been granted the opportunity to speak even if I could have found the words before she set about me with her deadly instrument.*

'These... spaces... are... for... mother... and... child... only!' Lou hissed venomously, each word accompanied by a heavy whack of her weapon of mass destruction. 'I... want... to... hear... you... apologise!'

'I've done nothing wrong!' he squealed in between smacks. 'Mum? Mum, tell her... Ouch, that hurt!' Malcolm couldn't believe how much a handbag used improperly in the wrong hands could hurt. 'Stop it. Ow!' *Why the hell doesn't she prod the woman with her stick or something?* Anything instead of just standing there and letting her attack him like this in broad daylight.

'Nothing wrong? You've ruined my life,' Lou screamed, all the pent up frustration of losing her car to the crusher blowing out of all proportion and erupting to the surface like the devil child from hell.

Ruined her life? Bit extreme isn't it? He'd only parked in the last parent and child bay. If she had really wanted it that badly, she only had to ask. Desperate to get away, Malcolm stepped back, but his foot caught on his mother's stick and as he fell and landed uncomfortably on the rough asphalt of the car park, it occurred to him in a flash. This was all just a clever ruse, and as the facts glared him in the face, he couldn't believe he hadn't seen it coming.

'She sent you, didn't she?' He shook his head, appalled that he hadn't realised it sooner. The mad bag woman was obviously some kind of hitwoman employed by Eileen to do her dirty work for her. He looked up at his mother in horror. Was she in on the conspiracy? Had Eileen somehow persuaded his own mother to be a party to his assassination? It all made sense now. The silly cow had obviously tripped him deliberately and this was the reason she made no attempt to help him in his moment of need.

Lou didn't answer. Instead, she just lunged at him once more with her weapon.

9

It was a crime of the greatest magnitude and Rita couldn't stand back and watch the abuse any longer. It was unclear whether the man had fallen or been pushed, but as he lay on the floor protecting his head with his hands and squealing like a child, Loopy Lou had stumbled forward, clearly still determined to slap him into submission. If Rita didn't act fast, it would be too late, the damage quite possibly irreparable.

She took a couple of cautionary steps towards them, well aware of how this might look to the small group of onlookers who had now created a small semi-circle around them. *Why doesn't someone do something?* It was inconceivable that they could all just stand there and watch the horror unfold.

Rita took a moment to study the boots more carefully, reasonably confident that they were slip-on and that the lace-up detail at the back was purely for decorative purposes only. *So disrespectful.* Designed with elegance in mind, for men to feast their eyes on and greedily consume the contents when a lady entered a room, they were not for thrashing about on the rough asphalt surface of the local car park. *The woman clearly doesn't deserve to own such magnificent exhibits,* she assured herself.

As Rita assessed her prey, she was confident that wrestling her to the ground would be easy enough. Lou was only small, but removing her boots without damaging them and managing to flee the scene without being caught was another matter altogether. Spasms of fear and adrenalin shot down the length of her spine as the memories of the last time played out in her head, but she couldn't help the way she was feeling. She didn't just *want* those boots, she *needed* them and nothing or nobody was going to stand in her way.

Now or never, the little voice nagged, and Rita took one last glance over her shoulder as she surveyed the car park for signs of the old bill, cocking an ear as she did so to listen out for any evidence of approaching sirens echoing in the distance. Swamped by pure and primitive desire, she then pounced at the smaller woman and Malcolm was barely able to register the commotion as she grappled the mad bag lady to the ground. Scrabbling backwards to avoid cushioning her fall, he crashed into the neatly stacked row of trolleys behind him and lay motionless, stunned as he watched the scene unfold.

Still none of the audience moved, the fear to get involved and dirty their hands clearly outweighing their desire to help. It was distracting having them there, but not enough to stop Rita finishing what she had started. She wasn't the baddie here after all, she was the hero, and as she wrestled with Lou, she was surprised at how easy it could be, even with so many people standing witness. If only the woman would stop wriggling and kicking out at her like an irritable child. *Does she not realise how difficult it is if she won't keep still?*

The unmistakeable wail of sirens in the distance resonated in Rita's ears then, and just as she was about to accept defeat and run, Malcolm appeared at her side.

'Here, I'll hold her still and you grab them.' Having already been viciously stabbed in the shin with one of the heels, Malcolm thought it was a stroke of absolute genius. By confiscating all lethal weapons, the mad cow would be stripped of the ability to cause any more injury while they waited for help to arrive.

Flinging her bag aside, he pinned Lou's shoulders firmly down against the floor and clambering aboard, he sat himself down on the back of her thighs to wedge her in place whilst Rita struggled to remove the offending items once and for all.

Seizing the opportunity to sneak a peek over his shoulder, Malcolm marvelled at Rita's athletic physique, every inch of it as fit and agile as his wife was horizontally challenged. As she caught him watching and held his eyes with her own for a split second longer than was strictly necessary, a sudden rush of blood smattered his cheeks and he looked away and stared at the floor in embarrassment.

If someone saves your life, aren't you then responsible for theirs? Malcolm was sure he had read that somewhere, which was why he made no effort to stop her when she got up and sprinted from the car park, boots firmly pressed to her chest seconds before the police arrived on the scene.

10

The water in the pool rippled gently and lapped against the sides as Eileen slowly waded towards the steps and climbed out. She couldn't believe she'd done it; she'd really gone and done it and better than that, she had enjoyed every single second of it.

Picking up her towel from the bench, she pulled it around her shoulders and shivered – a delicious combination of the warm air being kicked out from the heating system as it caressed her moist skin and the sight of her new swimming instructor Tod as, wearing a skimpy pair of briefs and little else, he made his way around the edge of the pool towards her.

'You're a natural,' he smiled, a web of wrinkles casting shadows around the corners of his dark black eyes as he sat down beside her, his bare leg grazing hers and sending a jolt of excitement shuddering through her body. Refusing to meet his gaze, she blushed and looked away coyly.

Tod meanwhile studied her closely, not quite able to believe his luck. When he had first clapped eyes on her, his mind had played tricks on him and convinced him that it was his mother finally back to make amends for her never-ending list of mistakes. Inexplicably drawn to her, he had approached gently, unsure what the protocol was for greeting a mother he hadn't seen in almost fifteen years. But then as he had got closer, he'd soon realised it was just a twisted optical illusion and that Eileen didn't even look that much like he remembered his mother after all. Which was just as well, since it had soon become apparent that he had another middle-aged lush looking for a bit of rough on his hands… and who was he to object?

Tod grinned at the earlier memory and the awkwardness of trying to engage in something so intimate: pressed up against the wall of the tiny changing room cubicle; the wet curtain sticking to their skin and threatening to give them away; their feet all the while slipping from beneath them on the soaking wet floor. Had his luck finally changed? The news about EJ had really knocked him for six and try as he might, he couldn't see any way out of his predicament without her. He had even considered breaking into her flat. She was sure to have some money stashed away in there somewhere, but with the pigs hanging around 24-7, the chances of gaining access were more than a little remote. But then, as though in a direct answer to his prayers, along came Eileen. He could literally smell her wealth oozing from every pore. All he had to do now was somehow convince her that she wanted to help him.

'I thought we could go to Majicks next Friday. Maybe book ourselves a room somewhere nice for a little afters?' As Eileen spoke, their eyes locked, Tod's dictating exactly what he'd like to eat, and she'd be willing to bet that what he had in mind wouldn't be on the restaurant menu. But then, the expression on his face changed and as he reached out and placed a hand on her thigh, the sheer gesture alone sent quivers of lust through her veins.

'I can't afford Majicks, Eileen. I can't even afford KFC right now. Bit of a cash flow problem.' *Eye contact,* he reminded himself. The golden rule. She'd fall for the puppy dog eyes eventually. They always did.

'Sssh,' Eileen placed her forefinger against his lips to silence him. 'Let me worry about all that.' With muscles bulging in places she'd only ever dared dream about, Eileen didn't care how much it cost for a repeat performance of earlier and unable to resist the temptation to glance at his groin as she stood up, she gave him a lingering look that she hoped was seductive rather than desperate. It had been a while since a man, any man except her husband, had shown any interest, and the ground between the two emotions felt distinctly muddied all of a sudden.

As Eileen turned and walked towards the changing rooms, all the while conscious of Tod's eyes burning into her behind, Tod meanwhile congratulated himself on his first-class performance. Come Friday, she'd be eating out of the palm of his hand, he felt sure of it. Come Saturday, play his cards right and he'd be eating out of her kitchen, his recent eviction worries nothing more than a bleak and distant memory.

11

The change in atmosphere and temperature from the upstairs offices to the holding cells below was palpable as Lucas made his thoughtful descent down the rear staircase to the ground floor. He held back whilst two PCs he didn't recognise made their way up the stairs in the opposite direction. Needing all the luck he could get right now, he didn't want to tempt fate. It was why he had dismissed the lift. The last time he had felt like this, the damned thing had broken down between the third and fourth floors, trapping him in the small box like a caged mouse for over an hour. Sweaty and claustrophobic, he had been left alone with only the maintenance workers for company as they yelled assurances up the hollow shaft that they would have him out in no time. *Never again.*

In his arms, Lucas clutched the pathologist's report and whilst they now knew without any doubt how EJ Mahoney had died, they still didn't have a single lead as to a possible motive or suspect. The Community Police Force AGM and Public Meeting was being held in less than a month's time and the higher powers that be were already getting twitchy, demanding results as though he could spring the answers they all so badly needed out of thin air.

Malcolm Muldoon. The name reverberated round and around in his mind, refusing to dissipate. Was he their killer? His relentless presence at recent crime scenes couldn't be ignored any more than the dark cloud of menace that seemed to shadow his every move. Lucas had spent the past few hours on the internal computer, scrolling through the catalogue of Malcolm's past misdemeanours. There were enough to fill a book, just not enough to confirm whether or not he was a serious contender for a murder charge.

Had Malcolm attacked Lou Wilson in the car park? She was currently downstairs claiming as much, but then so was Malcolm, claiming the complete opposite. One of his colleagues could have obtained the statements. It wasn't as though any charges could be issued at any rate since there were no forthcoming witnesses, leaving each with their word against the other, but Lucas wanted to see them both. Correction. He *wanted* to see Malcolm; he wanted to study the man carefully and see if his body language gave any clues as to what had really happened earlier today. And he *needed* to see Lou.

Nausea munched quietly at his insides and threatened to erupt to the surface as his mind wavered between Malcolm and what he had been unable to ascertain about the man's past, to Lou and whether they had any kind of future together (provided of course he could eventually locate his bollocks and tell her how he felt), before finally settling on EJ's final hours, the lethal concoction of household cleaning products slowly devouring every muscle and organ like a venomous, malignant cancer.

He stopped midway down the last flight, his knuckles turning white as he gripped the handrail with so much force; he half wondered whether if he were to apply yet more pressure still, it might snap under the weight. What if his suspicions about Malcolm were right? What then? Bile rose in his throat and he swallowed, grimacing as the acid burned in his chest.

And what about Lou? Would she be pleased to see him? She hadn't looked so keen the last time.

You were caught pissed up on her front steps at 4.38am talking through the letterbox to her cat! Not exactly his finest moment in history.

Six lousy months now since he'd last seen her. If you didn't count the fact that her face was the last thing he saw every night when he closed his eyes and the first thing he saw when he awoke every morning.

Six lousy months of following her. Watching, waiting, observing from a distance. Not that he'd be admitting that fact to anyone anytime soon.

12

Crouched alone in the loft hours later, the only source of light provided by a solitary fluorescent tube that hung precariously over his head, Lucas knelt on his hands and knees surrounded by old cardboard boxes riddled with damp and filled with memories no longer deemed worthy of living space. He hadn't been up here since his mother's death and even now, it felt as though she was watching – somehow disapproving of his every move. The boxes, soft to the touch, disintegrated before him as he carefully pushed several aside to allow himself the room he needed to progress deeper into the roof space.

Were his suspicions even conceivable? Even now he was in two minds, but there was only one way to find out for sure. It didn't take him long to spot what he was looking for and, careful not to trip over the clutter around him, he crawled as quickly as he could, stooped down on bended knee so as not to hit his head on the rafters. Standing only on the exposed beams that weren't hidden by insulation, he moved to the far back corner of the roof, where the ceiling sloped under the eaves. Underneath them, next to a tiny window heavily coated with a film of dust and cobwebs, lay the old-style school trunk.

Safely dragging the heavy container towards the loft entrance where there was more light to see what he was looking for wouldn't be possible, so he pulled the sleeve of his shirt down over his hand instead and wiped as much scum off the window as the linen would allow. It took a while, the years of grime resisting him at every turn, but still he persisted until it was clear that the remaining muck had formulated a part of the glass itself throughout the years of neglect.

He sat back on his heels then and embraced his shins with his arms. Resting his head on his knees, he closed his eyes, the trunk triggering memories that cast a web of fear and doubt so strong it threatened to suffocate him. Was he doing the right thing? Suddenly, he was back in the school car park, his father helping him across the courtyard to the locker room where all belongings were placed on arrival and thoroughly checked by a teacher before the students were permitted to unpack and put them in their rightful place.

'What people don't know, can't hurt 'em, son.' His voice was so powerful and real, Lucas had to turn and check his father wasn't stood behind him and he shook his head ruefully at his stupidity, a tear escaping and tickling his skin as it made its way down his cheek. It had been almost three years since his father's coffin had been lowered into the ground of the same churchyard where he had married Lucas' mother all those years previously, but the pain was still so raw; it might as well have been yesterday.

'But *I* know, Dad,' he sobbed. '*I* know.'

Lucas sat motionless awhile just staring at the trunk. Part of him desperate to open it and find what he was looking for, the other part of him insisting he turn and run – let sleeping dogs lie – just like his parents would have wanted.

Secrets: The sinner's staircase to Satan's soul.

The first time he had clapped eyes on Malcolm Muldoon, he had known deep down, the similarities too significant to ignore, but he didn't want this. He hadn't asked for it and he didn't want any part of it. He had thought that he could pretend otherwise, but then he found that he couldn't get him or the situation out of his mind and the more time that passed, the more Lucas needed to know for sure.

Discovering that his whole life as he knew it had quite possibly been a lie had been bad enough, but to live the rest of that life carrying that knowledge around with him didn't bear thinking about. He slowly released the clasps of the trunk and lifted the lid, careful to prop it gently against a rafter so as not to cause any unnecessary damage.

The letters were all addressed to his mother, the refusal to accept his responsibilities evident in each and every one, and Lucas instantly felt hatred for this man, the polar opposite of his real father. As he carefully fingered through the photographs, the mirror image likeness between them impossible to ignore – even back then when he was far too young for his features to have developed into their true self – Lucas found the anger slowly building within him.

All those times, he thought to himself, shaking his head in disbelief. All those times that a well-meaning relative or neighbour had said how much like his father he looked. And how his parents would nod and smile despite knowing damn well how stupid the observation had been since they both clearly knew that the sentiment was downright impossible.

Why am I even here? He didn't want to forge any kind of relationship with the man, that was for sure, and he certainly didn't want anyone to discover their connection. *Because he deserves to be punished for what he's done, that's why.* Selecting the letters and photographs he required, Lucas pocketed them before placing the rest back into the trunk.

Then, careful to close all the clasps securely he crawled back across the rafters to the hatch to make his exit and his way home. Except that he didn't want to go home. Right now the last place he wanted to be was home alone and as he turned off the light and clambered down the ladder, he knew exactly where he needed to be.

13

The clock had become Malcolm's enemy and as the time sprinted closer to the appointment, he was becoming more and more anxious with every second that passed, the fear about what his diagnosis might be slowly, but surely, devouring his insides.

Eileen had requested his presence in the kitchen more than half an hour ago. Said she wanted to talk and not daring to refuse for fear of the repercussions she might dish out, he had duly obliged. Not that they actually talked. Eileen did the talking, Malcolm just listened, all the while studying her over the top of his newspaper as she dunked biscuit after biscuit in her tea and droned on and on about what he should and shouldn't mention to the doctor. Soggy biscuits or dregs of tea swimming with soggy crumbs? He couldn't decide which was worse.

He still hadn't mentioned the lump to Eileen, nor the fact that he feared it could be something terminal. She had been so peculiar of late, he hadn't seemed able to find the right opportunity. Was there ever a good time to tell your wife that you thought you might be dying? *Especially when she wants you dead at any rate,* he thought to himself.

'You still haven't explained *why* they arrested you.' Eileen nodded knowingly at him as she spoke, the look on her face clearly implying that she held all the answers.

'They didn't arrest me. How many times? I went of my own volition and I left of my own volition.'

'But they think you had something to do with it, don't they?'

'With what?'

'EJ's death, what else?'

'Of course they don't!' Malcolm stuttered indignantly, wishing he had the courage of his convictions. That horrible little worm of a detective had asked so many questions the other day. Too many questions. The wrong questions and however many times he reiterated the fact that the woman had attacked him, it was clear that he didn't believe a word of it and was determined to implicate him in both that and EJ's death if he could. Malcolm had been tempted to feed him a few home truths of his own, but had thought better of it at the last minute.

'First EJ and now some random woman claims you attacked her in the car park. Is it any wonder they don't believe you?' Malcolm scowled at his wife, not liking the way she shook her head patronisingly at him as though she were admonishing a naughty child.

'EJ was already dead when I found her in case you forgot.' He was starting to think that the detective had also managed to conveniently forget that fact.

'Hmmm, says you.' Again that knowing nod of the head as though she could somehow coerce a confession out of him.

You should go and work for that lot down the nick. Right up your street, he thought to himself as Eileen blathered on and he tried to switch off and concentrate on his own problems. Did she already know that his days were numbered? It would certainly explain a lot: the healthy glow in her cheeks, the twinkle of excitement in her eyes. In fact, if he didn't know better, he'd say that his wife seemed happy for a change and that was odd. Very odd indeed.

Ever since his fortuitous escape the other day, Malcolm had been racking his brains as to what possible reason his wife could have for wanting him dead. He wouldn't pretend he was perfect. What person was? But overall, he wasn't far off and had always done his absolute best to be a good husband. There had been the occasional blip, of course there had, but never had he raised his voice, let alone his hand to her. Neither had he ever cheated on her, despite there being plenty of women who he felt sure would have relished the opportunity.

Had Eileen arranged for that woman to attack him in broad daylight? Judging by the smug expression on her face it stood to reason, but he wouldn't be giving her the satisfaction of sharing his suspicions. Instead he was going to find the woman. He was going to track her down and demand answers. He didn't care what it took, or what force he had to use. He was going to get to the bottom of why she did what she did if it was the last thing that he ever did.

Last night, unable to sleep, Malcolm had spent the majority of the night on the computer. He had wanted to see if Google could shed any light on whether or not it was *normal* for women of a certain age to fantasise about killing their husbands. The results had frankly been nothing short of alarming, women all over the globe apparently dreaming about exactly that. But then his attention had been drawn to Eileen's internet history, the proof right there on the screen in front of him that his wife almost certainly wanted him dead. Was the mad bag lady part of his wife's elaborate plan? She was going to be sorry if so. Very, very sorry!

As Eileen finally came up for air, Malcolm seized the moment and stood up, careful to push his chair tidily under the table just the way she liked as he shrugged his shoulders into his jacket. Sitting there analysing everything and listening to her bang on about sweet Fanny Adams was doing nothing for his self-confidence and everything to make matters seem worse.

'Dinner'll be six o'clock sharp. Don't be late,' she ordered, without so much as looking up at him as he opened the kitchen door to make his way out through the back garden.

Dinner. What was it with her and the need to feed him up all the time? Was she tampering with the ingredients? His mind flitted back to the contents of Eileen's search history on the computer.

'You haven't forgotten I'm needed at work tonight? Stocktake, or something or other.' Malcolm wasn't needed for any such thing, but Eileen didn't know that.

'No, Malcolm, I hadn't forgotten.' *I'm really rather looking forward to it. Tod's coming round later to roger me senseless in our bed.* A little wave of excitement fluttered in her belly at the prospect. 'You won't be wanting dinner before you go back in then?'

'Err, no. Thank you, dear, I'll be fine. Seems silly to come back and put you to all that trouble. We'll probably just get something out anyway.' Malcolm risked a glance at his wife, hoping she wouldn't see through his lies and was pleased to note that she seemed content with his response as she smiled and turned her attention to the newspaper he had discarded on the table only minutes previously.

14

Ronnie curiously eyed the man in the waiting room over the top of her spectacles as he fidgeted in his seat and continually crossed and uncrossed his legs and looked at his watch as though the gestures alone could somehow speed up the whole procedure. He didn't seem to have spotted her yet, but the mere notion that any minute now he was sure to was making her more than a little uncomfortable. Would he create a scene? He wouldn't like her being there any more than she liked him being there, that much was for certain.

Touché! she thought to herself as she idly scanned his notes on the screen in front of her and tried to ascertain the nature of his visit. Mind you, it wouldn't take a doctor to confirm that there was something very wrong with the man. So far as she was concerned, he was beyond help and nothing prescribed behind these closed doors was likely to make the faintest bit of difference.

As she studied him, the thin film of sweat shimmering on his skin under the artificial light, a prickling, crawling sensation tingled at the base of her neck as his head suddenly snapped upwards and his eyes locked on her own. She quickly looked away, but not fast enough to miss the sinister, menacing grin that spread across his features as he observed her for the first time.

★★★

Malcolm had stopped off first at the chemist to purchase an alcohol-based hand sanitizer – not that he actually intended to remove his hands from his pockets or touch anything for the duration of the appointment. After all, a room full of sickly individuals was quite possibly the worst place in the world he could go to get ill and what with Eileen secretly plotting to kill him, he needed to keep his strength up.

As he sat upright in his chair in the bland, whitewashed waiting room, he kept his hands very much to himself and patiently watched the seconds turn to minutes rather than encourage eye contact with the other occupants of the small room. *Frauds, the lot of them,* he thought to himself as one by one he witnessed the same conversation over and over again as somebody new entered the room.

'Hello, how are you?' the receptionist behind the counter would enquire and without fail, each and every one of them replied and said that they were fine. Was it any wonder it was such a struggle to get an appointment if perfectly healthy people were hogging all of the slots?

It was the receptionist's voice that had first grabbed his attention, but since she was the last person he was expecting to see in here of all places, it had taken a while for the recognition to dawn. He shuffled awkwardly in his seat, feeling overwhelmingly hot all of a sudden and as he glanced up surreptitiously for a better look, she caught his eye and left him in no doubt. *Ronnie.* Evil Ronnie who was always trying to poison his wife against him. He wouldn't put it past her to have put it in Eileen's head to try to kill him. Since when had she worked here? He gave her a little smile. Best to be polite given the circumstances, but rather than reciprocate she just hastily looked away and pretended to study the computer screen in front of her.

'Muldoon?' The doctor's voice snapped him out of his reverie and brought him back to the present and he looked up to find Death staring him in the face. Doctor De'ath, as he preferred to be called, gestured to the tiny room behind him and careful not to remove his hands from his pockets, Malcolm stood up and gave the man a curt nod by way of a greeting as he followed him through the dreaded door.

★★★

As the man followed the doctor into his office, Rita pretended to study her book intently and hoped above all else that he hadn't noticed her sat there on his way past. As if it wasn't bad enough to find Ronnie serving behind the counter, to see her partner in crime sitting in the same small space had been suffocatingly oppressive and suddenly she found herself questioning whether it was a good idea hanging around to see the doctor at all.

It was only a routine appointment, just her monthly check-up and prescription, but nonetheless she didn't want that damned woman knowing her business. *Totally unethical,* she thought angrily to herself. A little like selecting jurors, the doctors should be more careful when selecting potential employees. Surely they should not be employed if they knew any of the patients?

Trying to put Ronnie to the back of her mind was easier said than done when she knew that she was watching her over the desk, but nonetheless, Rita tried to concentrate on the man from the car park. Would he report her? Or worse still, had he already reported her? As the fear washed over her and threatened to drown her in a panic attack, so did the unbearable heat as it appeared out of nowhere and surged through her like a flaming furnace until she was struggling to breathe.

Air. She needed some fresh air and unable to bear it any longer, she grabbed her bag from beside her feet and made for the exit, painfully aware of everyone watching her – particularly

Ronnie, whose cold, calculating eyes currently seemed to be freezing pinpricks into the base of her burning skull.

Pausing for a moment on the pavement outside, Rita breathed deeply and wallowed in the cool air as it caressed her skin. Feeling instantly better, she perched on the window ledge directly outside the surgery and gave the matter some serious thought. Ronnie might be able to drive her away from the doctor, but there was no way she was driving her away from him as well. Fate had chucked them together in that room for a reason and if she didn't speak to him and find out what he intended to do, she would never know, always living in fear and expecting that knock on the door to arrest her for her crime.

Mind made up, she crossed the road and entered the coffee shop opposite the surgery and quickly reserved herself a table by the window. She'd wait for him to come out and speak to him, beg him if needs be. In fact, she would do whatever it took to convince him not to incriminate her.

★★★

As the doctor carried out his investigations, it suddenly occurred to Malcolm where he had seen the woman in the waiting room before. *Stop this instant, the lump can wait.* Unfortunately, being bent over with his pants around his ankles whilst Doctor De'ath carried out his internal rectal examination wasn't exactly conducive to taking control of a situation and barking out orders, so Malcolm kept his thoughts to himself.

Come on, come on, he inwardly urged. *I have to go!*

'If you could just relax, Sir,' the doctor requested. *Relax? Could you relax given the circumstances? Deep breaths, Malcolm. Yes, that's it. Relax. Sooner he's done, the sooner you're out of here.*

Less than ten minutes later, armed with his diagnosis and

a prescription to pick up from the chemist, Malcolm made his way to the surgery exit, all the while grateful that he had chosen to keep those hands of his firmly in his pockets if this kind of situation was typical of the doctor's day. He was also thankful that he wasn't going to die, of course he was, but right now, that was the furthest thing from his mind.

As he rushed through the waiting room, his eyes desperately scanned the room in vain and he paused a second as he contemplated asking at the reception whether or not she was still in the building. *Ronnie,* he thought, more irritated than ever by her unwanted presence here. Anyone else and he possibly could have, but not her. Not without having to explain himself to both her and no doubt Eileen later once the silly cow had finished telling tales on him.

As he stepped out onto the pavement outside, a small sob escaped his lips. The woman had quite possibly saved his life, but thanks to his own stupidity and self-obsession putting his health before her, he'd missed his chance. And then he spotted her. Crossing the road towards him in those magnificent boots that were so much more suited to her legs than the mad bag woman's.

15

Hannah leant on her elbows against the shop counter, chewing her sandwich thoughtfully as she watched her colleague 'tickle and titify' the window display as he liked to call it. She didn't like him, not one little bit; he gave her the eegie beegies. When she had expressed her concerns to her immediate supervisor earlier that day, the snotty cow had told her in no uncertain terms that 'ours is no such environment to air prejudiced grievances'. She wasn't prejudiced, for crying out loud, she was just realistic and the guy was a complete freak.

As though reading her mind, he suddenly turned away from his project and stared right at her, their eyes locking despite her best efforts to look away. She didn't even like the way he smiled, baring too many teeth like an aggressive dog about to sink its ivories into its prey. As he casually strolled over towards her, losing her appetite she stuffed the remains of her half-eaten sandwich below the counter and tried to avoid further eye contact with the unpleasant excuse for a man.

'So… Hannah.' His singsong voice rose a decibel as he pronounced her name. Han-Nah. Even that grated on her nerves and sent an involuntary shiver of disgust down the length of her spine. 'When are you going to put yourself out of your misery and agree to that drink with me? You know you want to,' he added, waggling his finger in her face and winking. At least she thought he was winking, but he did it a lot so it could be a nervous twitch, she supposed.

I'd rather sit down for a chinwag with Ted Bundy. Of course she didn't say this aloud and maybe not Ted Bundy. Tony Blair perhaps?

'I'm out with my *boyfriend* tonight.' She stressed the word 'boyfriend', as she always did, hoping above all else that he would finally get the message and stop hassling her.

'Maybe tomorrow then?'

Or maybe not. Talk about up himself. What was it with this guy? 'I'm kind of out with my boyfriend most nights,' she replied awkwardly, asking herself for the umpteenth time whether or not the job was really worth all this aggro. But yes, it was. Almost six months she'd been out of work before she had struck lucky and found someone who was finally prepared to take a chance on her and there was no way the likes of this idiot was going to stuff it up for her.

'Your loss.' He touched her arm and she jumped back as though scalded with a hot implement. 'You know, and I know,' he tapped the side of his nose knowingly, 'that it's only a matter of time before you give in to temptation.' Hannah stared at the top of the counter, terrified to catch his eye, yet knowing that his gaze was still firmly fixed upon her. *Don't be rude, don't be rude,* the little warning voice in her head echoed. *He might not be worth it, but the job is,* she reminded herself.

'I could give you a lift home if you like, only I've noticed you waiting for the bus and I pass your place on my way home.'

You pass my place? You've noticed me waiting for the bus? How the hell did he know where she lived anyway? She definitely hadn't told him. Had he been following her? Spying on her? Did Stalking Stanley here know that her imaginary boyfriend didn't even exist? She felt sick, the overwhelming sensation of foreboding gripping at her insides with all its might.

'I'm going to my *boyfriend's* tonight.' Never a good liar and knowing her face might give her away, Hannah was careful not to look at him. *What now?* Kill time in town until it goes dark and then spend the rest of the evening behind closed curtains?

'It's a date then, I'll see you later.' He grinned, ignoring her previous statement as though totally aware that she wasn't doing any such thing.

Not if I see you first. She didn't say the thought aloud. She didn't dare. If he was secretly spying on her and knew as much about her as he claimed, upsetting him would surely only exacerbate the situation.

16

arco's was a new eat-in delicatessen and coffee shop, which had recently sprung up on the retail park amongst the numerous other stores that now made the somewhat dated selection of branded shops and eateries that filled the high street seem blander than ever. Leather banquettes rose up from the oak veneered floors and lined the walls and walkways to create cosy nooks and crannies.

Whilst Ronnie approached the open bar to order their food and drinks, Eileen made a beeline for a booth in the far corner that offered one of the better views of the room as a whole. A man sat alone at the adjoining booth, nursing a mug of coffee and wrapped in a heavy-duty waterproof coat as though cold despite the warmth kicking out from the wall-mounted heaters. Determined to grab the best seats of the house before anyone else did, she didn't even notice him as she passed and sat down with her back to his enclosure.

As Eileen waited for Ronnie to return with the food, she allowed herself to lean back and relax in the plush leather upholstery and study the other occupants that weren't hidden from view. The eclectic mix of suits with briefcases, who met there every Friday, somehow clashed with the Zimmer brigade in the far corner. Nonetheless, each and every one of them seemed to relish the relaxed, unpretentious ambience and rich aroma of ground coffee and freshly baked pastries that hung in the air and radiated around the establishment. All of them, that was, except the man who sat alone in the trench coat and who seemed to be studying Ronnie's every move.

'So.' As Ronnie approached the table and set down the tray, they both spoke together before falling into companionable silence. Aware of Eileen's eyes on her, Ronnie placed her hands gratefully around the warm mug of coffee and watched, seemingly mesmerised by the small plume of steam that rose from the top. Eventually she looked up, her eyes locking on her friend as she tucked into her roasted butternut squash and cherry tomato salad as though terrified she would never eat again. She turned her attention to her own plate then, but her appetite seemed to have deserted her and she pushed the plate away.

'What's up, first day blues?' Eileen spoke between mouthfuls as she reached across and helped herself to some of the salad from Ronnie's plate.

'Malcolm came in.' Eileen stopped mid-chew. *Does she know something?* But reading her friend's mind, Ronnie just shrugged before continuing. 'I did try, but I don't have the password.'

'I could have killed him.' Eileen blurted the words out, immediately blushing and regretting being so open despite knowing Ronnie of old. Instead of reacting, however, her friend barely blinked as finally seeming to regain her appetite, she reached for a piece of bread and popped it into her mouth, relishing the taste as it slowly dissolved of its own accord on her tongue.

'Is that why you're upset?' Ronnie quipped as she swallowed the last of the bread. 'Because you didn't succeed?' She couldn't help herself. Malcolm was a poor excuse for a man and her oldest friend deserved better.

'Ronnie!' Eileen playfully kicked her friend under the table with her foot. 'I'm trying to be serious here.'

The bench provided the perfect cover and although he

could no longer see Ronnie since she had sat down, the man in the coat could hear every word perfectly and couldn't deny being more than a little intrigued.

'Typical.' Ronnie shook her head at her friend, surprised that even now after all these years, the insipid little man she'd had the misfortune to marry could still turn a situation around and make the poor woman somehow believe that she was to blame. 'Trying to make you out to be something you're not. So you tried to shut him up with a pillow. Big deal! Honestly, Eileen, he is *so* melodramatic.'

The man visibly bristled in his booth. *Typical,* more like, of Ronnie to play a situation down and make it all out to be someone else's fault, he thought to himself. Would she never learn?

'Did the doctor know what's wrong with him?' Eileen looked at her friend quizzically.

'Other than the fact he's a complete nut job and if he was a dog they'd suggest putting him down?' she sneered.

'It's not funny,' Eileen mumbled. 'I think he did it!' She looked up at Ronnie, her eyes brimming with unshed tears as she spoke. 'EJ, I mean. I think *they* think he did it as well. And he attacked some woman yesterday in the retail park. Said she attacked him, but what's the likelihood of that?'

Interesting, the man thought to himself as he drained the rest of his coffee. *Very likely,* as it happened since he was there. He could confirm everything. If he wanted to, which he didn't.

'Are the police involved?' Ronnie hoped so. The sooner Eileen's husband was locked up for good, the better.

The man sat motionless, afraid to breathe as he awaited Eileen's response. *Well? Are they? Come on, woman, we haven't got all day.*

'I don't think they believed him,' she shrugged helplessly.

The man let out the deep breath that he had been holding

and visibly relaxed. *Good.* Restorative justice was the best way to deal with situations such as what had occurred yesterday.

'*You-know-who* came in earlier as well!' Unsure how to reassure her friend, Ronnie deftly changed the subject and Eileen reached across the table for her hand, finally understanding why she seemed so *off* this morning. Eileen had never met Ronnie's ex, but she had heard more than enough about him to last a lifetime.

'No!'

Ronnie didn't speak, just nodded.

'And?' What was it with some people? Would the man ever get the message that she no longer wanted anything to do with him?

'And nothing really, just knocked me for six,' she shrugged. 'Like a bad smell, that one. Don't suppose I'll ever be truly rid. Anyway, enough of all that, how was the swimming lesson?' Ronnie reached for a fresh bread roll from the basket between them and chewed thoughtfully as she studied the grin that had spread across her friend's features. She'd recognise that look anywhere: the *I-got-laid* look.

'Tod's quite something,' Eileen giggled, blushing and picking at a loose thread on the corner of the tablecloth as she spoke.

'I'll bet he is. Come on, spill,' Ronnie laughed as she signalled to the waitress for a top-up. She couldn't be too late back, not on her first day, but this was the most animated she'd seen Eileen for weeks and she wanted to know everything there was to know about the man who had put the spring back into her friend's padding.

'I'm seeing him again tonight. Malcolm's not due home 'til late,' she confided. 'In fact,' she continued as she looked at her watch, 'I ought to make a move, but why don't you come to the next class? Well, actually,' she cackled, 'if Tod's teaching you, you'll definitely come!' They both laughed.

Sluts. The pair of them. Dirty, filthy whores! The man shifted in his seat and wrestled with his napkin under the table, squeezing and wringing the starched cotton in his hands. He closed his eyes so he could concentrate and better picture the image in his head, his hands all the while gripping the linen as hard as they could as he twisted them tightly around what he fantasised to be her neck.

17

He was excited. Very excited indeed and unable to concentrate on work, he had slipped away early. Tonight, he had a date. Correction: he had two dates. The first wouldn't take long, it was more an appointment that he was required to attend than a date, he supposed, but the other should be quite a drawn-out, leisurely affair. Nonetheless, he had a lot to do if he was going to successfully pull it off and effectively be in two places at once.

'Lots to do.' His eyes quickly scanned the room and he made a mental note of everything he needed to do. He hadn't been here for a while, to his own special place, and the amount of dust that had settled on the surfaces and skirtings in such a short period of time was quite alarming. Not to mention the occasional dead fly on the windowsills, meaning that the spiders had made his little hideaway their home and were nesting somewhere up above.

'Eurgh.' He hated spiders and he shivered instinctively at the prospect of removing them. The reflection in the mirror caught his attention then and he afforded himself one of his most encouraging smiles.

'Is tonight the night?' he asked.

'Yes,' he smiled kindly at his duplicate. 'I think it might be.' He smiled again, but it wasn't a pleasant smile – more the rictus grin of the Joker.

'Must get on,' he whispered as he swivelled on his heel

and made his way towards the bed where the photographs spilled from his satchel. He picked one up, his cock instantly hardening and straining against his trousers in its desperation to escape the confines of the material despite his best efforts to control himself. As though starving, his eyes greedily travelled the length of her body in the picture as he mentally stripped her of the tight fitted dress and black leather boots that encased her legs like a second skin and unable to contain his excitement any longer, he reached down and roughly grabbed his groin.

But now wasn't the time and he mentally admonished himself for his lack of patience. He'd waited long enough already, what difference did a few more hours make?

'All good things come to those who wait,' he reminded himself as he licked his lips and slowly, but deliberately, laid out the photographs one by one on the bed so he could appreciate them in all their glory.

He closed his eyes a moment and breathed the air deeply, relishing the first-hand memories. The photographs were all well and good, but nothing was ever going to take away the real thing and he fidgeted like an excited child as the image sprang to the forefront of his mind. *Those legs. Those endless, endless legs!* He had known it was wrong to take the pictures, but it wasn't as though he intended to do anything bad such as show anyone or plaster them all over the internet. *No, no. Good God no.* They were for his consumption only and he had no intention of sharing them with anyone. Just a few little mementos to be enjoyed in the privacy of his own home.

'Must get on,' he chastised himself. 'Busy, busy, lots to do.' And he did have lots to do.

'I've got a date,' he declared.

'A date? Wooooo, wooooooo,' he teased himself.

'A date with destiny,' he added knowledgeably, nudging the air knowingly with his elbow.

His mind flitted briefly to the argument with EJ. Even

now, despite having had the chance to calm down and wipe the whole sorry scenario from his mind once and for all, he couldn't. *Selfish.* Unbearably selfish and irrational, and she had made him do it. He squeezed his eyes tightly shut, but the image of her glaring at him defiantly as he in turn had studied her like a wary animal framed in the darkness as he waited for her to make the first move refused to budge. Eventually, he had lost patience. The first smack had been the hardest. From thereon, she had been incredibly subservient as it turned out and it had been remarkably easy. He had no regrets. Some people got everything they deserved in life. And in death, and EJ just happened to be one such person.

He turned his attention back to the job in hand and set about his preparations. Everything *must* be perfect. He changed the bed linen first. It was a silly little superstition since there was little chance she would see it, but better safe than sorry. He worked hard then, dusting and polishing each and every room that she was never likely to venture into at any rate within an inch of its life. And lastly, he hoovered throughout the house, only stopping briefly to treat himself to a light snack. He had worked up such an appetite, but didn't want to go overboard. Food tended to make him feel bloated and sluggish and he needed all the energy he'd got for later.

Selecting what he would wear should have been easy, but he had two dates let's not forget. Two dates, two very different venues, two different outfits almost certainly required. Besides, to wear the same to both would be lazy. Sloppy even, and he wanted to make an effort and look his best for both occasions.

Decisions, decisions, he mused, taking an age as he deliberated over which one he preferred for which event. The first was very colourful. *So gay.* He could almost hear the whispering as she belittled him behind his back. He wasn't gay. It was called fashion and the colour complemented his complexion perfectly. Even the saleswoman in the shop had said as much. *Nice.* She was real nice as it happened, even going to the trouble of selecting the perfect pair of shoes to match it. He decided to save this outfit for the second date, the more noteworthy of the two – the one he really wanted to make an impression for and leave his mark. He'd wear the blander outfit for the first.

Laying them both carefully on the bed so as not to crease them, he checked the time on the bedside clock. Another hour. Ample time. Picking up the box of hair dye from the dressing table, he read the instructions thoroughly one last time before applying the gloves, and then slowly and methodically set about combing in the highlights just as he had researched on Google. It was a risk, but so long as he followed the instructions to a tee, he felt confident that the end result would be worth it. Once he had waited for the recommended time, he entered the ensuite and carefully washed away the surplus dye before luxuriating in a long shower as he deliberately ran the razor across his chin, chest, legs, pubic area and underarms one last time. Girlfriends in the past had found it strange that he did this, but he didn't care. Stray hairs and stubble made him feel dirty and tonight he was determined to feel and look his absolute best.

Only once he felt totally fresh and rejuvenated did he finally step out from the shower and dry himself off. He then sat down once more at the dressing table and began to apply the absurdly expensive face and eye creams that he had been applying for a while now to keep the wrinkles at bay. He studied his reflection in the mirror, not convinced for one second that the creams actually worked and if he didn't see the results the packaging promised sometime soon, he fully intended to return them and demand a full refund.

18

The Beds 'R' Us store was much larger inside than Malcolm had envisaged from the exterior frontage and it was hard not to feel self-conscious as his new leather brogues clacked loudly on the hard, wooden floor and reverberated around the showroom as he entered through the main automatic doors.

Each individually designed bedroom set was lavished in sumptuous furnishings that blended seamlessly with the chosen accessories and Malcolm crept along on the tips of his toes between the tastefully partitioned sets in an effort to blend in and not draw any unnecessary attention to himself.

It didn't work. The saleswoman, who had been about to nip out the back and take advantage of the free WI-FI in the supervisor's office to check her Facebook newsfeed, had spotted him the second he had entered the shop. Or more to the point, she had spotted those ridiculously stiff-looking shoes on his feet that made him walk as though he'd had an accident and needed to change his underwear.

New money, she thought to herself. Before she had been made redundant and forced to spend almost six months claiming benefits, she had worked for a firm of accountants. She wasn't qualified herself, but nonetheless, over the years she had learned to spot the type a mile off. This man, in his posh new high-street suit and unforgiving shoes, oozed the *where-there's-a-will-there's-a-relative* kind of wealth – the worst kind in her mind. This type of individual had come into some money by chance, but deep down they still appreciated the value of it and would never flash their cash around unless it would make a direct difference to how people viewed them as a person. *Kippers and lace curtains,* she thought to herself. He'd have a nice house, nice car, sure, but she couldn't see him investing in something presumably only his wife (and mistress, she supposed) would ever see.

Based on her meagre commission, she needed the, *I've-got-more-money-than-sense* kind of wealth if she was ever going to persuade the bank to approve her for a mortgage of her own. That kind of customer didn't come in here very often so far as she could tell and she was starting to think that now she was finally back on the ladder, it might be time to look elsewhere for alternative work.

'Rita.' Malcolm cleared his throat and tilted his head, unsure whether the woman had even noticed him as she doodled on the notepad in front of her. 'I'm looking for Rita?'

'Aren't we all?' she responded, chomping on her gum and clearly bored as she continued to engrave a work of art into the paper.

'Is she in?' The woman's blatant disinterest was starting to irritate him. It was a simple question, worthy of a simple answer.

'Rita is *definitely* out.' The woman finally looked up from her masterpiece, flashing him a set of crooked teeth, and he found himself wondering whether she was going to share the private joke she was so obviously relishing.

'But she was supposed to meet me.' Malcolm shuffled from foot to foot on the spot, anger and disappointment mingling in his gut and threatening to overwhelm him. *She stood me up!* A promise was a promise and she had promised to go for a drink with him after her shift. *She broke her promise!*

'We had a date,' he mumbled under his breath. How could she do this to him? He'd been on tenterhooks all afternoon and had gone to so much effort to look his best. He tried not to panic. There must surely be a simple reason for her absence and so he turned his attention to the display behind him, determined to distract himself whilst he waited for her to show up and put him out of his misery.

'My wife would like that one,' he smiled at the assistant as he pointed to the biggest bed he had ever seen. Maybe if he could make a friend of her as he waited, she would divulge a little more about Rita's whereabouts.

'Hmmmm?' *Here we go again,* she thought as she glanced at her watch. She had heard the joke a hundred times before. *Five more minutes.* Then she could kick him out.

'Size apparently matters and all that.' Malcolm winked and chuckled at his little joke.

So much for befriending her, he thought to himself less than five minutes later as she ushered him towards the exit of the store. *Bitch!*

'I *have* to ask you to leave now, I *need* to close up,' he imitated in his best girlish, singsong voice. She didn't *have* to do any such thing. She didn't *need* to do any such thing. She could have helped him if she wanted to. Incandescent with rage, Malcolm stormed back to his car to wait. That silly little cow in there might be able to kick him out of the store, but he was going nowhere until he found out what Rita was up to.

'Nobody stands Malcolm up and lives to tell the tale,' he muttered determinedly to himself, as he frantically jabbed at the keypad of his mobile phone in search of her number.

19

Lucas was careful to park a safe distance from the building, aware of how it would look if she were to catch him spying on her, but turning off all the feelings, hopes and dreams that he had carried around with him over the past year was proving easier said than done. Being here was crazy, he knew that, but not as crazy as convincing himself all this time that they had a future together.

He leant forward and banged his forehead on the steering wheel, gently at first, then a little harder as he idly wondered whether it would be possible to hurt himself enough that the searing pain that currently ran amok through his heart would pale in significance.

How could this be happening? He had thought they had finally turned a corner and that his patience had paid off. When she had agreed to a drink after work, he had even dared to imagine the scenario when one day not so far from now, he could truly say that she belonged to him. *Stupid, stupid, stupid!* He banged his head on the steering wheel again, harder this time, and instantly winced at the pain he'd brought upon himself.

He had waited ages, almost an hour past the time they had arranged to meet. Not for one second did it cross his mind that she might have a change of heart and leave him stood there like a jilted groom at the altar. Eventually, unable to bear the suspense any longer and assuming there would be a perfectly sensible excuse as to why she hadn't turned up, he had plucked up the courage and queued at the reception desk to enquire as to her whereabouts.

You're a cop, he kept telling himself. *Cops don't need to explain the reasons for their actions.*

'Left ages ago with some bloke.' The disinterested woman behind the counter had barely looked up from her keyboard as she spoke.

Some bloke? What bloke? Frustration gnawed at his insides. He was supposed to be a detective, yet right now, it was quite apparent he couldn't even detect whether or not Lou reciprocated his feelings correctly and he mentally kicked himself for being such an unobservant idiot. He had made it his business to make sure that he knew everything he needed to know, yet somehow some bloke, as this woman had referred to him, had totally slipped his radar.

Lucas knew he had to deal with it. That he had obviously lost the fight. He had failed to man up and tell her how he felt when he had the chance and now it was too late. The inevitable had happened and he needed to let go. Except that he couldn't let go. He wasn't sure that he ever could.

I won't stay long, he promised himself. *Just long enough to see her one last time. Then I'll let it go. I'll stop this once and for all.* Except that he wouldn't, he knew he wouldn't because he couldn't. Lou was his addiction and like a drug addict desperate for his next fix, Lucas permanently craved the next sighting of her. At first, her Facebook account had been enough and every time he logged in as her, convinced her suspicions would eventually be aroused and she would have changed her password, he couldn't believe his luck when the account allowed him access. A little like having the benefit of hindsight without the hindsight, the luxury to get to know her inside out had proved invaluable.

He reached for his mobile. Still no missed calls or messages and he felt the anger bubbling in his gut once more as he logged into her Facebook account to see if that could shed any light as to her whereabouts.

20

R ude. *Very, very rude!* He banged his fist on the steering wheel and glanced at the clock on the dash for the umpteenth time in as many minutes. He hadn't been that angry at first. Convinced there was some kind of mistake and that they would go for their drink as arranged, he had been prepared to sit it out. He was a patient person after all. Never one to lose his temper without good reason. He yanked down the visor and glared angrily at his reflection in the mirror.

'We had a date! Where the hell is she?'

'On her way to hell at this rate.' The man in the mirror smiled at him and he returned the gesture. Such a knowledgeable chap. He liked him. He liked him a lot.

'I was looking forward to it,' he whined, finding it hard not to be upset. 'I thought this one was different.' Six o'clock on the dot. They had agreed. He'd only been two minutes late, if that – an unplanned anomaly, which couldn't be helped. She should have waited. He looked at the clock again. 18.49. He couldn't wait all night. Did she have any idea how busy he was? Places to be, people to see.

'You know what they say, don't you?' the reflection asked him.

'No, I don't know what they say. What do they say?' he responded.

'Bad behaviour breeds bad behaviour.'

'Oh yes, I'd forgotten that,' he chuckled. 'She has been

very, very bad, so now I'm allowed to be very, very bad.'

Shaking with a combination of anger and excitement, after all, he was effectively being invited to dish out a worthy punishment, he climbed from behind the wheel and made his way towards the wine bar where he had envisaged spending the rest of the evening luxuriating over a bottle of something nice on ice with his second rendezvous. He'd only have the one glass. Alcohol tended to make his brain fuzzy and render him incapable of thinking straight and he was still optimistic he would make his second appointment. Besides, it wouldn't do to be pie-eyed in charge of a vehicle.

'I-am-not-drunk-I-am-not-drunk-I-am-not-drunk,' he chanted to himself an hour later as he clambered once more from behind the wheel. And he wasn't. Well, maybe just a little. The liquid had slipped down a touch too easily and he now felt somewhat lightheaded.

'Naughty, naughty feet,' he admonished, giggling at their disobedience as they seemingly developed a mind of their own and dragged him towards her building.

'Are you there? Come out, come out, wherever you are,' he sang as he hung around in the shadows and desperately scanned the nearby windows for a glimpse or clue that she might be inside. About to give up, his mobile phone vibrated in his pocket. *Voicemail,* but before he had the chance to check it, a movement out of the corner of his eye caught his attention.

21

Sprawled naked on the bed, Tod leaned back against the pillows and stared up at the ceiling, a lazy smile playing out on his face. He couldn't believe how easy it had been. One minute his landlord giving him notice for non-payment of rent and then the next, the fox had entered his life and lured him into her den.

Reaching across to the bedside cabinet, he reached for his cigarettes and carefully unwrapping the cellophane from the packet, he placed two between his lips. Lighting both, he inhaled deeply before blowing a perfect smoke ring. Passing one across the bed, Eileen gratefully accepted, puffing deeply on the end as though the chemicals within it held the answer to the river of emotions that were currently flooding through her. No sooner had she accepted it, however, she discarded it with disgust in the lid of one of her moisturising creams, the only item in the vicinity of the bed that would pass as an emergency ashtray. What the hell was wrong with her? Suddenly, she didn't know which was worse: her blatant lack of self-control resisting a drug addiction she had defied for near on thirty years, or her inability to abstain from the first sign of temptation no sooner had trouble reared its ugly head within her marriage.

'Poison of life, love.' Although only fleeting, Tod hadn't missed the glimpse of regret in her eyes and didn't like it one little bit. It wasn't part of the plan.

'What's that?' Eileen had heard him as clear as day, but she needed to hear him say it again.

'Remorse. Poison of life.' Tod dragged hard on his cigarette and stared at the ceiling, determined to avoid eye contact despite her best efforts to persuade him otherwise. Why was she being so weird all of a sudden? It was like being in a room with two different people, the contrast so stark it was starting to unnerve him.

'Didn't have you down as a Brontë fan,' Eileen observed, irritated with herself for being so patronising, but more annoyed with the fact that he refused to look at her and even more aggravated still that she had been so weak as to fall for his charms in the first place.

'So, can we do this again?' Deep down, Tod already knew the answer but he had to try. He had to somehow persuade her to get rid of that idiot husband of hers, or else he'd be out on his ear. *Wants rid of you first more like.* The words rumbled in his ears and intent on remaining calm, he lay back on the pillows and closed his eyes as he awaited her response.

As Tod lay there, despite her best endeavours Eileen's eyes navigated his bare chest once more, her body instantly responding and rebelling against her mind-set. The man had certainly been a well-earned treat. Her husband was more of a *wham-bam-thank-you-mam* kind of man, but in direct contrast, Tod had taken his time, genuinely seeming to enjoy the process and care that she did too.

But no, deep down she still wanted him to go. Now. Before she did something she would later regret. Was that so wrong? She had wanted a fling, a bit of fun, not someone who was going to cling on well past their use-by date. She wished now that she had gone to the expense of a hotel after all. Bringing him here, to her home, had been a stupid idea.

'You have to go now, my husband will be home soon.' Malcolm should have been home ages ago if the truth be known and the thought of him bursting in and catching them like this didn't bear thinking about.

Tod flinched, the words hitting him like an out-of-control truck on the motorway that didn't care about the carnage or aftermath it would cause. *No. Who the fuck does she think she is?* After all his hard work, he wasn't going anywhere until he got what she owed him.

'Get rid of him,' he ordered, turning on his side and propping himself up on an elbow and resting the side of his head on his hand as he studied her reaction.

Excuse me? The mere suggestion was absurd and Eileen could barely believe her ears. Anyone would think he was discussing a mouldy item of food in the fridge as opposed to her husband of twenty-five years.

'And how exactly do you propose I do that?' She had no intention of doing any such thing, but was curious nonetheless to hear Tod's disillusioned thoughts on the matter.

'I dunno, divorce him, kick him out, who cares?' Tod certainly didn't. His mother had seemed to find moving on from man to man easy enough so he couldn't understand what Eileen's problem was. If you wanted something badly enough in life, you fought for it. End of.

Sex. Twice. Admittedly good sex, but was he deluded? Did he really think she would replace her husband over one quick fumble at the swimming baths followed up with a session of dicky doctors at home? Judging by the look of sheer conviction written all over his face, that was exactly what he thought and she shifted uncomfortably under the dead weight of his arm, which now lay possessively across her waist. This man in her bed, in her husband's bed, spelled D.A.N.G.E.R. How had she not seen this coming? She had to make him leave. Now.

'I can't just kick him out, Tod,' she snapped as she extracted herself from his embrace. 'It's his house for starters,' she muttered as she walked to the ensuite, desperate to wash every last bit of filth of him from her body.

Eileen's attitude was starting to make him feel twitchy. Did she really think someone like him would be interested in someone like her without good reason? Any day now, he would be homeless. She owed him. Climbing from the bed, Tod followed her into the bathroom and pressed his nakedness up against hers from behind. As his hands wandered down her body, he gently nuzzled the back of her neck the way he knew she liked and sure enough, she soon leaned back against him and gasped.

'We could kill him,' he whispered in her ear, his tongue gently tickling her lobe as he did so, but then she pushed him away. The fucking bitch just shoved him away like he was nothing and his eyes scanned the bathroom shelves for something – anything he could use to threaten her with and make her see sense.

'Have you completely lost your mind?' Eileen glared incredulously at her lover, their nudity now feeling totally inappropriate and giving her a vulnerability she didn't much care for. Pushing him aside, she reached to the back of the bathroom door and grabbed both towelling robes. Chucking the first at him, she hastily shrugged herself into the other.

Deep breaths, deep breaths. Listening to the voice in his head, Tod duly obliged. *Talk her round. Make her see sense.* He licked his lips before continuing, aware that he needed to word the next part carefully if he were going to persuade her to go along with his plan.

'You'd be surprised how easy it is to accidentally consume something toxic, Eileen. You could kill a whole football team with the contents from under your kitchen sink alone.' He reached out to touch her arm, but she yanked it away.

Jesus Christ! Who in their right mind even knew this kind of stuff, let alone considered utilising that knowledge?

As though reading her thoughts, he carried on. 'I Googled it. Downstairs on your computer the other day.'

When? How? Oh dear God. The other day when he'd dropped in unannounced. Said he was just passing. She'd left him alone in the room to his own devices whilst she made him a coffee. She now stared at the only man beside her husband that she had ever allowed into her marital bed with absolute horror. *Love is blind.* That was the saying, wasn't it? Well, lust clearly didn't help you to think all that straight either as it turned out, she thought to herself.

'And once we've killed him, what then?' she demanded. Tod looked up at her, encouraged that she seemed to be coming around to the idea, but then she continued, unable to hide the contempt from her voice. 'They seize the bloody computer for analysis, that's what. Find out what you've done and bingo. We go down for life. For God's sake, Tod, how could you be so stupid?' she spat. 'Now get out.'

Shocked at her tone and the emotions it created inside him, Tod didn't move. She was just like his mother after all, standing there screaming and treating him like an idiot. *How dare you do this to me?* He trembled with rage, his cheeks flushed with an angry crimson as he glared at the floor. Scared to blink for fear of releasing the tears of fury and years of frustration that welled deep inside him and threatened to escape, he waited in vain for an apology.

'I said, GET OUT!' Eileen yelled, jabbing her finger towards the door and as though registering her venom for the first time, Tod rushed from the bathroom and retrieving his discarded clothing from around the bedroom, he dressed as quickly as he could. How had it all gone so wrong? Why didn't she want him? After his earlier performance, she was supposed to beg him to stay. Flashbacks of his mother screaming at him and telling him how useless he was bounced uncontrollably around his brain like a pinball. She hadn't loved him either.

As the self-pity overwhelmed him, the floodgates opened and once the tears started, they wouldn't stop.

Sensing his pain, Buddy slunk up beside him and nudged him with his muzzle as though trying to reassure him and Tod knelt down on the floor a moment, almost childlike as he buried his face in the dog's fur and squeezed him tight. It felt good, therapeutic, and after a while, once his sobs had died down and his breathing returned to normal, Tod lifted his face from Buddy's neck and wiped at the remaining tears with the back of his sleeve.

And then he spotted it. The heel of one of Eileen's shoes poking out from under the bed and he lunged forward and grabbed it, groping around with his free hand until it settled on the other. It wasn't much, but it would at least be something to remind him of what could have been when he lay in bed alone later in the dark, empty squalor of his bedsit. He might even sell them. Raise some funds that way since selling EJ's shoes was no longer an option.

Eyeing Buddy conspiratorially, content in the knowledge that he couldn't tell on him even if he wanted to, Tod slowly raised a shoe to his face and inhaled deeply, wallowing for a second in Eileen's comforting scent as it caressed his nostrils. The click of the bathroom lock indicated that she was coming then, spurring him on. Tucking the shoes firmly under one arm, Tod gave the dog one last gentle pat as he rushed from the room and down the stairs without so much as a final backward glance.

22

No sooner had he positioned himself back behind the wheel, a movement out of the corner of his eye caught his attention and Lucas glanced sideways to see Lou marching purposefully down the small path and out onto the street. She looked angry, upset even, and he sat and watched a moment, unsure as to what he should do and whether or not he should intervene at all.

As though on auto pilot, he turned the key in the ignition and putting the car into first gear, pulled slowly out from his hiding place and crawled gently behind her, careful to keep a safe distance whilst he tried to figure out what to do for the best. Explaining his presence here wasn't going to be easy, but what choice did he have? If she had turned up to meet him as arranged, none of this would have been necessary.

Driver's window now fully open, Lucas slowed down and quietly trailed behind her as she continued her course down the pavement, seemingly so preoccupied she didn't even notice that she was being followed. *Worrying. One woman murdered, the killer still at large. She should be more careful.* As though reading his mind, Lou sped up her step and worried he might have scared her, he called out.

'Pssst. Lou, it's me.' She stopped and turned and to his utter horror and dismay, he realised she'd been crying. 'Lou?' He unclipped his belt and climbed from the car as fast as he could, placing a sympathetic hand on her shoulder as he guided her towards the passenger seat. Opening the door and helping her in, he fastened her belt before making his way back to the driver's side. They both sat there a moment, lost in their own thoughts until Lucas finally broke the silence.

'Want to talk about it?'

'Not really,' she sniffed, yanking her headphones from her head and wrapping the lead tightly around them before stuffing them in her coat pocket.

Please God… let the new boyfriend have fucked up. Lucas wasn't sure he even believed in God, but what harm could praying to him do at any rate? Nothing ventured, nothing gained.

'Still up for that beer?' *Better late than never.*

She wrinkled her nose in disgust and he cringed as it occurred to him how little he truly knew about her. He didn't even know what she liked to drink, or how many sugars, if any, she took in her tea. She didn't discuss that kind of thing on Facebook.

'Or something,' he added, hoping that she would still take the bait.

She did. 'If you like,' she shrugged, and feeling a swell of relief threaten to implode in his chest, he pressed down hard on the accelerator and headed in the general direction of town. Lucas didn't actually care where they went, just so long as she went with him, and was determined to get there as soon as possible before she had the chance to change her mind.

'I'm sorry about your mum.' As she spoke, she reached out and placed a hand on his thigh, a tiny current of hope running through his soul as she did so. He didn't move, instead opting to concentrate on the road ahead, terrified to react for fear of destroying the moment. At face value, the passing comment was extremely ordinary under the circumstances, but there was no doubt in his mind that her apology ran much deeper. Almost twelve months ago now, his mother had passed away in the hospital where Lou worked as a cleaner. It was Lou who had accidentally unplugged the machine that was keeping his mother alive in preference of the hoover.

'Thanks.' He cringed at the mindless comment that carried a separate underlying meaning. *Is this how it's going to be from now on?* Stilted sentences and dwelling on the past? Lucas hadn't wanted his mother to die, of course he hadn't, but nobody should be kept alive against their will. What proud and self-respecting woman would choose to be mentally and physically dependent on their only child? Not his mother, of that he was certain, and her unexpected release from that pain and fear was everything he could have wished for and more.

They drove the rest of the journey in silence, both lost in their own thoughts until after what seemed like an eternity, music pumping out into the evening air from a large building up ahead signalled that it would be as good a place as any to stop.

The pub was heaving, bodies pushing and shoving awkwardly at the bar like groupies at a concert in their desperation to be served next, and the odour of stale beer and sweat soaked into the atmosphere and lingered in the air. A band of four youths, none of whom looked old enough to be in the joint and all of whom looked like they were off their faces on drugs, desperately clutched at their guitars and microphones as they performed a peculiar mix of rock and soul that frankly didn't work on the improvised stage in the far corner. Lucas took a hold of Lou's arm for fear he'd lose her in the crowd and fought his way in the general direction of the bar, wishing above all else that he had taken her somewhere quieter.

Ten minutes later, as she pressed her body up against his in an effort to avoid being shoved from behind by a drunken reveller carrying four pints in his hands and spilling half of the contents across the already tacky floor as he approached his drinking buddies, Lucas decided that coming here hadn't been such a bad idea after all. It felt good just being here with her, knowing that this room full of strangers would automatically assume that they were a couple and he possessively placed a hand on the base of her spine as though to somehow confirm the fact to anyone who might be intending to make an unwanted approach.

With each drink that she consumed, Lou visibly relaxed more. As she slowly moved her hips in time to the music, she was clearly enjoying herself, not even seeming to mind that every now and then an unwitting member of the crowd jostled her into his arms. As she sipped at her drink and smiled up at him, Lucas had never wanted something or someone so much in all his life. The urge to take her in his arms, to touch her skin with his own and to taste her lips grew, but he knew he must wait. Finally, he decided to broach the subject of why they were here.

'What happened, Lou?'

'He ruined my life!' she declared, the venom in her voice taking him by surprise.

'Who?' *The new boyfriend?* A flash of envy stabbed at his heart, the burning flare of hatred for this imposter competing with the tiny dash of hope that he was in with a chance after all. 'Is this about your new boyfriend?' He finally trusted himself to mention him.

'Boyfriend? What boyfriend?' Her hot breath as her lips lightly brushed his ear was incredibly arousing as she leaned in and shouted over the music.

'But the woman behind the reception said you left with some bloke.' Lucas shook his head in confusion.

'Peter,' she interrupted. 'I finished early so Peter kindly offered me a lift.'

'Who's Peter?' Lucas was doing his best to keep the jealousy at bay, but the mere mention of his competitor was all it took for the little green-eyed monster to erupt to the surface once more.

'A friend, he works there. I think.'

'You think?' Lucas was seething. How could the man possibly be a friend if she didn't even know where he worked?

'I did call, Lucas. I left you a voicemail and everything. I wasn't comfortable hanging around. Peter reckoned he'd seen some bloke waiting outside the exit and after what happened the other day, I freaked. He couldn't wait with me because he had elsewhere he needed to be, so he thought it best to drop me home. That's why I was so upset. I was really looking forward to tonight, but I was scared. Convinced that freak was biding his time before he attacked me again.'

Voicemail. What with everything else, being so angry and upset when he thought she'd stood him up, he'd forgotten he had a message. Had Malcolm been lurking around outside the hospital waiting for her? He'd bloody kill him if he found out that he had. Determined to put the evening back on track, he reached forward and placed a hand on the side of her waist, gently stroking his thumb backwards and forwards against her stomach. His breath caught in his chest and he could have danced a little happy dance right there and then when she made no attempt to pull away or remove it.

'Have you arrested him yet?' Lou meanwhile wanted answers. It was a risk lying to Lucas, but the parking pig needed to be punished and she could see no other way.

Malcolm Muldoon. The name reverberated around his skull. No sooner did he get it out of his head, someone or something put it right back. *As though it somehow belongs there.*

'He's claiming you attacked him. I know, I know,' Lucas continued, holding the palms of his hands up to her as though making a symbolic gesture of surrender. 'It's crazy. He's crazy, but without witnesses, there's little we can do.'

'There was a witness. The bitch who stole my boots,' Lou spat, her cheeks flushing an angry crimson as she looked down and concentrated intently on her vodka and coke. *What if the other witnesses come forward and tell him the truth?*

'A witness whose face you never saw!' He reached forward and gingerly tucked a strand of hair that had fallen free from the restraints of its tie behind her ear with his fingers. He wanted to help, really he did, but what did she expect him to do without so much as a description of this other person who Malcolm was claiming was a figment of her imagination?

Has he figured out the truth? Is that why he isn't helping? Panic gripped at Lou's guts. If she didn't do something, if Lucas didn't do something, the man was going to walk free. After everything he had done. *Over my dead body*, she thought to herself vehemently. She needed to up her game, that's what she needed to do – make him want to help her.

Idiot. Furious with himself, Lucas shook his head bitterly. *Why wasn't I there to protect her? I'm always there to protect her!* But then Lou slowly leaned towards him and gently touched his lips with her own. Terrified he might have misread the moment and of being rejected, he didn't respond at first but then her lips found his again. He couldn't breathe, nor did he dare move for fear he would spoil the moment and break the spell, but unable to control himself a moment longer as her lips grazed his own he eventually groaned quietly before responding. Gently at first until no longer able to control the swelling in his chest and throbbing in his groin, he pulled her closer to him and forced his lips down hard on hers as his tongue explored her mouth in search of hers.

23

It had been a busy, if not productive, few hours and as Rita rushed to the appointed rendezvous, she hoped above all else that Malcolm would have waited. That Malcolm would have considered she was worth the wait. As she rounded the bend in her new Jimmy Choo boots, which she knew only too well he would appreciate in all of their glory, she wasn't to be disappointed.

'Darling, I can't apologise enough.' She leaned forward on tippy-toe and gave him a lingering peck on each cheek.

'Mwah… Mwah.' She stood back then, holding him at arm's length as her eyes digested him from head to foot. *Very swish.* She liked a man who took care of his appearance. 'Did you get my message?' she whispered provocatively at him, her lips just millimetres away from his own.

Is she drunk? She seems a little strange. Still, he couldn't exactly judge. He'd downed a few himself over the past couple of hours by way of Dutch courage. Malcolm hopped nervously from foot to foot and flushed with embarrassment at her extravagantly affectionate gesture. 'I did, I did,' he exclaimed, her earlier tardiness instantly forgotten.

'Shall we?' She cupped her arm, inviting him to link his own with hers as they made their way down towards the high street and the thriving nightlife beyond.

Twenty minutes later, sat in the far corner of one of the new bistros that Malcolm had been reading about in the local rag, their appointed table benefited from a superior view of the restaurant and out onto the lit-up street beyond. Not that it mattered personally to Malcolm. He was more than content with the view that sat opposite him at the table. A bottle of iced Chablis sat in the bucket between them, half consumed glasses apiece in front of them, and he nervously studied the beads of condensation that trickled down the sides and formed small pools of damp on the linen tablecloth as he desperately tried to think of the best way to broach the subject.

'What's she like?' It was eventually Rita who broke the silence.

Malcolm reached into his jacket pocket and retrieving his wallet, he produced a small photograph and pushed it across the table towards her. Rita stared down at the faded picture. It had clearly been taken years ago, but still, there was no mistaking the youthful innocence and exuberance that radiated back at her from the crumpled page.

'She's not like I pictured,' she responded, a stab of unexpected jealousy piercing her chest as she studied the woman's features closely. When Malcolm had blurted out the sordid details of his predicament earlier in the street, Rita didn't know what she had expected, but it wasn't this. The woman seemed positively *normal*. 'She doesn't look like a murderer,' she stuttered indignantly, unable to hide her disappointment.

'Tracie Andrews. Rose West. The Giggling Granny. None of them were branded with the words *I'm a killer* on their foreheads either.' Malcolm shuffled awkwardly in his seat and licked his lips nervously as he studied Rita's face and tried to decide whether or not now was a good time to broach his plan with her.

'What will you do?'

What will I do? Not wishing to voice the words aloud for fear of any future witness coming forward and claiming to have overheard him say them, he extracted the note he had prepared earlier from his jacket pocket and pressed the paper with his fingers as though to iron out the folds before placing it on the table in front of her.

'You're going to kill your wife?' Rita exclaimed loudly, too loudly, and Malcolm fidgeted uncomfortably in his chair and glared angrily at her.

'Sssh. Keep your voice down,' he hissed as he spotted the waitress approach the table. Looking away guiltily he scratched vigorously with his finger at an invisible mark on the tablecloth.

The waitress, meanwhile, having overheard the whole exchange, almost spilled the contents of the sharing platter of salami and chorizo with home-baked breads and dipping sauces on the table in her haste to extract herself from the strange couple as soon as she could.

They sat in awkward silence until the waitress had disappeared from earshot, and Rita reached for her glass of wine and downed the contents in one large gulp. The ice-cold liquid created a burning sensation in her chest and sent a much-needed hit to her brain. Eventually she trusted herself to speak.

'You're going to kill your wife?' She whispered the words this time, unable to resist checking over her shoulder that no one was within hearing distance. As she turned her attention back to Malcolm, she studied his face for a reaction, desperate for some kind of indication as to whether he was all talk, or in fact actually capable of the cold-blooded murder of his wife.

Conscious of the thin layer of sweat forming on his forehead and upper lip, Malcolm reached for the bottle of wine and dutifully replenished her glass. *I need you, Rita. Without you, I'll be the number one suspect. With you, I'll have an irrefutable alibi.* He chose his words carefully.

'You said it yourself. What choice do I have if she's intent on killing me?'

Rita didn't recall saying any such thing, but she let it go. Was it so bad? It wasn't as though she had to be personally involved and if the man was intent on killing his wife, who was she to stand in his way? It wasn't as though she could stop him even if she wanted to, after all. Was this the opportunity she had waited her whole lifetime for? She'd seen the Mercedes. She'd seen the way he flashed his cash around as though money were no object. Fate had seemingly chucked them together and just when she had finally come to accept that she would never be allowed to be truly happy, there was every possibility she could be just that.

Only if Eileen is removed from the equation, the voice nagged. Was it really possible to want something so much you would be prepared to go to any levels to achieve it? Rita wasn't physically attracted to Malcolm, she never would be. He quite simply wasn't her type. *You wouldn't have to live with him,* she assured herself. Plenty of couples lived perfectly healthy lives apart these days, didn't they? No doubt they also recognised the fact that there was far more to life and maintaining a solid relationship than sex.

Money doesn't buy happiness, dear. Her mother's words echoed in her mind and she scoffed inwardly. *Well, lack of it hasn't made me very happy either, Mother.* Suddenly, the knowledge that Malcolm had the ability to give her everything she had ever craved was so overwhelming, it was suffocating. Was she finally being offered the chance of a lifestyle she'd only ever dared dream about? A lifestyle that she deserved.

Only if Eileen is removed from the equation, the voice echoed.

24

Crunching his way through a tube of Extra Strong Mints as a preventative measure in case he was stopped by the police, Malcolm traversed his car through the back country lanes in the dark as he made his alternative detour home.

He felt ridiculously light-headed and had no idea whether he was drunk on the euphoria or because he'd had one too many glasses of wine. Either way, he probably should have ordered a taxi home instead of electing to drive when he finally dragged his reluctant feet from under the table he had shared with Rita. He couldn't believe how angry with her he had been and felt exceptionally foolish now about his little outburst, particularly since, as it turned out, she had made several attempts to contact him and let him know that she was running late.

Corked, the spit and sawdust-style bistro come wine bar where they had spent the evening, had been a most peculiar place – not his cup of tea at all – but entering the establishment with such a spectacular-looking woman attached to his arm had soon alleviated any concerns that he might have otherwise had. Besides, nothing had been normal about the past few days and so doing something completely different and out of character had seemed like the most natural thing in the world.

Lightning never strikes twice. Meet Joe Black, wasn't it? He liked that film. He liked it a lot. Anthony Hopkins played a great part – not as slick or as smart as Hannibal Lecter in

Silence of the Lambs, but extremely exciting nonetheless. 'I'm having an old friend for dinner.' His shoulders shook as he chuckled at the memory. *Lightning could strike*. Was that it? He couldn't remember the exact saying now, but no matter. Both were correct. Lightning had struck and within minutes in Rita's company, Malcolm had known that she was the one: the woman he wanted to spend the rest of his life and grow old with. His feelings for Eileen had literally paled in significance. Eileen was a mere rumble of thunder compared to the tempestuous tornado that swirled through his veins and groin every time he so much as thought about Rita.

And the feeling was mutual. He shuffled in his seat like an overexcited child. 'The feeling is actually mutual!' he declared, as though to reiterate the fact and make it more definite. But Rita was a lady, make no mistake. When Malcolm had suggested checking into a hotel, she had wanted to, he could tell by the look on her face. But she had declined. Said it was too soon and she was right of course. *All good things come to those that wait,* he reminded himself.

The trouble was, much as he had enjoyed every last minute of his time with Rita, he was now feeling increasingly frustrated, a situation that wasn't helped by the fact that Eileen had been starving him of his basic marital entitlements. Malcolm wasn't an impulsive man, never had been. He preferred a daily agenda to adhere to with no room for unscheduled deviations, but in that split second of madness, there was no denying how deliciously reckless he felt as he indicated left and pulled into the lay-by to relieve himself.

Rita exceeded his expectations, as he had known that she would. Riding him like a competitive jockey determined to come first, about to pass the winning line, Malcolm failed to notice the glare of headlights reflecting in his rear-view mirror. Neither did he notice the face pressed up against the driver's window until, completely throwing him off his stride at the crucial moment, a solitary knuckle rapped hard against it.

It was little solace to Malcolm that the police officer didn't breathalyse him. The whole sorry episode had instantly sobered him up at any rate and receiving a warning for indecent exposure in a public place was more than enough embarrassment for one night. Not to mention the trouble he would be in if Eileen ever got wind of the incident.

As he pulled into the driveway, gravel crunching beneath his tyres and alerting her to the fact that he was finally home, Malcolm couldn't miss the unmistakeable twitch of the curtains, which only served to confirm that his latest misdemeanour was the least of his problems. Taking his time, he slowly walked towards the front door and quietly let himself in.

25

True to form, Malcolm hadn't even had time to hang up his jacket on the back of the chair before Eileen started on him.

'Your dinner's in the dog,' she spat angrily as she took another slug from her glass, the tell-tale line of deep purple around the rim of her lips a good indication that she had already had more than her recommended daily allowance.

Obviously didn't tamper with it if it was good enough for the dog to eat, he thought to himself. 'We discussed this earlier, my love. I was eating out with my colleagues, remember?' He spoke through gritted teeth, furious with his wife for attempting to spoil what had been such a perfect evening.

Of course she remembered, did he think she was senile? If Eileen was entirely honest with herself, it wasn't Malcolm she was actually angry with at all, just the fact that he had inadvertently caused the whole argument with Tod in the first place. The truth was, she was spoiling for a fight. She wanted somebody to blame and her husband fitted the bill perfectly. Had he been a proper husband over the past few months, none of this would have happened.

'Well?' she asked indignantly.

'Well, what?' Malcolm snapped, reaching for a glass from the cupboard over the sink and quickly pouring himself a large measure. He didn't want another drink. He wanted to take himself off to bed and dream sweet thoughts about Rita, but if his wife was determined to have a confrontation, masking any remaining smell of alcohol lingering on his breath would be a good idea. Reducing her consumption levels for the evening would of course also be an added bonus.

'What did the doctor say?'

The doctor. What with everything else, he'd completely forgotten about him.

'I'll live.'

'More's the pity.' There she went again, mumbling under her breath. Did she think he was deaf?

'What else did he say? That can't be it.' Eileen took another large swig of wine, failing to notice that she had spilled half of it down the front of her blouse as she glared at him, her eyes demanding the answers he was terrified to disclose.

'He gave me a prescription. One capsule, twice a day for seven days and if I'm no better, he wants me to make another appointment.'

'And does this mystery illness of yours that's affecting you and everyone else around you have a name?' Eileen studied her husband, the look of disappointment and disdain written all over her face, and Malcolm braced himself. She wasn't going to like it. Not one little bit.

'Piles, Eileen,' he said. 'I've got piles.'

***

Half an hour later, hands shaking with anger, Malcolm poured a large tumbler of brandy and swiftly downed the contents before promptly refilling the glass with another equally generous measure. Well aware that Eileen's glass was once again empty, he didn't bother to offer her a top-up. She had clearly had more than enough already.

How could she be so bloody unreasonable? Any proper, self-respecting wife would be pleased that their husband was suffering with piles, but not Eileen. *Oh no!* God forbid she be grateful that it was nothing more serious.

He glared menacingly at her from across the room, the blood pumping from his brain and pounding loudly in his ears as the realisation dawned on him once more. *She wants me dead.* Eileen wanted him dead and what Eileen wanted, Eileen usually got. He wouldn't be surprised if Ronnie had already filled her in on all the sordid details earlier and this was why she was in such a mood – because now she would have to do the dirty deed herself.

Malcolm eyed her suspiciously as she stood up. She swayed awkwardly on her feet until she caught her balance, all the while gripping the neck of the bottle tightly as though it were a weapon as she made her way towards where he stood, framed between a chair and the sink. He stroked the back of the chair nervously, Rita's words of earlier echoing in his ears.

'You're going to kill your wife.' Of course, she'd posed the statement as a question, but the underlying assertion hadn't been lost on him. He felt his heartbeat speed up and his breath lodge somewhere in his chest as Eileen approached, the only audible sounds now the soothing whir of the refrigerator, followed by the tell-tale clunk as she leaned across him and discarded the bottle in the sink with the others before turning to leave the room.

Malcolm didn't move at first, not even sure that his feet would have obeyed even if he wanted them to. Instead, he stood stock still, listening to each ominous footfall as she commenced her deliberate ascent up the stairs, each step that she made echoing the hammering in his chest.

As though in slow motion, he watched Buddy lift himself from his basket and quietly slink from the room in search of his mistress, but still Malcolm didn't move, lacking the confidence that she wouldn't have a change of heart and thunder back down the stairs to attack him. Only when the sound of plumbing running through the pipes as she prepared herself for bed stopped and the house took on a deathly quiet did he finally dare to slip through the darkness towards his office, pushing the door hard towards the hinges to prevent them creaking and awaking her.

She wants you dead. The words vibrated over and over in his brain, everything suddenly falling into place and making perfect sense: her recent behaviour; the cool, calculating way she had been treating him; the failed murder attempt with the pillow; the search history on the computer; and the affair – *oh yes, I know all about that, thank you very much!* He couldn't lie down beside her and get a good night's sleep now if he tried.

Rita had advised turning to Google for assistance and so that was what he did. Working solidly throughout the night, his face illuminated by the soft glow that emanated from the computer screen, he carried out his research. Only when the first light of day broke and the birds started to sing did Malcolm finally sit back and assess his list one final time before he logged off and shut down the computer.

26

Hands firmly ensconced in his trouser pockets, Lucas rocked back and forth on the heels of his shoes and tried to rid his concerns about Lou from his mind by concentrating instead on the job in hand. The building was a dump, no two ways about it, and the urge to heave was immense as the foul concoction of piss, stale tobacco and skunk assaulted his nostrils. With no maintenance having been carried out for months if not longer, it didn't bode well for the lift that was currently rumbling behind the walls as it clattered its course to the ground floor. Where were the stairs at any rate? He felt sure there must be some. It would be totally illegal to have no proper means of escape from fire, but then judging by the state of the rest of the building, Lucas couldn't help but wonder whether the landlord gave a damn about such a minor technicality.

Another victim. Another corpse with underwear strung carelessly around her neck as though to imply strangulation. Another person inadvertently connected to Malcolm Muldoon. Coincidence? Lucas didn't believe such a thing existed. Neither did his colleague Sam, and he for one was looking forward to hearing her thoughts when she got wind of Malcolm's connection to this latest victim.

Some little old lady in the flat opposite, a Doris Dowell, had apparently made the gruesome discovery. Over the course of the weekend, her cat had gone missing. Doris claimed that she had knocked on the victim's door to no avail several times over the past forty-eight hours. It was still unclear why, or even how, Doris came to discover that the door was unlocked, or what had eventually made her enter the flat without invitation during the early hours of the morning.

Grinding his teeth nervously, Lucas tried to focus on the mildew painted patterns that fought against the nicotine stained walls for pride of place as he deliberately avoided catching the eye of what must surely be Britain's most heavily tattooed man who stood eyeing him curiously as they both awaited the lift. His mind inexplicably wandered back to Lou. He couldn't seem to help it, and however hard he tried to dismiss the thoughts, they just kept popping back. Was there something going on that he didn't know about? Last night, he had tried to broach the subject of Peter again, but she had just got all defensive and accused him of being ridiculous. *She doth protest too much!* Lucas wasn't sure whether it was good old-fashioned gut instinct or copper's nose, but he knew when he was being lied to, and Lou was lying.

As he stepped into the lift and the doors juddered angrily behind him and his travelling companion, Lucas tried not to let his nerves get the better of him but it was impossible. *What if it breaks down again?* He brushed irritably at the thin film of sweat forming on his upper lip with the back of his sleeve and tried to ignore the set of eyes that bore a pair of holes into his forehead as they studied him from the other side of their small prison.

'You wiv' the filth?' It came as no surprise when the man finally spoke. It had been written all over his face that he had been itching to say something since he'd joined him on the ground floor, and Lucas couldn't help but think it had probably taken him all that time to string the sentence together in his head. Not liking to agree to such a derogatory term, Lucas chose not to speak. Instead, he simply nodded as he gazed vacantly at the rotten threadbare carpet and tried not to think too hard about what he might be about to witness in flat number 203.

'Dreadful business,' the man continued, shaking his head from side to side.

'You knew the victim?' The last thing Lucas wanted to do was strike up a conversation with this dreadful man, but if he had something to say, he would prefer he just spat it out now than have to hunt him down for questioning at a later date.

'Nah. Not sure no one knew Hannah as it goes. Kept herself to herself like... although...' the man added as an afterthought.

'Although what?' *What did you see?* There was something about the look on the man's face that told Lucas he wasn't messing with him. Something had occurred to him and he needed to know what. Only then could he decide whether or not it was information he should be sharing with the rest of the team.

'There was this one woman, started coming 'ere... ooh, now let me think about that a sec.'

A woman? Not what he had been expecting. Lucas breathed deeply and tried not to let his impatience get the better of him as he waited for the man to continue.

'A week or so it'd be she started hanging around... maybe more,' the man continued. 'Couple of weeks maybe. Yeah, that's more like it. Never came in, mind, just hung around outside in the shadows waiting for Hannah.' He winked knowingly at Lucas and nudged him with his elbow before continuing. 'Thought she might be, well, you know...' He leant in and whispered as though he was about to swear. 'One of them minge munchers. Wasn't like you ever saw Hannah wiv' a boyfriend or nuffin' so it stood to reason.'

Eloquent. Lucas eyed the man with distaste as the lift finally landed on the twelfth floor with a huge thud and wobbled, reminding him of an aeroplane experiencing turbulence. Thanking him for the information, he noted down the man's name and flat number before making his way towards the victim's apartment. It wasn't hard to find, the blue and white tape that cordoned off the entrance to keep curious neighbours who might risk contaminating the scene at bay standing out like a flashing neon sign in a dark, deserted street.

Even from the other end of the hallway, Lucas could make out Sam. Beyond her, he could also just about see two scenes-of-crime officers working within the flat itself. He stepped forward and walked purposely towards them, all the while daring to hope that the victim's final hours hadn't got too messy. Even after all this time, Lucas had never quite been able to develop the stomach for studying a murdered body close up.

'Ello? Oy, you!' The raised voice calling from the other end of the corridor behind him made Lucas stop dead in his tracks. *What does the bigoted little prick want now?* He turned, swinging himself around on the heels of his shoes, but made no effort to walk back towards the man who he had dared to hope he'd seen the last of as he had exited the lift just seconds before.

'Can I help… Sir?' His tongue jammed against his teeth at the inappropriateness of the last word. To call this man Sir was tantamount to calling that Vicky Pollard creature from *Little Britain* a lady.

'I just remembered…' The man scratched at his privates as he ambled down the corridor towards Lucas, the mere gesture alone making Lucas develop a nervous itch of his own. 'Can't believe I almost forgot, to be honest. Like I said, Hannah never 'ad man friends, so to speak, but now's I come to think about it, there was a bloke.'

A bloke? Now that *was* what he had been expecting. *Come on, come on,* he urged the man to continue. *Did he, or did he not fit the description of Malcolm Muldoon?*

'Nice chap he was, friendly enough.' *No accounting for taste,* Lucas supposed.

'Thursday night I'think it was, or it might have been Wednesday. Or was it Friday? Well, I don't suppose it matters in the grand scheme of things, but I thought I'd best mention it.'

Was this guy for real? Of course it mattered. The victim was last seen alive on Friday. If a man was seen loitering around her flat on the very same evening, it mattered a great deal. Notebook in hand, Lucas started to jot down details. He was a bit sketchy with some of them whilst elaborating on others, but since the guy seemed to be struggling to remember, he didn't see that becoming too much of a problem.

'Anything you can tell me about this man? Distinguishing features?' he asked pointedly.

'Well, yeah, now you come to mention it. He had a hat on, one of them beanie things. And jeans. And a T-shirt. Yeah, that's right, a navy T-shirt, or it might have been dark purple, black even, I'm a bit colour blind see, but it struck me as strange. What with it being as cold as it's been of late.'

Lucas dutifully made a note on his pad. It was surprising what you thought you would remember only to find that you had completely forgotten at the crucial moment. *Hat: Fedora? Trilby? Panama? Medium build. Approx. 50 yrs of age. Smartly dressed: overcoat, suit and tie.*

It was hardly the stuff of *Mastermind* since the information could fit at least half of the male population in the country let alone Cliffborough Cross, but just so long as the detail also applied to Malcolm Muldoon, that was all that really mattered. So what if it wasn't true? Malcolm was obviously responsible and the only witness to date was clearly an imbecile. If it took a little helping hand to convince his colleagues of Malcolm's guilt, then so be it.

The heavy wooden fire door to number 203 was propped

open by a dusty old fire extinguisher borrowed from a bracket from the adjoining wall, and out of curiosity Lucas couldn't resist a peek at the servicing information on the small, wilted label that was peeling from the smooth surface. Almost three years since it had been attended to – not that this came as any surprise given the state of the rest of the place – and he had a good mind to register a formal complaint with the Fire Authority. But for now, he had more pressing matters to attend to.

Quickly sliding into the obligatory protective suit and Tyvek shoes, Lucas slipped on a set of Latex gloves and tentatively stepped over the threshold and into the depths of the small apartment, instantly struck by the overall cleanliness of it in stark contrast to the filth of the corridors just a few metres away. In fact, it was fair to say that the only out-of-place item that made the otherwise immaculate living space look untidy was the woman's dead body, which was now currently being prepared for its transfer to the morgue.

The victim looked peaceful, so much so that she could just have been sleeping or resting her eyes. Something he supposed would provide little solace to her nearest and dearest, one of whom in particular would be required to formally identify the body in due course. Lucas looked up to see Sam approach in her own set of mandatory protective gear that mirrored his own.

'Alright.' They both spoke in unison, before Lucas continued.

'Please tell me we haven't got a serial killer on our hands.' He didn't look at her as he spoke, his brain too busy as it greedily stored every last piece of evidence available to his eyes.

'No can do.' Sam shook her head ruefully at him before continuing. 'Way the pathologist's talking, I think you'll find we might have exactly that.'

Lucas felt his guts gurgle and bowels loosen at the news. If he was going to put Malcolm in the frame, he was going to need a lot more than a flimsy description from a forgetful neighbour for evidence.

'What do we know?' *Ladies first.* See what Sam had discovered about the situation then he would decide what information he would or wouldn't impart.

'He was careful,' Sam replied. 'The boys are turning the place inside out for prints. Not looking good mind, look at the place.' Sam waved her hands around the small but immaculate space as though to make her point. 'No sign of a struggle, no sign of any sexual interference, no sign of fucking anything except we've got ourselves another stiff with underwear – this time a bra wrapped around her neck.'

He. The word bellowed in his eardrums. What about the lady friend? Was this lady friend also a lady-killer?

'Poison?' he asked. Thallium, a known component of rat poison, which was also more commonly found in household items such as hair removal creams and kitchen cleaning products, had been responsible for EJ's death. It was still unknown whether the killer strangled for kicks or as a feeble attempt to cover up the actual cause of death.

Sam nodded towards the pathologist before continuing. 'Reckon so, but she's not saying much 'til they've got her back to the lab.' Lucas' eyes wavered to Erika. He wasn't a personal fan and was confident that the feeling was mutual.

'Time of death?'

'You know what she's like.' Sam nudged her head in Erika's direction as she spoke. 'Won't be specific at this stage, only that it was definitely sometime on Friday evening.'

'What do we know about the victim?'

'Hannah Gregory. Thirty-five years old. Lived alone. No boyfriend, no girlfriend, no nothing.'

There may have been both. Lucas opened his mouth to speak

but thought better of it. Perhaps it was best to see where the investigation led them before sending the team on a wild goose chase involving an unreliable witness who couldn't even remember what day of the week he may have seen the possible suspects.

'Mother died last year – car crash.' Sam raised an eyebrow before continuing. 'Literally.' Car crash had always been their code for a messy death. 'Victim clearly inherited some money but presumably didn't trust the banks with it or didn't want to lose her benefits. Been claiming up until recently when she got a job at the retail park.'

Retail park. So his colleague had already ascertained where she worked. How long before she realised that Malcolm Muldoon also worked in the vicinity and was a very likely candidate for the crime? Lucas remained silent, hoping to glean as much as he could in the little time afforded to them.

'Father's Colin Gregory. Name ring a bell?' Sam shook her head ruefully at Lucas as she spoke. 'The one Mad Muldoon locked in the basement over the conservatory wrangle.' *Not very long at all 'til she suspects Malcolm,* he thought to himself, unable to disguise the small wry smile at the prospect.

They would pay the store a visit next, that was standard procedure and maybe, just maybe, they could pop in and see Malcolm personally whilst they were on the estate. See what he had to say for himself and ascertain his whereabouts during the estimated time of death. Perhaps even shock him so badly by turning up when he would least be expecting them that he would cave in and confess his involvement.

'How much money was there?' Lucas asked, as a thought occurred to him.

'They're still counting it.' Sam gestured towards the two officers across the far end of the lounge. 'Almost two grand so far. Hid it all under there.' She pointed to the sofa that lined the far wall as she spoke.

'So we know it wasn't a sexual or financially motivated crime.' Exasperation and hatred devoured his intestines. *Malcolm Muldoon.* Once again, the name thundered through his brain, making it ache. *You wouldn't kill for money would you, Malcolm? You wouldn't need to. Not anymore.*

27

Eileen eyed her husband suspiciously as he flapped around the stove preparing the brunch, humming and rhythmically tapping his foot in sync to the music as it streamed effortlessly into the room from the integrated system in the hall. She had no idea who the artist was, but the words were frankly most inappropriate and sipping from her glass of juice, she frowned as though hearing them for the first time.

Sliced her up and buried her? Permitting such a blatant confession on live radio to the gruesome murder of one's wife was surely, totally unethical?

Is he having an affair? It wasn't the first time that the thought had occurred to her over the past couple of days. After all, she had caved in to temptation, so why not him? So many little idiosyncrasies that by themselves amounted to nothing, but when you put them all together, the end result equalled trouble. He didn't even ask for sex anymore, which was fine, better than fine in fact, but it did beg the question: *Why* hadn't Malcolm asked for sex?

Her mind wandered to Tod who had been haranguing her with calls and voicemails all weekend, each one slightly more aggressive and accusing than the previous and serving as a new poignant reminder as to the grave mistake that she had made. Hopefully he would eventually get the hint. She didn't much fancy having to pay him a visit to shut him up once and for all.

As she studied the veritable feast that her husband was

preparing, Eileen felt encouraged that at least his appetite seemed to have returned. Over the weekend, he had refused point blank to eat the food that she put on the table, seemingly oblivious to the fact that she had slaved away for hours preparing it. Fed up with the waste of food, time and effort, she had eventually challenged him about it, but rather than be remotely remorseful, he had instead become quite unpleasant and behaved like a sulky child being admonished for not eating his greens.

'How would you like your eggs, dear?' Malcolm's voice interrupted her thoughts.

'Mmmmm? Oh, scrambled would be nice for a change.'

'They're fried. How do you want them cooked?'

Fried or fried? Honestly, sometimes he was impossible! 'I'll have fried then please, love,' she answered through gritted teeth, wondering how long they would have to wait for a second opinion from the doctor. *Piles!* She had never heard anything so ridiculous and would be requesting someone with more experience next time.

As Malcolm jigged in time to the music, he barely even noticed Eileen's sarcasm. He was far too excited about what today held and couldn't really care less how she wanted her eggs cooked. If she was incapable of giving him a sensible answer, she could have them sunny side up whether she liked it or not and without further ado, he cracked four eggs in succession into the bubbling pan of oil.

Cooking a late breakfast had been Rita's idea, one that would ensure that Eileen wouldn't have the opportunity to tamper with any of the ingredients, and hopefully encourage her to agree to spend some time with him so he could get on and execute the first item on his list.

'I thought we could go to the garden centre this afternoon,' he suggested. Eileen loved nothing more than to trudge around the exotic gardens attached to the centre, admiring all the shrubs and vegetation, and to lose herself for hours in the large glasshouses as she selected plant after plant for their own garden.

Spending the afternoon with his wife, pretending to like her let alone the plants, would be onerous to say the least, but the end would surely justify the means and even though he would normally shiver with horror at the prospect, he found himself shivering instead with excitement at the possibilities.

He'd actually wanted to go yesterday, get it over and done with, but Rita had pointed out that it would quite possibly be the worst conceivable time. *Sunday drivers with nothing better to do,* she had said and of course she was right. A Monday afternoon would be much better. Much quieter. Even his supervisor seemed to think it was a good idea, telling him to take as much time as he needed when he'd phoned in sick earlier. *Oh, I will,* he grinned to himself.

The lake he had in mind lay within woodland at the far edge of the centre. According to the website, the area was secluded and surrounded by greenery and views that were to die for. *I sincerely hope so,* Malcolm thought to himself. *A pity though,* he supposed, *to have such a tragic accident so soon after she'd finally decided to take the plunge and learn to swim.*

28

T od stared pitifully at the three large bin bags crammed with his clothes and possessions that were piled in the hallway outside his bedsit door. Or what *was* his bedsit door. Apparently, it now belonged to a big black man called Leroy who hadn't taken kindly to him trying to kick the door in ten minutes previously.

He wandered aimlessly, his eyes barely taking in the dirty threadbare carpet beneath his feet or the grubby walls that were well overdue a lick of paint, towards the payphone, which hung precariously from the wall in the alcove beneath the stairs. It went against everything he believed in to use the damned thing, especially now that the bastard had turfed him out on the street with nowhere to go. But with no credit on his mobile, greasing the man's grubby little paws one final time seemed almost inevitable.

He dialled Eileen's number again, but after four rings it went straight to voicemail. He tried again, but still it diverted to the automated answering service. Anger getting the better of him, he decided to try the landline. *Let her explain who I am,* he thought to himself bitterly, but yet again, it just rang out until the answering machine kicked in. He tried again. And again, but each and every time, rather than pick up, he was subjected to Malcolm's dulcet tones informing him that nobody was home and to leave a message or try again later. *Where the hell is she?* Would she even care about his latest predicament when he did catch up with her? After the argument about getting rid of Malcolm, she had been impossible. He knew he had little choice but to take a step back and bide his time. Except that time was a luxury he could no longer afford.

Tod sat down on the bottom step. He stretched his legs out in front of him and rubbed his hands wearily over his face. He hadn't mentioned any of his financial problems or the rent arrears to Eileen for fear she would automatically jump to conclusions and assume the worst of him. Even now, however much he tried to dress the situation up as he mentally composed his version of events, he still couldn't see her agreeing to put him up.

'He can't do that!' Tod could literally hear her indignant protests. 'It's against the law.' Except of course, he could. His landlord had just proved that he could do exactly that and with Leroy now in residence, there was seemingly bugger all he could do about it.

Anger started to well in the pit of his gut at the injustice of it all. Was a little financial assistance until he could get himself sorted, from the woman who seemingly had more money than sense, really too much to ask? Only the other day, Eileen had proudly boasted about a ridiculously overpriced handbag that she had purchased on a whim. Who in their right mind paid over one grand for a poxy bag, for crying out loud? A grand that would have put a roof over his head and food in his mouth for at least three months.

And as for being backed into a corner by his landlord... one day the man was going to pay for that mistake. *By God, he'll pay!* The click of a door as it opened overhead behind him jolted him out of his trance and Tod turned hopefully towards the source. Excluding the little disagreement with EJ, he had always got on reasonably well with his neighbours. Maybe one of them could help him out? It needn't be for long. Just a night or two until he could convince Eileen to do the right thing and cough up some dough to get him out from between the rock and hard place he suddenly found himself in.

His eyes travelled up the stairwell and settled nervously on the guy who had effectively stolen the roof from over his head and all but climbed into his bed before it had even had the chance to go cold. Hatred, and something more sinister that Tod couldn't immediately identify, danced in his pupils as he glowered at him over the handrail.

'Time's up, white boy. Got myself visitors and you hanging round making my place look dirty ain't part of the deal, you get me?' *Cocaine.* The guy was so high he was floating amongst the clouds. Tod flinched then as Leroy picked up the first of the three bags and hauled it over the bannister before releasing it into the air and letting it free fall down the gap to the bottom, narrowly missing hitting him by inches.

'Watch it.' He jerked aside as the other two bags followed suit and landed in a heap at the base of the stairs. His whole life stuffed into three solitary bin liners. *How sad is that?* He shook his head ruefully, but aware of Leroy's robotic eyes burning a hole into the base of his skull, he quickly grabbed the ties to the bags and dragged them towards the door.

'Tosser,' he muttered as soon as he was sure he was a safe enough distance away to make himself feel better for standing up for himself, but far enough that the big man wouldn't actually hear him and retaliate.

Staying here had been a stupid idea at any rate. He had hoped they'd have moved on by now, but ever since EJ's death, the pigs had been buzzing around the joint day and night like flies round shit and he really didn't need that kind of aggro on his doorstep. *Mind you,* he suddenly thought to himself as he turned back and looked up the stairwell towards both of their old abodes, *no sign today.* So typical of his luck that the one day he could have done with their interference, they were nowhere to be seen.

Hauling the bags through the main entrance doors of the building, Tod stood outside on the steps and took a second to contemplate his options. He was tempted to get a cab but with less than one hundred quid to his name until he could rub Eileen up for a temporary loan, he thought better of it. Instead, he lugged the three bags as best he could in the direction of the bus stop, mindful not to allow the bottoms to drag on the floor any more than absolutely necessary for fear of ripping them.

He would get a bus to the pool to ditch his stuff first. Five lockers should do it, and it sure as hell beat carting the damned things half way across town to Eileen's. Besides, it was free storage for as long as he needed it since nobody, himself included, ever bothered to check they were emptied at the end of the day like they were supposed to.

29

R ita had spotted them before they even entered the store. She could detect them a mile off, sometimes sensing their presence before she even saw them. Ever since... she shivered at the memories: the shared cell with the apoplectic monster Maxine who had attacked her husband with an axe and insisted upon being called Mad-Axe-Max; the faeces-encrusted toilet that had seen neither bleach nor brush in years; and the humourless clowns who had handcuffed and chucked her in the back of their vehicle, treating her like a common criminal rather than see the situation for what it was: a simple, innocent misunderstanding.

'Little girls' room's calling. Won't be long,' she announced over her shoulder to her colleague behind the till before making her way out the back to the staff toilets, just as the two cops made their way into the store through the main entrance. One was unfamiliar but she'd recognise the other a mile off: the weird detective who was always hanging around spying on Loopy Lou when he thought no one could see him.

Aware that the clock was ticking and that it was only a matter of time before they wanted to speak with her, Rita gazed vacantly at her reflection in the restroom mirror as she tried to make sense of the situation and figure out what to do. Had Loopy Lou sent them here? She'd heard it on good authority that she had involved the police, claiming that Malcolm attacked her and demanding his arrest in the process.

Having watched the whole fracas unravel, she knew for a fact that he hadn't done any such thing, but how on earth could she possibly admit as much without implicating herself in the process?

She glared down at the Jimmy Choos on her feet, suddenly hating them with a passion. If it wasn't for them, she wouldn't be in this mess at all, and unfastening them as quickly as her shaking hands would allow, she ripped them from her feet and stuffed them as best she could into her bag.

They didn't fit and try as she might there was no way to disguise them and so, holding the bag protectively in her arms as though cradling a baby for fear they would fall out at the crucial moment, Rita hurriedly left the ladies' room.

'Could I have a word?' The female detective was standing so close to the door as she blocked the toilet exit, it was nothing short of a miracle that Rita hadn't crashed into her in her haste. 'If you'd like to follow me.' *No. No, I wouldn't, not one little bit.* Her eyes scanned the corridor desperately for somewhere to stash the boots, but what then? Would it not seem stranger still if she was barefoot? Pausing briefly, she slipped her feet back into them as fast as she could and followed the detective towards the staff kitchen.

As Sam held the door open and followed Rita into the kitchen, Lucas found his eyes inexplicably drawn to Rita's long, muscular legs encased in the tight, black leather of the knee-high boots. She wasn't his usual type. Anything but. The woman was kind of strange looking, as though she had been born in the wrong body, yet the magnetic force the boots had on him yielded it impossible to tear his eyes away. They wouldn't have been cheap and it begged the question how a sales assistant could afford such expensive clobber in the first place, let alone run the risk of damaging them at work. He also found it surprising that her employer allowed such provocative attire to be worn at all, but then he supposed she would certainly attract people inside the otherwise rather mundane store.

Squeezing his temples between his thumb and middle finger thoughtfully whilst Sam made the coffee, Lucas willed the nagging something in the back of his brain that he couldn't identify to make a proper appearance. And then it occurred to him. Was it possible, or just completely ridiculous, that he thought he recognised the boots? He quickly dismissed the idea. The boots could wait. Catching Hannah's killer, and quite possibly EJ's if the two deaths were connected, which all the evidence would suggest that they were, couldn't.

'How well did you know Hannah Gregory?' Lucas asked, careful to watch Rita's facial expression as she reacted to the question. It was amazing how many mouths could tell one story, only for the face to tell another.

'Hannah?' *Of course, Hannah!* Rita shook her head and did her best to look thoughtful, relief flooding her veins that this wasn't about the boots and the attack on Lou. Anything else they wanted to suspect her of would be pure conjecture and they wouldn't be able to prove otherwise.

'Well, I didn't,' Rita continued. 'Not really. You ask anyone. Hannah was a loner. Didn't mingle, you know?' Gratefully accepting the cup of coffee from Sam, she placed it on the table in front of her as she spoke. 'Don't think she even liked me if the truth be known,' she whispered conspiratorially.

The supervisor and other staff had all pretty much said the same and helping himself to a biscuit, Lucas chewed thoughtfully as he shrugged at Sam. *Alibi and out,* he mouthed to her between mouthfuls. They had far bigger fish to fry, namely Malcolm Muldoon.

'Could you confirm your whereabouts from six o'clock on Friday evening until midnight, Rita?' The biometric time attendance system set in place at the store had recorded the victim leaving work at precisely 18.00 hours. Her movements thereafter were, however, a mystery, and Sam was frankly still flabbergasted that the car park operators had opted for dummy cameras instead of a proper, fully functional system.

'Am I a suspect?' Rita fidgeted in her seat, trying her best to look indignant as she brushed away an imaginary speck of fluff from her skirt.

'Not at all, Madam,' Sam responded as though on autopilot, an assurance she must have made a million times before.

I am! I'm a suspect, she panicked, her mouth suddenly arid, and she reached for the cup of coffee and downed the tepid contents in one mouthful. Sam meanwhile pretended to doodle on the notepad in front of her as she awaited Rita's response. No one ever liked this question. It was as though the mere concept threatened their integrity and somehow confirmed their guilt.

'We'll be interviewing everyone on the estate,' Lucas interjected, noticing the nervous expression on Rita's face. It was, in his experience, a common reaction and he wasn't concerned, but the sooner she answered their questions, the sooner they could pay Malcolm a visit. 'We're working our way through all the retail outlets. It's just standard procedure to eliminate you from our enquiries.'

All the retail outlets? So Malcolm's a suspect too! Rita knew she shouldn't lie, especially about something so serious, but she couldn't tell them where she had been. They would never understand. It was a hasty decision. One she had no idea whether or not she would live to regret, but in that split second it made sense.

'I was with Malcolm. Malcolm Muldoon.' It wasn't a total lie after all. She had been with Malcolm for much of the evening. Rita paused a moment as she caught the male detective staring at her and giving her a look she couldn't quite decipher. It looked distinctly like a mixture of dismay verging on disbelief and her eyes skidded away from his and concentrated instead on the empty mug of coffee on the table in front of her. 'He works...'

'We know where he works,' Lucas interrupted, raising an eyebrow at Sam and trying not to feel too dejected by the news. If Malcolm was Rita's alibi, Rita was Malcolm's alibi. So much for paying him a surprise visit and shocking him into submission.

30

'Eileen?' Malcolm called out nervously. 'Eileen, are you alright, dear?' Having pushed her down the stairs only seconds previously he certainly hoped not, but it was best to go through the motions in case she could hear him and subsequently made a full recovery.

The resounding smack that had reverberated around the otherwise deadly quiet house as her head hit the wall at the foot of the stairwell had certainly sounded extremely promising. *So did the fact she didn't immediately resurface from the bottom of the lake and look how that turned out,* he thought to himself. Rather than leave the garden centre the mourning widower, Malcolm had been forced to endure a record-breaking ear bashing that had lasted the whole journey home. *You pushed me! No I didn't. Did. Didn't. Did. Didn't. My favourite cashmere. Ruined!* On and on and on. Was it any wonder he felt the need to shut her up once and for all?

As Malcolm digested the scene in front of him, Eileen groaned quietly as she slowly but deliberately tried to pull herself up using the bottom stair as a lever, but with neither the strength nor the energy to complete the manoeuvre, she soon collapsed back into a crumpled heap at the base of the stairs. He shook his head ruefully. Why couldn't something go right for him for a change? Time and time again, circumstantial events seemed to be ganging up against him most vindictively.

Eileen's eyelids fluttered as she attempted once more to

move, her arms and fingers reaching out blindly for the nearest object – anything she could grab and use as a hoist to lift her from the floor. As Malcolm watched on, as though suddenly realising the graveness of the situation before him, he rushed to the foot of the stairs and collapsed to his knees beside his wife's body.

'How could you do this to her?' he cried out, but was met only by silence as he madly tried to extract the canvas from her grip. His very own *Godiva Unmasked*, the naked painting that reminded him so much of Rita, ripped from its fastenings on the wall and totally ruined by his wife's carelessness. Furious, he rushed to the kitchen to search for something that would remove the stain from the fabric before it seeped through and caused irreparable damage.

As he rooted through the kitchen cupboards, Malcolm was so preoccupied with the job in hand that he didn't even hear the tell-tale crunch of gravel underfoot as Lucas approached the back door. Neither did he register the loud rattle as a set of knuckles tapped at the glass as he hauled out cleaning products from under the sink in search of something – anything – that would be suitable to remove the blood from his beloved picture before it was too late.

Lucas meanwhile stood awkwardly at the door, still unsure as to whether or not confronting the man was a good idea. What was it they said? *Never approach a bull by the horns, a horse from the rear, or an idiot from any direction.* Maybe he should just go? When Malcolm's colleagues had informed them that he had called in sick earlier that morning, Sam had suggested speaking with him tomorrow. *Not an immediate suspect.* How could she be so blind? He absently fingered the photograph and letters in his jacket pocket as though they could somehow provide him with the strength and courage of his convictions to see it through. *A wayward sperm. You'd ruin everything over one stray that got away? I don't intend to ruin anything… except Malcolm Muldoon and he hardly counts!*

Lucas trembled as a fresh wave of anger embraced him and he glanced back towards the front of the house where Malcolm's Mercedes sat on the expansive driveway, the bonnet still warm. *Where are you, Malcolm?* As though reading his mind, a shadow moved out of the corner of his eye and caught his attention. Pressing his nose up against the glass for a better look, Lucas could see Malcolm on his hands and knees on the kitchen floor surrounded by cleaning products. What was he doing? It was clear the man was in a state of panic as he seemingly searched for something in particular.

As Lucas stood and watched through the pane of glass, his mind wandered back to Operation Cross, the new official case name for the murders of EJ Mahoney and Hannah Gregory. What was it about Malcolm's behaviour? Something he was doing now that was slowly but surely devouring his mind. *Bam!* All of a sudden the connection hit him in the chest like a stray bullet. Erika had called earlier and confirmed that Hannah Gregory had also died from consuming a lethal concoction of cleaning products. No longer able to see Malcolm from where he was stood, Lucas clenched his fist and banged repeatedly on the glass, no longer caring whether or not the fragile material shattered with the force of the action. Still no response.

He stood still a moment, wrestling to juggle and assemble into some kind of order the deluge of thoughts as they crashed through his mind before deciding to take a wander around the side of the house, checking out the windows as he went to see if he could see any other signs of life in the house.

It wasn't until the third window that Lucas saw what he had both been expecting and dreading: Malcolm's wife's listless body at the base of the stairs and Malcolm himself leaning over her doing... *Doing what? Administering his lethal concoction of cleaning products?* Lucas sprinted the rest of the distance from the side path leading back to the front of the house and unsuccessful at first, he repeatedly chucked the full weight of his body at the solid oak door until finally, the aged wooden surround cracked and gave way to the full force of the load.

As Lucas staggered through the door and grabbed the balustrade to steady himself, his eyes slowly digested the scene in front of him with total disbelief: Eileen lying motionless in a pool of her own blood at the base of the stairs and Malcolm, seemingly oblivious to her plight as he scrubbed at… *What the hell is that?* Despite the urgency of the situation, Lucas couldn't help but lean closer to scrutinise what was quite possibly the ugliest picture he had ever seen.

'What have you done?' Tearing his eyes from the freak show in front of him, Lucas dropped to his knees and checked Eileen's neck and wrist for a pulse.

'I know, she's completely ruined it!' Malcolm continued to scrub incessantly at the picture as he spoke as though nothing else mattered.

'Are you mad?' *Is that why you behave the way you do?* There wasn't a jury in the land who wouldn't believe a clinically insane plea if they could see the man right now.

'Furious!' Malcolm didn't even look up as he doused his cloth in more liquid and continued to rub vigorously at the painting.

'Call an ambulance,' Lucas commanded, glancing up in disgust at Malcolm as he continued to obsess over his ridiculous painting, but he may as well have been speaking to himself for all the effect it had on him. Reaching for his mobile phone from his pocket, Lucas hurriedly dialled the emergency services himself, before turning his attention back to Malcolm. He didn't want to rise to the bait, nor did he want to enter into any kind of conversation with him at that particular moment in time, but when push came to shove, he found he couldn't help himself.

'What have you given her?'

Finally, Malcolm stopped rubbing at the bloodstains on the picture and turned his attention to Lucas, unable to disguise the curiosity from his voice.

'What on earth you on about, lad? She fell.'

'I saw you, Malcolm. Just now, in the kitchen.' Lucas glared threateningly at him, determined to make him spill and confess before the paramedics arrived, otherwise it might be too late.

'I was trying to sort *this*,' he scoffed, holding the picture up in front of him as though it held the answers to his insanity. Self-doubt started to flood Lucas' judgement. Could he really put this madman in the frame for the heinous crimes that littered his desk and his mind, or would the mere notion be laughed out of court?

'Did you push her?' Malcolm didn't respond immediately, his silence speaking volumes, but Lucas needed to hear the words for himself, so he tried again. 'Did you?'

'Of course I didn't.'

'He did.' Eileen's voice, a dull groan and barely audible was most welcome, and Lucas gently stroked the matted hair caked with blood away from her face.

31

Rita had fancied a walk, a breath of fresh air. She also hadn't been able to get hold of Malcolm on his mobile, which was most unlike him – unheard of in fact – and there was the little matter of the alibi that she needed to discuss with him. So out of character was his silence that, unable to even settle in front of her favourite television show, she had decided to take a walk past his house and see if she could shed any light on what might have caused this sudden communication blackout.

The slope leading to his house was steeper than she had imagined, so her progress was slow and she found herself pausing every now and then to catch her breath before pushing forwards once more, determined to get to the bottom of what was going on. Up ahead, she could just about make out the rhythmic strobes of light from emergency vehicles as they pulsated in the distance against the dusky sky, but with the exception of the occasional rumble of tyres on the highway as commuters made their way home, the air oozed an eerie silence.

She slowed her pace as a thought suddenly occurred to her. Had he actually gone and done it? When Malcolm had first confided his plans to her, she hadn't for one second believed he would go through with it, but now, she wasn't so sure. In fact, the more that she came to think about it, it was all starting to make sense. His determination to get rid of his wife, his silence and refusal to answer her calls and the flashing lights of the emergency vehicles up ahead.

Rita pulled the hood of her coat further over her head, determined to disguise her identity from any curious drivers who might later be able to identify her presence in the vicinity if his silence should turn out to be related to Eileen's death. She then increased her pace as much as was physically possible, painfully aware of the tightness spreading across her chest at this sudden and unexpected strain that she was placing upon herself.

After what seemed like an eternity, she reached the top of the hill and paused to take several deep breaths in rapid succession. The house was more impressive than she had anticipated and she glanced up to admire the Victorian façade in all its splendour, standing proud and magnificent behind the tall iron gates presumably put in place to keep the local riff-raff at bay. *Home.* She was looking at her future and a small wave of excitement cartwheeled in her belly at the prospect.

Muffled voices reverberated in the air from the direction of the front door and she tentatively tiptoed forwards through the open gates, desperate to get a better view of what was going on but also terrified of being caught. An ambulance sat parked up on the drive, its nose facing the road and rear doors flung open towards the front door completely obliterating any view that she otherwise may have had of what was occurring and she struggled to contain the immense feeling of irritation that threatened to overwhelm her.

What's yours is mine now, Eileen. Totally ahead of herself, she dared to allow a small tremor of exhilaration to shudder through her body at the prospect. The voices she had heard a moment ago increased in their intensity as they approached the emergency vehicle and Rita ducked behind one of the large stone pillars that reinforced the gates, holding her breath in order to better hear what was being said.

'It's procedure with a head injury, Ma'am,' a voice, presumably one of the paramedics, was saying. 'Don't want us getting into no trouble for not doing our job right, now do you?'

'But really, I'm absolutely fine. Just a silly fall.'

Eileen? A wave of fury enveloped Rita, wrapping its extensive arms around her body and smothering the breath from her lungs. *You had better bloody not be fine – you're supposed to be dead!* The unfairness of the situation clawed at her skin like a wild animal attacking its prey and she rubbed irritably at herself, as though the action alone could erase the sensation. It took every ounce of willpower she possessed to stay put, the urge to spring from her hiding place and expose herself and demand to know what was going on immense.

One simple task, Malcolm! One simple task and you can't even get that right.

32

Trouble was making a nasty little habit of following Tod around and he couldn't remember ever feeling this scared or alone in all his life. What the hell had happened back there? And why was Eileen still playing hard to get with his calls? *Eileen's dead.* When he had climbed from the bus at the bottom of her street and noticed the emergency lights reverberating in the otherwise unlit sky, the answer had hit him head on. That mad husband of hers must have done something stupid. Tod was trying not to panic, but it was easier said than done. How would she be able to help him if they were already preparing to hammer the nails into her coffin? And what if they suspected him of killing her?

He fingered the mobile phone in his pocket as he tried to figure out the other implications. There was sure to be a trace of his calls to Eileen, of that much he was certain. How many times did he call her from the payphone in the hall? He couldn't remember. Only that if they could trace them, it was too many. Granted he no longer lived there, but it wouldn't take a genius to put two and two together and come up with the dreaded magic number.

And what about pay-as-you-go? Could they trace that back to him? Only that afternoon, he had topped up his credit in the local shop opposite the leisure centre. Did they have CCTV? He had no idea. He hadn't thought to check. And what about caller display? He hadn't left any messages on the voicemail, but the likes of Malcolm and Eileen were sure to have it. His brain fired round after round of questions like an out-of-control machine gun popping out bullets at the enemy, and rather than eventually dissipate, if anything they just seemed to gain in their momentum. He didn't have any of the answers he so badly needed, but the thought of finding out brought another unwelcome spurt of acidic bile to his mouth. If they could trace the calls back to him, it also wouldn't take them long to work out that the same mobile phone had been used to text EJ on the evening of her death. To *threaten* EJ on the evening of her death.

He should never have lied about her, he knew that now, but when the pigs had first come knocking, he'd panicked and before he knew where he was at, he had told them he didn't know her. He had even elaborated on his stupid lie by pretending he didn't think her flat was occupied. *Why? How could I have been so stupid?* He should have ditched the phone then; he knew it and he'd wanted to, but a part of him also knew that whilst he wasn't a suspect it was safer to hold onto it.

Shit. He promptly panicked as something else occurred to him. He looked down at his rucksack and pulled it up from the floor and onto his lap as though suddenly afraid to let it out of his sight for even a second. Running his hands agitatedly through his hair, he tried to think. The only sensible answer was to get rid of them. But where? How? If getting rid of the mobile phone had been too risky, safely disposing of the shoes would prove near on impossible.

Fingerprints. Tod felt sick, properly sick now, the paltry contents of his stomach rebelling against the corner he had inadvertently backed himself into. In films, they would rub the object with a cloth to remove them. Did that really work? He had absolutely no idea and wasn't sure he dared take the risk finding out. But what was the alternative? Get caught with them in his possession? *Not likely!*

He looked down at the empty pint glasses on the table in front of him. Getting blinding drunk had seemed like the obvious solution earlier, but now, as the alcohol started to merge with the adrenalin already flooding his veins, and as the acidity of the bile reacted angrily against the bitterness of the beer, the doubts and paranoia threatened to take over and his body convulsed spasmodically with each empty violent retch and heave it produced.

Dragging himself up from the table, he began the unsteady walk to the rear entrance of the pub that adjoined the bogs. He had been out several times already that evening to suss out the joint and given his current state, there was no reason for the bar staff to realise he didn't plan on either using them, or returning to settle his tab until he was well and truly on his way.

33

Prison wasn't at all like Malcolm had envisaged it would be. He had hoped for a room with a view. Nothing too extravagant, just perhaps a window spliced with thick bars that overlooked an occasional patch of lawn and maybe out towards the razor-topped walls that he imagined surrounded the perimeter of the grounds. Instead, he got a dark, dingy box of a room with paper-thin walls, a concrete slab to sleep on, a small cracked basin that dripped water permanently from the tap, and with only a nine-inch gap between the edge of the toilet and the adjoining wall, he needed to be some kind of contortionist to carry out his morning business.

He had read an article about prison once. They reckoned prisoners were ignoring perfectly good opportunities to escape because the accommodation was superior to what one might expect from a five-star hotel. Right now, he was struggling to see this argument through their eyes, but he supposed that no two prison cells were the same – each and every one probably as unique as the fingerprints of the people inside them. That said, when he came to think about it, this place did bear some remarkable similarities to the hotel where he and Eileen had spent their honeymoon. That had been a complete shithole as well and it beggared belief that the owners hadn't made it disappear in a cloud of dust years ago. But if he had to choose between the two, the décor in the Grand Hotel was slightly more tasteful, the furnishings more luxurious and the liquid refreshments courtesy of the house were definitely a little more lively than the shitty brown sludge they served up in here.

He still couldn't believe that they had arrested him at all, let alone held him overnight. Eileen had confirmed that it was all her own fault and that she had tripped over those silly fluffy slippers of hers. Nonetheless, they had still abducted him, cuffing and dragging him across the gravel to their vehicle like a convicted criminal.

The young detective bothered him for more reasons than he cared to mention. Unable to give a satisfactory answer as to why he was lurking around his property in the first place, he had simply laughed in his face when Malcolm had demanded answers. It was a laugh that Malcolm was all too familiar with: a cocky, self-appreciating snigger that lacked genuine humour or feeling, but instead boasted power and a lack of remorse. Ever since witnessing it first hand and his subsequent incarceration, Malcolm had tried to find out what the man's interest was in him but no one seemed prepared to tell him anything.

'You'll find out soon enough,' was all that had been said when he had asked the jailer, or whatever he was called as he stuffed the inedible meal through the serving hatch in the door the previous evening.

'But I haven't done anything.' The whole place had started to remind Malcolm of boarding school and as the first tear escaped his eye, he soon found there was no stopping himself.

'No one ever has, mate, now shut it.' The serving grate had been snapped firmly shut then and as Malcolm had listened to his footsteps disappear down the corridor, he had sat down on the floor and tried to make the best of a bad situation. *Need to keep your strength up*, the voice in his head warned him as he pushed the food around the plate and tried to find something – anything – that looked appetising enough to put in his mouth.

He glanced across at the now empty tray on the floor.

He couldn't believe in the end he had even licked the plate. Just went to show that if you were hungry enough, you really would eat anything. Was it twenty-four hours they could hold him without charge? He couldn't remember, not that it really mattered. Having confiscated all his personal items to include his wristwatch, Malcolm had no idea how long he had been here, let alone how much time they had left.

His mind wandered to Rita who was bound to be beside herself with worry. He had all but begged for the opportunity to make a phone call, but each and every request fell on deaf ears, the officers responsible for holding him hostage seemingly more concerned with *who* he intended to call. *None of your bloody business,* he'd thought to himself although he hadn't dared speak the words aloud and antagonise them further. In the movies, criminals (although he most certainly didn't branch himself in that bracket) were entitled to a phone call, but this was all so typical of the British justice system. *One rule for them and one for the rest of us,* he thought, shaking his head with disappointment.

Lastly, somewhat belatedly, Malcolm thought of Eileen who would probably be every bit as smug as she was indifferent to the fact that he had been forced to spend the night luxuriating at Her Majesty's pleasure. *And furious,* he thought to himself wryly. The plethora of emotions would undoubtedly be fighting for pride of place in her brain: smug that she'd got one over on him; indifferent to his absence just so long as she had Buddy for company; giddy with excitement at the prospect of being rid of him for a while; and presumably also fuming with rage that he wasn't available to carry out any household chores as and when she deemed fit.

What had she done last night in his absence? Held a party to celebrate? He wouldn't put it past her and didn't doubt that the second she was discharged from the hospital she would have run off to her fancy man and got drunk, the pair of them all the while berating him and plotting his downfall.

Malcolm looked around his tiny cell with disdain. He certainly couldn't recommend prison and he definitely wouldn't be hurrying back. The accommodation and amenities were seriously lacking, the quality of service was next to nil, and with only drug addicts and rent boys for company, the overall ambience left a lot to be desired. Upon his release, he fully intended to write to the Prime Minister about the whole sorry situation.

34

L ucas was thoughtful as he sat in his office, arms folded
behind his head as he leaned back in his chair and crossed
his legs on the desk in front of him. His presence had been
requested at the briefing regarding the forthcoming public
conference, but the meeting was a nonsense and when push
came to shove, he simply couldn't be bothered. *Don't mention
this. Don't disclose that. Never give sixpence if a penny will do.* An
hour of his life he would never claw back and in truth, Lucas
already knew exactly what he should say. *Nothing.* Because
nothing was precisely what he had managed to glean about EJ
and Hannah's deaths to date.

His eyes travelled to the small sample on the desk in front
of him, a tiny little piece of Malcolm Muldoon that would
hopefully confirm his suspicions beyond all reasonable doubt.
It was a dirty world, full of people with filthy habits even if
they were unaware of them most of the time. Smoking. Nail
biting. Nose, scab, skin, teeth picking. Malcolm's weakness, as
it turned out, was putting foreign objects in his mouth.

It still riled Lucas that the man had been discharged at
all, but with his wife refusing to press charges and Rita Tate
from the Beds 'R' Us store providing him with an alibi for the
evening of Hannah Gregory's death, they had little choice but
to release him back onto the streets. *To kill again.* The words
hounded his every waking thought, but despite the fact that
the internal computer held a list long enough to write a book

about Malcolm's numerous escapades and misdemeanours, there was nothing powerful or incriminating enough to justify keeping him.

Would Eileen Muldoon think differently if she heard the tapes? The urge to make a copy and secretly show her was immense. *Your wife will live, Malcolm.* The image of him as he responded, his shoulders shaking as he chuckled at his private little joke, only serving to confirm how dangerous the man actually was. *More's the pity.* That's what he had replied and even now, Lucas shook his head at the incredulity of it all. Arrested for the attempted murder of his own wife, questioned about the murders of EJ and Hannah, and rather than show any remorse, Malcolm had simply joked about his lack of success.

His mind wandered to the assistant from the Beds 'R' Us store. Rita Tate was clearly lying, but why? What hold could Malcolm possibly have over the woman? Frustration gnawed at his insides. Malcolm Muldoon had the word 'guilty' written all over him, but a volatile temperament and a connection to both victims wasn't enough.

'Why did you attack Lou Wilson in the car park, Malcolm?' Whilst the man had been trapped between the four walls of the interview room, Lucas hadn't been able to resist confronting him about the matter.

'How many times? She attacked me!' Malcolm had spat back, his upper lip curling over his teeth in a grimace as he spoke. 'She'll pay for that. You mark my words, she's going to pay for what she did.'

Even then, despite everything, the man didn't care. He refused to show any remorse or empathy for his behaviour, and Lucas had felt the blood in his veins gurgle as he'd assessed the evil oozing from every pore of the specimen sat in front of him. *No, you'll pay, Malcolm,* he had thought to himself, shaking with anger as the words spilled into his brain. *If it's the last thing I ever do, I'm going to make you pay!*

35

ucas' arm was chucked carelessly across Lou's waist as she lay in bed and listened to the gentle whistle of his breathing whilst considering the irony of her situation. *This is what you wanted*, the voice reprimanded. *No. It's not. I wanted to feel loved and protected, who doesn't? But not like this.*

As though sensing her discomfort, Lucas stirred in his sleep and she held her breath as she stared intently at the first signs of morning light as they wrestled for space through the curtains in the otherwise dark room. *Not yet, please not yet*, she urged. She needed time to think. Time to consider the much talked about fine line between love and hate. Something that wouldn't – couldn't – happen if he was breathing down her neck and questioning her every move.

How was it possible to want something so badly, only to not want it at all the second you had it? Oh yes, on the surface, Lucas was the perfect catch. The youngest detective to ever serve at Cliffborough Cross, he might not be stereotypically tall, dark and handsome, but he did at least have the kind of athletic physique that was guaranteed to make women's heads turn from a hundred paces. Not to mention an easy-going manner that seemed to attract children and the elderly alike. But there was clearly also a more sinister side to Lucas. A trait he kept well hidden from unsuspecting eyes until he felt ready to disclose it.

What was it they said? *Beauty is only skin deep.* Lou realised now that in Lucas' case, never a truer word had ever been spoken. Knowing relatively little about him, she couldn't deny that he had worked wonders for her self-confidence, but what woman wouldn't be flattered that such an outwardly charming and successful man had set his sights on her? Everywhere Lou turned, people around her seemed to be settling down: old school friends, work colleagues, actresses on the television. Was it any wonder she had started to develop a fear of somehow being left behind? And so, yes, when Lucas had come along, she had given herself a quick dust down and jumped from the shelf feet first, not even thinking to question the character that lay beneath what she now knew to be a flimsy layer of exterior charm.

If she was honest with herself, the doubts had started to creep in that very first night, but determined to make it work, she had deliberately blanked them from her mind. The fact that he had so magnanimously protected her over that whole unfortunate incident surrounding his mother's death had only served to exaggerate her feelings, but in truth she realised now that she had simply felt indebted to him. An emotion that had perhaps been muddied and construed by her heart as attraction, but there was no denying any longer *what* and *who* she had deliberately allowed into her life.

The dull crunching sound as Lucas slowly ground his teeth signalled that he was about to wake up and Lou squeezed her eyes tightly closed, determined to shut out the confrontation she felt sure was about to follow.

'So where were you?' Groggy from sleep, his voice was muffled and the stench of sleep filled the air.

Despite the fact that she had been expecting it, Lou still froze under his arm. *None of your bloody business,* she thought to herself. They had only been dating five minutes and already it was like he wanted to take over and control everything she did – to include being made aware of her whereabouts every second of every day.

'Well?' he demanded when she didn't respond. *Does she have any idea? A lunatic is currently stalking the streets hunting for prey and she decides to go walkabout without even bothering to let me know where she is.*

Lou breathed deeply and filled her lungs with as much air as physically possible as she tried to keep her anger at bay. *Why can't he just leave it?* How had she not seen him for what he really was: a jealous, possessive monster lurking behind a genial façade?

'It was just a drink after work,' she responded irritably. 'I thought we'd been through all this already.' Had the argument when she had got in last night not been enough to satisfy his anger? She certainly didn't have the energy for another fight. *Takes two to fight.* The words reverberated angrily around her skull. *What kind of man does his talking with his fists?*

'Was *Peter* there?' Lucas emphasised the name through gritted teeth as he spoke.

Peter. What was it with his morbid fascination with a guy who she barely even knew? *He's not my type and I'm certainly not his, you fool!* She kept the thought to herself, not wanting to get into the whole pointless argument all over again. The one-way shouting match when she had arrived home last night had been more than enough and she shuddered instinctively as the images flashed through her mind… No sooner had she opened the door, he'd pounced. Venom spewing from his lips like lava, seconds before his fist connected with her jaw.

Retrieving her arm from beneath the duvet, Lou gingerly touched her chin and winced as a spasm of pain jerked through her at the touch. How would she explain this at work? Surrounded by medical experts, she somehow doubted they would swallow the old *I-walked-into-a-door* routine.

Her mind flitted back to the argument. Lucas dressing up his violence as concern as he had sat on the floor afterwards, his arms wrapped tightly around his knees and huddled to his chest as he rocked back and forth on his buttocks and cried and begged for her forgiveness. Chanting his apologies over and over as though it would somehow make everything okay. Well, it didn't. Lou didn't forgive him. She didn't even pity him. The only emotion running through her veins right now was repulsion and the sooner he left, the better.

'Are you shagging him?' The mattress sank under his weight as he swung his legs over the side of the bed and used it to push himself up.

'Well?' His bare feet slapped against the hard floor and Lou shrank back under the duvet as it occurred to her that he might lash out again. He didn't. Instead, he just stood and glared at her, eyes flashing with anger and fists curled aggressively at his sides when she didn't respond. *Guilty as charged,* he thought to himself. Her silence screamed out her affirmation so far as he was concerned and the fact that she refused to so much as look him in the eye only served to exacerbate the situation.

Still Lou didn't speak. Instead, she turned her back on him and pulled the duvet up over her head as she prayed above all else that he would do the right thing this time and leave. Despite holding her breath, she couldn't hear a sound but, terrified of antagonising him further, she just lay there motionless under the quilt for what felt like an eternity until eventually she heard the unmistakeable sound of the catch snapping loudly on the front door as he let himself out.

36

'What were you thinking?' Rita hissed into Malcolm's face, a tiny glob of saliva hitting him full pelt in the eyeball. Pinning him up against the wall, she was a lot stronger than she looked and her dark eyes, angry slits of fury, bore invisible holes into his own. Malcolm wasn't sure he could find the words, let alone the breath to respond even if he had the answers she demanded.

'It wasn't my fault,' he pleaded. 'Please... darling.' He stroked her hip tenderly, totally at odds with this demented woman masquerading as his Rita and desperately hoped he could snap her out of this peculiar trance that was so out of character.

'I saw the detective,' she spat, pushing away his hand, which tingled her skin as though an army of tiny insects were crawling beneath the fabric.

'He just turned up, I don't know why. I still don't know why. Please, my love.' His hand hovered awkwardly mid-air as he wrestled internally as to whether or not he should try again to stroke her into submission. It tended to work with Buddy after all. He warily placed his hand on her shoulder, so gently that Rita couldn't even feel it resting there, and as she studied his eyes closely for tell-tale signs that he was lying, she eventually relaxed her grip.

'I'm sorry.' Finally Rita spoke, her voice muffled against his shirt as she rested her face against his chest and Malcolm pulled her closer into him in an embrace. When she had spotted the detective that was always hanging around spying on Loopy Lou at the house, she had automatically panicked. Knowing about Malcolm's plans to kill his wife, she had put two and two together, created twenty-two and convinced herself that she would somehow be implicated in the crime.

'He knew. I could see it in his eyes,' Malcolm muttered quietly, and Rita stiffened in his arms and pushed him away.

'What do you mean, *he knew*? Knew what?' Panic churned in her belly once more. What the hell had he got her into? She knew she shouldn't have trusted him. She should have walked away the second he had confided his plans to her.

'The alibi,' he declared emphatically. 'The Gregory woman.' Malcolm still couldn't believe that they had both had the foresight to use one another as an alibi for the full time in question without running it past each other first. *Fate!* What other possible explanation could there be? 'He knew, but he can't prove it,' he continued. He pulled her tighter into another embrace. Now wasn't the time to admit that he suspected the detective knew he had tried to kill Eileen. 'Great minds think alike, eh.' He grinned madly and hoped she would let the matter drop.

As the fear pounded in her eardrums and reverberated in her chest, Rita didn't reciprocate his delight. How could she have been so stupid as to think a man like Malcolm could protect her from the police? Looking at him now, the childlike mannerisms radiating from within, it was quite apparent the man couldn't escape from a Jehovah's Witness, let alone the murder squad if they suspected him of anything untoward.

'We both needed an alibi,' she eventually conceded.

'We did, my darling, we did,' Malcolm exclaimed as he gleefully planted a big kiss on her forehead. It was a very wet kiss. Most unpleasant in truth and it took everything Rita had got, not to reach to the spot and wipe it away with the palm of her hand. 'And now, we're in the clear,' he continued, 'which just leaves the rather unpleasant matter of *that woman* to deal with.'

'Head like a conker.' Rita shook her head ruefully. How on earth his wife had managed to survive that kind of impact remained a mystery.

'Well, yes, there's her, of course there is, but I was referring to the other specimen. The one with the big headphones and even bigger temper.' Malcolm still felt a bitter taste coat his tongue and sting the back of his throat every time he thought about the woman and what she had done to him. And as for then trying to have *him* arrested and charged. *Bloody cheek!* It was like he'd told the cocky detective earlier. She would pay for that mistake.

'Spent most of his time trying to trip me up and make me admit I attacked her,' he continued. 'Treated me like a common criminal.' Malcolm couldn't wait to fill in the blanks and bring the man down a peg or two and he grinned inanely at the prospect.

'What? But I thought…'

'Yes, so did I,' Malcolm interrupted. 'One minute I'm being questioned about my wife's dreadful *little mishap*,' he smiled and winked before continuing. 'Next thing you know, he's harping on about that stupid woman – and the others. No, let me finish.' Seeing she was about to interrupt, he placed a finger on her lips as he spoke. 'It's like he's trying to set me up. Get me to admit I attacked her and put me in the frame for these murders.'

Rita tried to swallow the lump that had appeared in the back of her throat but it wouldn't budge as the fear wrestled with her intestines once more and threatened to wreak havoc with her bladder. Why oh why had she got herself involved when she could have just walked away? An image of the glorious boots flashed before her eyes and she knew, without a doubt, that if she had her time again, she would do exactly the same all over again.

'Little bitch needs silencing.' Rita spat out the words before she even had the chance to engage her brain, the anger that roared beneath the surface surprising even her, and Malcolm raised an unsuspecting eyebrow in her direction before pulling her towards him and squeezing her tightly once more. *Too tightly,* but they were both on tenterhooks, she knew that, and so even though she was struggling to breathe, she did her best and tried to settle into the embrace rather than push him away.

'Sssh.' Malcolm continued to squeeze and Rita continued to struggle to breathe until eventually he released his grip as he spoke.

'Eileen. Mad bag lady. The detective. None of them are going to spoil our happiness.' He planted another kiss on her forehead, this time on her hair, which absorbed most of the excess saliva so it didn't feel anywhere near as unpleasant as the last one.

'Tonight we'll go again,' he continued.

We? Don't drag me into it. But then again, if she didn't keep an eye on him, he was sure to mess it all up. Possibly even implicate her in the process. That much was quite obvious from his previous escapades and there was no denying she'd be happier once his wife and Loopy Lou were out of the equation once and for all. Only then could she finally have the type of life she craved. The type of life that she deserved.

'I've got a little something for you.' As though reading her mind, Malcolm interrupted her thoughts and she eyed him warily as he side stepped around her and walked over to the sideboard that sat against the far side of the other wall in the hall.

'For me?' Rita's eyes lit up as he produced the small box and she grabbed at it greedily, ripping the paper that surrounded it like a spoiled child.

Infinitely better, Malcolm thought to himself. He wasn't sure he liked Rita all that much when she was angry and vowed to get on and get rid of Eileen at the first available opportunity for fear of a repeat episode of this afternoon.

As Rita walked up and down the hall, studying herself in the full-length mirror, Malcolm stood and watched, admiring the way the shoes accentuated her long, toned legs. Despite being determined to honour her wishes and not force the issue, a stab of desire shot straight through his abdomen and settled in his groin. He couldn't remember ever wanting something as much as he wanted her right now and the more she taunted and teased and made him wait, the more his desire seemed to grow.

As she came to a standstill and studied her reflection, he approached from behind and pressed himself firmly up against her. Eyes locked on hers in the mirror, he swayed his hips gently, pulling her back into him firmly as he did so. He was determined to finally persuade her to give up this silly notion of waiting until Eileen was out of the picture before cementing their relationship.

Rita turned towards him then, grabbing his testicles with her hand through the thin material of his trousers. As she kneaded them like dough, he gasped, unable to contain himself a moment longer.

'Please,' he begged. He was so excited he was ready to explode.

'Soon,' she teased and he felt himself soften slightly as she let him down, yet again. 'When it's me that shares your bed, we'll have all the time in the world,' she promised, kissing him gently on the lips and stroking his cheek with her thumb before stepping back and retrieving her bag and surplus shoes from the floor.

'I must go.' She blew him a kiss as she opened the door. 'Call me when it's done.'

Malcolm stood and watched her go, his rock-hard erection pressing uncomfortably once more against the fabric of his underwear. *When it's me that shares your bed,* the words bounced violently around his brain and he could barely control his excitement.

37

As Eileen slowed the vehicle to make the right turn at the top of the hill into their driveway, it was hard to miss Rita as she fought to keep her ankles upright on the gravel surface and struggled in the heels towards the road. *Are they my new Manolos?* She would be willing to bet that they were.

Any doubts that she had misread the signals that Malcolm had been giving off dissolved quicker than an effervescent in water in that one split second. *Marriage-wrecking bitch!* She didn't want to watch, but mesmerised by this woman who seemed to think nothing of crashing into their lives and taking whatever she saw fit, Eileen couldn't help herself. *Including my shoes,* she thought indignantly.

She knew it was hypocritical in some respects. After all, she had thought nothing of a little extracurricular activity with Tod, but her recent fall had put all of that business into perspective in her mind. That was where she had been the past few hours: trying to locate him and put an end to their little dalliance. She hadn't wanted to see him in person, only too aware of the temptation it would create, but having spent the better part of the morning trying in vain to contact him on his mobile, her options were limited. In the end she had decided to call round and break the news to him face to face.

As it happened, the trip across town had been a complete waste of time. Not only was Tod not there, but a peculiar-acting Jamaican gentleman had taken up residence instead. She cringed at the memory of him inviting her into his 'crib'. *Big mistake* and within seconds of entering, she had found herself backing her way back out of the door to make her escape.

As Rita paused on the pavement as though unsure which direction to take, Eileen turned her attention back to the problem at hand. *What else have you taken? Is my husband not enough, you've started on my wardrobe too?* Furious and determined to have it out with Malcolm once and for all, Eileen pressed her foot down hard against the accelerator, gravel flying in her midst as she sped up the drive. Taking one last glance in the rear-view mirror, she dared to hope above all else that a piece of stone might flip up from the tread of the tyres and hit Rita right where it would hurt the most.

Has she also been in my bed? The thought came to her in a flash, jealousy scratching at her intestines. She might not want her husband in that way any longer, but she certainly didn't want anybody else abusing the privilege either. Absolutely not, and if that middle-aged floozy who clearly couldn't find a husband of her own thought she was going to sit back and allow her to crash in with her bulldozer and demolish something that had taken almost thirty years to build, she had another think coming. 'Over my dead body,' she muttered angrily.

As Eileen entered the house, she allowed the door to slam behind her and the latch snapped loudly into place. Her heels clacked noisily on the hall floor, echoing off the walls as she marched headlong into the kitchen to confront him, but as she opened the door and assessed the room, Malcolm was nowhere to be seen. Chucking her bag onto the kitchen table, she surveyed the unwashed dishes in the sink and the cardboard food packaging discarded on the sideboard beside it, crushed and ready to be taken out to the recycling bin that sat in the back yard. Where on earth was he? Noticing steam rising from the kettle, she walked over and aimlessly touched the side of it with the palm of her hand. Just boiled, so he couldn't be far away.

She pressed on through the house, checking each room one by one but there was no sign of him. *Upstairs?* Fear at what this could mean surged through her veins, but it made perfect sense. If the pair of them had been at it like rabbits while she was out, where else would he possibly be? Careful to make as little noise as possible now, determined to catch him out, Eileen crept slowly up the stairs, careful to avoid the third and ninth steps which always creaked and might give her away. She didn't know what she hoped to find – after all, only minutes previously she had witnessed his lover leaving this very building with her own eyes. Nonetheless, she had known her husband long enough to be confident of her conviction that if he was up here, he was clearly up to no good.

As she reached the landing and hovered awkwardly outside the bedroom door, Eileen took one final deep breath before shoving the door violently, the hinges squeaking in protest as she barged into the room. And then she stopped dead, unable to find the words to speak as she stared in shock at her husband. *The rabbit.* Only this time, the rabbit had been well and truly caught in the headlights.

'What the hell?' she mumbled, eventually finding her voice. Feeling giddy, Eileen grabbed frantically at the door surround as her knees threatened to give way under the weight. 'How could you?' she squeaked, vaguely aware that her voice didn't sound like her own at all as she surveyed her husband, crouched on the floor with his pants around his ankles as he relieved himself over that dreadful picture he had insisted on hanging in the hall the other day.

'It's not how it looks,' Malcolm stuttered, scrabbling to his feet and wrestling his pants and trousers back over his knees.

He's a monster! You married a sexually depraved deviant. Unable to contain her disgust, Eileen turned about foot and staggered, blinded by furious tears, from the room, almost tripping over Buddy who eagerly awaited his mistress the other side of the door. *She's welcome to you,* she thought as she stormed down the stairs into the kitchen, Buddy close on her heels.

Spotting an open bottle of wine on the draining board, she grabbed it and plonking herself down in the nearest available chair, she started to swig the contents straight from the bottle.

38

Lucas sat motionless behind the wheel and stared at the clock on the dashboard: 21.29. Precisely twelve hours and twelve minutes since he had left the house at Lou's behest. He didn't care if it took another twelve hours; he wasn't moving or going anywhere until he saw her. *Or him.* His stomach growled in angry protest. All good engines needed fuel and it must be approaching twenty-four hours since he'd last eaten. *Soon.* He rubbed his belly as though to console it. *Just as soon as I've seen what she's up to.*

However hard Lucas tried, he couldn't evict the image of Peter – this imposter – from his brain. In his mind-set, Peter was a well-built man, tall and slender with muscles that swelled and rippled beneath his taut skin as he moved. He was handsome too, with chiselled features and a sprinkling of designer stubble on his chin. And *fuck-me* eyes. Let's not forget the eyes, and rage boiled in Lucas' chest once more as the vision of him and Lou embroiled in a passionate embrace played out in his brain.

What does she want? The million-dollar question that he couldn't answer. He had thought he could and had gone to huge lengths to prove his commitment to the cause but instead of gratitude, she had chucked it all back in his face. And for what? Some bloke she barely even knew who could never love her as much as he did. Peter, he was sure of it, was the kind of opponent that no man ever wanted to find themselves up against. The man needed removing from the equation, simple as, and Lucas wasn't prepared to give up until he had done exactly that.

As images of their first night together flashed through his mind, he leaned back into the comfort of the leather seat to enjoy the spectacle. It was nice to watch from the outside. Like watching a movie in which he played a lead part. It was all too easy to miss things in the heat of the moment but he could see everything clearly now and there was no way a person could put on a performance such as Lou's unless they too were deeply mentally and physically involved.

But she told you to go. She didn't mean it. She looked like she did. She was angry. His emotions bickered amongst themselves inside him again, the endless contradictions as they bounced around his skull grating on his nerves and rendering it impossible to think logically. *She doesn't want you, she wants him. Peter. She wants… ENOUGH!* Determined to shut up the voices once and for all, Lucas slammed his fist on the steering wheel in anger.

Possessive and controlling. That's what she had said. Okay, so he shouldn't have hit her. He regretted that big time, but it was a one off. He would never do it again, but she only had herself to blame. If she hadn't left him pacing back and forth like a frantic caged animal, frightened and scared with no idea when, if ever, she would come home to him, it would never have happened. Lucas shook his head ruefully. He couldn't win. His last girlfriend had said that he didn't care enough. Disrespectful and ignorant she'd called him when he had tried to behave indifferently to her behaviour. *Women.* They were all the same deep down, and he was damned if he did and damned if he didn't.

Who and where are you, Peter? Only once Lucas knew a little more about the man could he ascertain the level of risk. *I've waited too long for this. If I can't have her, as sure as God made little apples neither can you!* A surname or an address would do – anything more than *something-stinks-about-the-bloke* that would justify him digging deeper. Copper's nose. The unwritten sin that all officers on the force were warned against acting on, but in all his time working for the police, Lucas had never had a hunch that had let him down.

The sound of a door slamming interrupted his reverie and Lucas looked up to see Lou walking down the path. Wearing only a skimpy dress which clung to her toned body like a second skin and a pair of matching silver heels that clacked sharply against the hard floor, there was no doubt in his mind that she was dressed to impress. Lucas ducked down in his seat behind the wheel as far as the limited space would allow and obscured his face with his fingers as he peeped through the gaps like a child cheating at a game of hide and seek.

Slut! 'Off to meet lover boy, are we?' he grumbled, furious with her for her earlier sanctimonious piousness. About to climb out from behind the wheel to confront her, a thought occurred to him and his legs remained stubbornly rooted to the well of the car as though deliberately refusing to answer his silent requests to move. She'd only deny it, but if he followed her, he would be able to find out once and for all what she was up to.

He waited patiently until he was confident she hadn't spotted him and then he quickly fastened his seatbelt and turned the key in the ignition. He cringed as the motor sprang to life, but if she heard it, she made no sign of alarm. Putting the car into gear, he gently pulled away from the side of the road and crawled at a safe distance behind her, far enough away not to draw attention to himself, but close enough not to lose sight of her.

39

Eileen opened her eyes, oblivious to anything untoward except perhaps the darkness that surrounded her. She glanced sideways to check the time on the bedside clock. *Odd.* She couldn't see it. *Power cut maybe?* She tried to stretch out her limbs, arms first, then her legs, but they felt disjointed, as though they no longer belonged to her body as they lightly scraped against a solid wall of cold metal.

She twisted uncomfortably, willing her eyes to adjust to the lack of light. Rain battered against the ceiling above her head and echoed around the cramped, hollow space and she shivered involuntarily. *Cold. So very, very cold.* A bloody scab on her forehead pinched at her skin and stretched it to unbearable proportions. She impulsively reached to scratch it, but instantly regretted the decision as she felt the blood trickle down her temple. *Thirsty.* Her tongue stuck to the roof of her mouth and she tried in vain to pool saliva so she could swallow and shift whatever it was that had lodged itself in her throat that was causing so much discomfort.

Eileen lay in silence as she tried to pinpoint the source of the distant rumble that resonated from somewhere below. The cage juddered then, and a cattle grid clattered loudly beneath her, creating a wave of panic that washed over her and squeezed her chest in its vice-like grip as realisation dawned. Her fingers groped around in the darkness as though needing reassurance she was somehow mistaken, but as they singled out various objects one by one, there was no remaining doubt. As the fear mingled with anger, Eileen clenched her fists into tight little balls and hammered against the aluminium ceiling that engulfed her.

'Malcolm?... Malcolm!' Her cries were met only by silence and the crunch of tyres on the surface beneath her and so she tried again. 'Malcolm! Let... me... out!' She banged furiously on the roof now, but still, either he couldn't hear her, or he was deliberately pretending that he couldn't. The car braked hard before surging forwards once more and Eileen was thrust violently against the rear panel. She clawed around in the dark, feeling each surface with her fingers in vain as she tried to find something to grip onto to steady herself.

Malcolm meanwhile was so preoccupied with his own thoughts that he was only marginally aware of the strange banging coming from the back of the vehicle as he leaned over and turned up the volume on his special playlist. Now wasn't the time to be worrying about whether or not the vehicle was due a service. A few more hours and it wouldn't require one at any rate.

As 'Ding Dong! The Witch is Dead' blared from the speakers, Malcolm sang out heartily, wiggling in his seat like an over-excited child. He couldn't believe Eileen had been so unreasonable. He had needs. Needs that she was neglecting and as such, she had nobody to blame but herself for the predicament she now found herself in.

That detective the other day had given him the idea. As had Eileen's internet search history. It was so simple, yet the thought would never have crossed his mind had they not been considerate enough to put it there in the first place. The support site that he had subsequently joined on Google for further advice on the subject had also been very informative. Particularly in relation to everyday household products that Eileen could accidentally consume that wouldn't cause immediate asphyxiation, but that would instead cause her to become delusional and disorientated. Just a little something to make her behave out of character and do silly things, before finally claiming each and every last breath from her.

'Slowly, slowly, catchy monkey,' he whispered to himself.

Administering the poison had been far easier than he had anticipated. When Eileen had barged in so unexpectedly earlier and quite literally caught him with his pants down, Malcolm hadn't been able to think of one single sensible reason to excuse his predicament. Nonetheless, he had dressed himself in record time and rushed down the stairs after her. When he had clapped eyes on his wife, sat at the kitchen table swigging from the very bottle of wine that he had spiked only hours earlier, he could barely believe his luck.

The only issue remaining now was rigor mortis, but none of his allies had been able to be specific about this particular matter. His wife had always been difficult in life so there was no doubt in his mind that she would be equally awkward in death, and it was frankly all well and good to suggest approximate times, but Eileen had never been a woman of a patient disposition.

'Right turn ahead,' the Sat Nav advised, breaking into his thoughts, and Malcolm glanced at the screen before slowing to almost a standstill as he manipulated the car onto the narrow beaten track. He cringed out of habit as the wheels violently clunked a pothole and something beneath the car, possibly the spoiler, scratched the road surface below, but then he remembered that it didn't matter. This was Eileen's car, not his, and since it would soon be mangled around the trunk of the biggest tree he could find, a few little surface scratches here and there were of no consequence whatsoever.

40

Walking home in the early hours of the morning, dressed in little else except the low-cut, strapless dress and matching silver diamante heels that she had blown the majority of her last wage packet on specifically to impress Lucas, wasn't one of her best ideas. *Neither was trying to impress Lucas,* Lou thought to herself bitterly as she staggered out from the club, blinded by tears and a little worse for wear courtesy of one too many apple-flavoured shots that she hadn't even enjoyed.

But, what choice did she have? With the exception of five pieces of shrapnel and two second-class stamps, which she couldn't see any taxi-driver viewing as acceptable currency, her purse was bare. Wasn't alcohol supposed to numb pain? It didn't. The image of Lucas pressed up against her in the dimly lit hallway as he demanded to know where she had been, the force he had used to roughly shove her to the floor, and the ominous crack as his fist attached itself to her jawbone all played havoc with her sanity once more.

Bastard! Her feet were killing, so she paused a moment and yanked off the shoes, not even bothering to undo the straps. Holding them firmly in her hand, she marched determinedly in the direction of the main road, but then she stopped and looked back in the direction of the club, and then again in front of her as though unable to make up her mind. She had no intention of going back in there, it wasn't that. Playing gooseberry with Nat from work and the bloke she'd picked up at the bar a couple of hours previously held no appeal. She just couldn't decide whether it was safer to stick to the main road, or whether she was less likely to be noticed or draw attention to herself if she took the slightly longer, but quieter route home.

The figure sat quietly behind the steering wheel watching her every move, silently willing her to do the right thing. Eventually, his prayers were answered and Lou turned and walked towards the gate that led to the old canal. *Good girl.*

'Think you're invincible, do you? DO YOU?' he demanded even though he knew she couldn't hear him. Would she never learn? He sat and watched as she continued her unsteady path towards the old canal.

'Time somebody taught her a lesson.' He nodded knowingly at his reflection in the rear-view mirror. 'I think I know just the person,' he added and emitted a low throaty chuckle of delight.

He waited for her to disappear from view and then slowly moved the Volvo from its sheltered position and headed in the opposite direction. There was no particular hurry. The path only led to one place and he would be there in plenty of time before she had even managed to walk half the distance in her state.

41

inally, Malcolm found what he was looking for and turning off the headlights for fear of drawing any unnecessary attention to himself, he pulled the vehicle off the poorly maintained feeder road that had once served the old canal and the disused site behind it. Despite his lack of speed, the crunch of grit and old crumbling asphalt beneath the tyres echoed loudly against the deathly quiet backdrop as he manoeuvred as carefully as he could between the neglected boats and machinery that now littered the yard.

Turning off the ignition, he climbed out from behind the wheel to stretch his legs. He stared up at the decaying, crumbling walls of the derelict warehouses that loomed large against the tarmac, their reflection dancing eerily in the moonlight against the water's edge behind him. It still bothered him that the police would question what Eileen was doing here in the first place when her body was found, but he needed somewhere quiet and unobserved to carry out his task. And she was a woman, after all. Did anything they ever did make any sense?

Leaving the driver's door ajar for fear of making any unnecessary noise, Malcolm slowly crept down through the shrubbery towards the canal, eyeing up the aged trees that separated the site from the towpath until his eyes finally settled on one he liked the look of. Although actually, if the truth be known, he didn't like the look of it at all since he was required to drive into it head first at any moment. But unlike the ancient buildings behind him it looked sturdy enough and its presence alone was testimony that it could stand the test of time and whatever – in this case two tonnes of metal – was chucked at it.

As he stepped forward to get a better look, he shivered inadvertently, the ice-cold breeze enveloping him in its suffocating embrace as he spotted what looked like a parked car, camouflaged from sight within the shadow of the branches. The cluster of trees blocked out what little light there was and it took a moment for his vision to further adjust as he moved towards it and nervously pressed his face up against the driver's window. His warm breath instantly fogged the cold glass and he stepped back and took a deep breath before leaning in once more to study the interior, his eyes fixing in alarm on what contents he could make out.

Why? It made no sense. His eyes darted around nervously in the darkness, as though half expecting the occupant to step out of the bushes and surprise him at any moment, but there was nothing. No movement, no sound, no nothing and he slowly crept around the vehicle to get a better look. *Coincidence maybe?* His eyes settled on the registration plate. Something about the letters KS nagged in the back of his mind but however much he tried, he couldn't envisage the coinciding plate he wished to mentally compare. He looked around again before leaning forward and pressing the palm of his hand on the bonnet. *Warm.* The driver must be close by.

A movement by the canal caught his eye then and he stopped dead, straining his eyes into the distance, but whatever he had seen was now blocked from sight behind the vegetation. Malcolm stood motionless and held his breath, unsure why really, other than that the slightest sound might give him away. He waited and sure enough, within seconds the object was once again in his line of sight.

What on earth? He watched transfixed as the figure stumbled along the path towards the tunnel, clearly struggling with the undergrowth underfoot. *Mad bag lady.* He'd recognise her a mile off. Malcolm watched awhile, curious, the thought flitting through his mind that he could kill two birds with one stone. *Two birds.* Unable to suppress his amusement, he cackled uncontrollably. He rather liked that analogy.

Rigor mortis, he reminded himself. The condition bothered him far more than he would care to admit. What if he'd left it too late? It would all be so typical of Eileen to make life difficult for him. He glanced at his wrist, the screen of his watch lighting up instantly and assuring him. Yes. If his informants on Google were right – and for now he was just going to have to hope that they were – Eileen could wait.

He crept further down the slope towards the canal, ominously aware of each and every squelch and crunch of mud and debris under foot as he did so. He needed to move fast now before the owner returned for their car. *The car.* Was he imagining it? He didn't think so, but now wasn't the time to get embroiled in the mystery.

42

The disused towpath to the old canal was rough and uneven underfoot, and the tiny pebbles compacted in mud needlessly assaulted the balls of Lou's feet as they rebelled angrily against the alien surface. Nonetheless, she knew from past experience that it was preferable to the grassy verge with its hidden weeds and thistles that lulled a person into a false sense of security only to then viciously attack them when they were least expecting it.

The light was better than she remembered it: an eerie, effervescent glow emanating from the street lamps that lined the housing estate directly behind the path. Not that it would have mattered at any rate. She knew the route like the back of her hand. Abandoned take-away packets and Styrofoam containers littered the walkway and she paused outside the tunnel entrance that served the railway above it to admire what she could see of the graffiti-lined walls, slightly in awe of the raw artistic talent of the unknown expert behind the design.

And that was when she heard it: a rustling noise, followed by the sharp snap of a twig underfoot. Exaggerated ten-fold by the surrounding silence, Lou turned sharply, her eyes darting back and forth as they carefully digested the shadows of the trees that whispered in the cool breeze and danced rhythmically against the water's surface. Content that there was nothing untoward, she turned back and slowly crept towards the tunnel, her heart still working overtime as her mind raced with possible terrifying scenarios.

As the noose was lassoed around her neck with the expertise of a rodeo rider roping his calf, Lou thought she had imagined the feeling of rough fabric against her skin at first, but then it was yanked tight, reining her in and demanding subservience. *Too tight.* She clawed at her neck with her fingers as she desperately tried to get purchase under the material and release it from its wrenching grip on her throat, but the hands holding it in place were too strong.

'Help!' she cried out, vaguely aware that no sound escaped her lips except for a harsh, gravelly whisper that was unrecognisable from her ordinary tones. The cloth pinched at her skin and dug into her larynx and she heaved, but as the hold on the material increased she pleaded with her attacker once more.

'Please.' She had no idea whether she was speaking aloud or hallucinating now. 'I have money.' She didn't, but her parents did and despite their recent differences, she couldn't see them refusing given the circumstances.

'Sssh.' The breath was hot on her ear as the voice ordered her to be quiet and she stopped struggling. Hadn't she read somewhere that a victim should befriend their assailant, or was that in a movie she'd seen? Lou couldn't remember, but as she wrestled in and out of consciousness she dared to hope that if she complied, it might somehow make them release their grasp on the material that was smothering every last breath from her body before it was too late.

They both stood still a moment as though reaching a peculiar sense of stalemate. Would she die without further ado or would the killer be forced to apply more pressure until she no longer had it in her to resist? Lou held her breath and awaited her fate, the only audible sound now the fear as the adrenalin pumped through her veins and pounded in her ears.

'Say you're sorry,' the voice hissed in her ear and Lou recoiled as the spray of saliva washed over her skin.

Sorry? She didn't understand, but she recognised the voice. But how? Who? If only she could get him to relax his grip, she might be able to concentrate. *Talk to me. Tell me who you are and what you want.*

'Please, I'm sorry.' It was agony to speak, her vocal chords damaged by the pressure of the rough fabric as it gripped her neck, but still she persisted. 'Let me go, we can talk. I'll do whatever you want. Please, I'm sorry.'

He didn't speak again, instead opting to simply stiffen the grip on the snare around her neck once more, but she was ready now. As ready as she ever would be for death to welcome her into its fold, and as the fight dissolved from her body, she physically relaxed. She wanted to die now. She wanted the fear and pain over with, but why was it taking so long? As she eased into death and accepted the sentence that destiny had served her, Lou's legs buckled beneath her and caved in under the pressure of having to hold up the deadweight of a body without a functioning brain to instruct them as to what was expected of them.

At some point she must also have wet herself, but that hadn't been a conscious decision. It hadn't even been something that she had realised she had done until she felt the warm liquid trickle down the inside of her thigh. Collapsing to the floor, the world as she knew it turned black and smothered her in a cloak of darkness. Lou no longer felt afraid. Instead, she relaxed into her fate and concentrated as the slideshow of images of her life started to play out in her mind.

Until a person experiences death, they have no way of knowing how it will feel. How their final moments will ultimately play out. But as Lou breathed her final breaths, it occurred to her in those short seconds that it actually wasn't half as bad as she had imagined that it would one day be. She had expected excruciating pain. Days, maybe even weeks, grieving for the life she was about to lose, but it hadn't been like that at all. The terror of what might happen and the fear of the unknown were what had made her final moments so dreadful. The injustice of being taken from a place she belonged before her time would be the role for her grieving family to play.

The pathologist would later describe Lou as lucky. A word that seemed completely at odds with the way that her life had so needlessly been brought to an early conclusion. The fact that her heart chose to give up and allow death to claim her before the vicious beating that followed could probably be classed as such, but this was still of little consolation to her family when they were called to do what no parent should ever have to do: identify the mutilated cadaver that was once their healthy child.

43

The figure sat on the small bench visibly shaking, the upper half of his body huddled over his knees. Like a desperate drug-addict finally getting their fix, it was supposed to provide a release and make all these dreadful thoughts and feelings of pent-up anger and resentment disappear, but if anything, it had only exacerbated the whole situation. Of course, the violence hadn't helped. That had all been so unnecessary to the proceedings but the woman clearly had the most unpleasant ability to bring out the worst in people.

Nevertheless, things had been allowed to get out of hand and that was very wrong. He should never have allowed himself to stoop to her level. As soon as it had all blown over and the dust had settled, a visit to Lou's graveside to apologise would be in order. There wouldn't be an apology for killing her though. That part had been absolutely essential, not to mention perfectly executed to cause the minimum amount of fuss and discomfort.

Picking up the small bundle from beside him with trembling hands that were cut and grazed from the commotion, he slowly peeled away the soiled, bloodied fabric to reveal the silver shoes. Slightly scuffed during the fracas, they were still exquisite nonetheless. It was always the same afterwards, the shoes bringing to mind a book he had once read that attempted to profile serial killers and put them all away, nice and tidily in a little box. The author had implied that all killers were the same and of a certain 'type'. The author was obviously an idiot who clearly didn't know what he was talking about and one day he fully intended to write to him and tell him as much.

The shoes weren't his trophies, at least not in the way that the writer claimed. To suggest that a killer removed items from a crime scene because they wanted a tangible scrapbook of souvenirs to remind them of their crimes was nothing short of ridiculous. Did the writer not realise that reminders were the last thing that some of them wanted? That there was nothing remotely pleasant about watching a person breathe their very last breath before death claimed them?

He glanced down at himself. His new top was caked in a grubby green lichen substance that he assumed had rubbed off from the tunnel walls during the initial scuffle and a bloodied crud had anchored itself beneath the tips of his fingernails. More than enough reminder of those final moments. Of course he would have to scrap his clothing now. A fact that displeased him no end.

A shadow moving out of the corner of his eye caught his attention and he glanced at his watch. 01.33am. *Strange. Why would anyone be loitering at the entrance to the canal at this time of the morning? Except me. I've got a very good reason for being here.* His eyes scanned the dark, hunting for the source of the movement and he started to question whether or not the whole thing had just been a figment of his imagination. The darkness, the ominous silence that filled the air, the knowledge of what lay in the tunnel, and the fear of being caught all contriving together to convince him that he was doomed.

Eyes peeled on the verge and hedgerow for signs of life, he stood up slowly and gently crept forward, cringing inwardly at the dull crunch of leaves and debris underfoot. Something moved then in his line of vision to the right. *Animal? Too tall.* Paralysed with fear, the deafening silence that screamed back at him was every inch oppressive as it was eerie. He had to kill it – the silence – before it killed him.

'Hello.' *Hello,* the voice echoed back over the water. *Idiot!* Calling out was a stupid idea. *Now they know you're here!*

'Pssst.' He jerked towards the source of the sound, just in time to see a man stagger out from the undergrowth and directly into his path.

You? There was no mistaking the figure as it stepped towards him.

'Got any change, mate? I'm thirsty.'

Drunk more like. A large rucksack and countless discarded cans of lager lay just inches from the man's feet and nose wrinkled in disgust, he slowly inched closer towards him. This wasn't part of the plan. It was totally inconvenient, but what other choice was there? Reliable witness he might not be but what if he recognised him too? It was too big a risk to let him go. Killing him was the only option. There really was no other way.

44

A s Malcolm rushed back up the slope towards the car as fast as he could, a shrill wail reverberated in the distance and caught his attention. He paused and strained to listen for the source of the sound. *Animal?* It was difficult to tell but the noise was definitely coming from the direction he'd left moments previously.

As he approached the main yard and spotted Eileen's car exactly where he'd left it, he relaxed a notch but then another noise grabbed his attention – a clank this time as though metal had been disturbed. The place was starting to give him the creeps and as he looked at the decrepit old buildings that loomed up ahead, he trembled instinctively. Were there ghosts here? People from the past watching his every move, waiting to pounce and seek some form of revenge of their own? If he listened carefully enough, he could almost hear their cries – the pained sound of death screaming out at him from behind the crumbling walls. His hair stood to attention on his skin and sent tiny little shivers crawling up and down the nape of his neck at the prospect.

Leave me alone. I want to be alone. Oh dear God, the last thing I want is to be alone. The conflicting emotions squabbled in his mind. *You aren't alone,* the voice warned him and he lurched sideways, scanning the yard for movement before reassuring himself it was just his mind playing tricks on him. *Get a grip, Malcolm,* he admonished as he scrabbled around the back of the car looking for a suitable weapon to defend himself just in case.

Another muffled squeal whistled across the water and he faltered, his ears on full alert as they tried to locate the source. *Eileen? Eileen's dead,* he reminded himself as his fingers settled on the small compact umbrella that had fallen behind one of the seats. Crawling backwards out of the car, he made his way gingerly towards the boot, careful to watch his step as he hurried awkwardly in his haste on the wet, muddy surface beneath his feet. He needed to move fast now. Get the dirty deed over and done with before rigor mortis set in, but then the unmistakeable sound of the boot latch as it was released from the locking mechanism stopped him dead in his tracks once more.

Why wasn't she dead? Why did she always have to go and spoil absolutely everything he tried to do? Malcolm moved as quickly and quietly as he could back to the front of the vehicle. Clambering behind the wheel, he engaged the central locking so that she, or anyone else come to that who might be lurking around the creepy site, couldn't get to him. How angry was Eileen likely to be? His wife could be quite calculating at times, vicious even when she felt wronged, so right now there was a good chance she would be lethal if she did get her hands on him.

Having finally managed to pick the lock, Eileen lay motionless and held her breath to listen as the cold air washed over her and flooded her prison. What was he doing? Only the tiniest of rustling sounds gave him away. She moved awkwardly as she attempted to loosen her joints enough to climb from the cramped space. *Easy does it.* She stretched one leg over the ledge first and once she felt the blood return to her feet, she did the same with the other.

About to manoeuvre her body over the side, a bloodcurdling scream from beyond the trees to her left pierced into the night, gliding across the water and settling directly upon the point where she lay. *Fox?* She stopped what she was doing to listen, fear knocking the wind from her lungs at the ominous sound of heavy footsteps as they urgently thundered towards the car. Terrified of what she might see, the need to know what was happening was stronger and she sat up as best she could to look towards the source of the noise. Squinting in the darkness, she could just about make out an approaching silhouette as it sprinted towards her from the tunnel that ran along the side of the canal.

The car surged forwards then, the lid above her cracking shut and her body jolted as the wheels hit something hard. Blinded by terrified tears and the lack of light, Eileen fumbled around madly in the pitch-black space for something to grip onto as she was thrown from one side of the boot to the other.

'Malcolm,' she screamed. 'MALCOLM!' Dear God, surely he wasn't going to drive home without first releasing her from this cage? As though in direct response to her question, the car accelerated and Eileen pressed the palms of her hands down hard on the metal floor as she desperately tried to stop herself from being tossed around.

45

The four sisters – shit, shower, shave and sleep – were calling but as Lucas climbed wearily into his car and slammed the door gratefully against the elements, his mobile let off a series of bleeps. Retrieving his phone from his jacket pocket he turned his attention to the screen, his heart sinking at what it revealed. Eight missed calls from the station. One call for every hour he'd been missing from shift could mean only one thing: the superintendent was on the warpath and wanted answers as to his whereabouts.

Where are you, Lou? It had been exactly 22.02 when he had lost sight of her. She had taken a short cut down the alley behind Lake Street and by the time Lucas had managed to manoeuvre around the parked cars that littered the adjoining side roads that backed on to the alley there had been no sign of her. Despite spending relentless hours thereafter hunting the streets and every available pub he could think of, he had drawn a blank. She wasn't at home either; that's where he had spent the rest of the night, camped outside on the doorstep waiting for her.

Turning the key in the ignition, the windscreen wipers immediately sprang into action, furiously clunking back and forth as they fought the onslaught attacking it and he sat and stared a moment, transfixed by the hypnotising motion. Picking up his mobile once more, his finger hovered awkwardly over the keypad a split second longer than was absolutely necessary before he hit redial. Counting the endless unanswered rings, he tapped his fingers impatiently on the steering wheel as he waited for someone to pick up.

On the verge of hanging up, the monotone voice of Derek Matthews finally greeted him and resounded around the vehicle as the hands-free system kicked in.

'Cliffborough Cross CID.'

'Derek, it's Lucas.' He pulled away from the side of the road and joined the heavy queue waiting to cross the traffic lights up ahead.

'Welcome back, good holiday?'

Sarcastic little shit. Lucas grinned. He liked Derek. He was one of the good guys. 'You called?' he responded, all the while gritting his teeth at the prospect of what he felt sure was coming next. Derek had a habit of communicating by song and sure enough, he didn't disappoint.

Lucas shook his head. It was a toss-up, which was worse, the rendition of Stevie Wonder or Brenda Lee's 'You're in the Doghouse,' both of which were about as welcome as a shit in a wetsuit, but he couldn't help laughing anyway.

'Don't ever give up the day job will you, mate?'

Seemingly happy to dispense with the jokes as quickly as he had started them, Derek pressed on. 'We've got the body of an IC1 female, badly beaten and dumped in the tunnel on the old cycle path adjoining the canal.'

The grinding started up almost immediately, gnawing at the inside of his brain like a horde of mice munching their way through something they shouldn't. *IC1 female. Old cycle path. What's that from Lake Street, ten minutes?* Had another victim fallen foul of the Cross Killer? *Lou? Please God no,* he pleaded internally. *Badly beaten.* Derek's words reverberated in his ears. *Malcolm Muldoon.* Again, the name that was never far from the forefront of his mind. What was it the man had said when questioned about the attack on Lou? *She's going to pay.* Is that what had happened? Had Malcolm attacked her again? Served up his promised punishment?

'Cause of death? Suspects? Has the victim been identified?' Lucas' mouth raced in time with his brain and as he pulled up at the next junction, his leg jigged impatiently under the wheel as he waited for a sympathetic driver to allow him into the relentless queue of angry commuters.

'Tut, tut, Lucas, you know the score. Act on fact, never overreact or detract.' The unwritten rule in the unpublished handbook of policing that was rammed down their throats at pretty much every staff meeting and briefing. Lucas slammed his fist down hard on the steering wheel in frustration, a thin layer of bile coating his tongue, and he retched as the bitter taste stuck in his throat as he tried to swallow. He needed to know if the victim was Lou. Or more to the point, he needed to know that the victim wasn't Lou.

'Sure they'll fill you in just as soon as you stop yapping and get your arse down there. I'll tell you this much for nothing though,' Derek continued, 'hers wasn't the only body.'

Gobsmacked at this latest little snippet of information and needing to concentrate, Lucas put on his hazards and engaged the handbrake. 'Two women?' Incredulous, he was totally oblivious to the obstruction he was causing and the angry blares from motorists' horns as they struggled with the oncoming traffic to pass his stationary vehicle on the narrow stretch of road.

'Is that what I said?' Derek didn't wait for an answer before continuing. 'The body of an IC1 male was found a short distance from the other.' Derek paused, clearly enjoying divulging the news to the young detective. 'The way they're talking, you might just have your killer.'

'Yes!' Lucas made to punch the air in victory, but stopped short of completing the gesture as the meaning of the words filtered into his brain. 'How can he be the perpetrator if he's dead? He's not dead, is that it?' he added as an afterthought.

'You've got to stop jumping to conclusions, Lucas, that's not what I said.'

'Well stop talking in riddles then.' Lucas shook his head in confusion, wishing Derek would just get to the point and spit it out. 'You're not making sense. If he's our killer, he can't be dead.'

'Well, you know me, I ain't one for conjecture.' Lucas smirked as he spoke. Derek loved hearsay more than life itself. 'But between you, me and the gatepost, they're saying the killer and the latest victim are one and the same.'

'A suicide killing?' Feeling suddenly impatient, Lucas released the handbrake and nudged the car forwards, hoping to persuade someone in the queue to give him a break and let him join the mainstream flow of traffic.

'Someone killed him alright, but there's no escaping the fact he had several suspect items on his person when he died.'

'Planted?' It was the obvious explanation and Lucas was starting to think that his superiors might have a point about acting on fact.

'That's your department… *Detective.*' Derek chuckled, the cogs as they whirred in Lucas' brain almost audible down the phone line.

'Derek, I've got a call waiting I need to take.' It was a blatant lie, but the conversation was going nowhere and Lucas needed to think.

'One other thing,' Derek pushed on urgently, aware that he was just about to hang up, 'you're needed where the poorly people live.'

The hospital? *Lou's hospital?* If Lou needed him at the hospital, she must be okay? The combination of need and fear simultaneously crushed the air from his lungs and he struggled to breathe.

'Why?' he asked, finally finding his voice.

'Some woman, Veronica Higgins,' Derek read from

his notes. 'Admitted several hours ago, badly beaten by all accounts.'

Badly beaten? Once again, the words echoed in his ears. Why did he suddenly have a bad feeling about all of this? 'Please tell me this isn't anything to do with our killings, Derek.'

'This isn't anything to do with our killings.' Lucas frowned. Another of Derek's little quips, or was he legit this time?

'Can't uniform deal with it?' he asked, deflated that it wasn't Lou. Of course the last thing he wanted was for her to be hurt, but hurt was frankly better than dead. If this attack had nothing to do with Lou, his time could be better served at the murder scene where he could satisfy himself once and for all that the victim wasn't her.

'Don't shoot the messenger, lad. The order for you to attend came from the higher powers that be.'

The superintendent. His punishment for going AWOL no doubt. 'But surely she can wait? I need to visit the crime scene first.' *Then I'll shove a broom up my arse and sweep the hospital corridors if that's what makes him happy,* he thought irritably.

'Have it your own way, only I heard you have a particular interest in Malcolm Muldoon.' *Can't kid a kidder.* Derek had been quietly observing Lucas' blatant fascination with the man for days now.

'Malcolm Muldoon?' Lucas sat bolt upright in his seat. 'Are you saying Muldoon's involved?' The man attacked Lou, so why not this other woman? He nibbled his lower lip impatiently as he awaited Derek's response.

'Act on fact, never...'

'Yeah, yeah, yeah,' Lucas interrupted. 'Come on, Derek, spill.'

'I didn't tell you this, right.' Derek leaned into the phone conspiratorially as he spoke. 'Word has it, this Veronica – Ronnie she calls herself – is pointing the finger at Muldoon's wife.'

'Eileen Muldoon?' Lucas brushed his hand through his hair in confusion. 'I don't understand.'

'Nor do the rest of them. Look, son,' he continued, 'get yourself down the hospital and speak to her. There's nothing you can do for the other victims so they're hardly likely to hold your absence against you.'

As a sympathetic driver finally chose to let him out of the junction, Derek's last words hit home and he turned a sharp right in the direction of the hospital. If there was any possibility that this potential witness could point him in Malcolm's direction, he wouldn't miss it for the world.

46

The double doors swung forcefully behind him as Lucas entered the hospital and he paused a moment to wrestle with his demons. *Perfuming the pig*, he thought to himself as the stench of disinfectant mingled with the overpowering trashy floral scent being pumped into the air-conditioning system assaulted his nostrils. The place stank of the foul concoction and instantly brought back memories he would rather leave buried with his mother in the churchyard.

Determined to block both his sense of smell and his mind of stuff he would rather forget, he took a deep breath and strolled purposefully towards the reception and joined the line. The staff positioned behind the front desk were all too preoccupied to notice him, camouflaged by queues of patients and visitors all demanding their attention and so he stood a moment, careful to avoid any unwanted eye-contact as he absently observed the floor and feet of his comrades as they slowly moved forward and signalled it would soon be his turn.

Shoes. The thought struck him out of nowhere and he pulled his mobile from his pocket and dialled his colleague Sam. Her phone went directly to voicemail, so without leaving a message he dialled the station instead, determined to ignore the filthy look from the woman behind him as she huffed and puffed and pointed angrily to a sign forbidding the use of mobile phones.

'Derek, it's me again. Get hold of the inventories for

Hannah Gregory and EJ Mahoney's properties. If there's no shoes on the list, I want to be the first to know.'

'What's the magic word?' Derek teased.

'Now.' Lucas replaced the phone in his pocket without further ado and smiled apologetically at the busybody behind him before moving forward to the desk and flashing his warrant card to the receptionist.

Ten minutes later, having navigated the maze of stairs and corridors to avoid using the lift, Lucas stood outside the main doors to the Griffiths Ward. He took a moment to compose himself and figure out how he was going to play it. *Why Eileen Muldoon?* It made no sense, but Malcolm on the other hand had history. Not only had he attacked Lou, he'd also threatened to make her pay. And now here he was, about to speak to a victim who not only knew Malcolm but who also, by her own admission, was loathed by the man.

Had Malcolm carried out the attack on this Ronnie Higgins and somehow managed to frame his wife in the process? *Desperate people do desperate things,* he reminded himself, and after what he had witnessed the other day at the house, there was no doubt in his mind that the man would go to any levels to put himself and his needs before those of his wife. Lucas started to feel sick again, the fear that Lou was dead feasting on his nerves and quietly devouring his mind. *I'll bloody kill you, Malcolm. So help me God, I'll kill you with my own hands if you so much as laid a finger on her!*

As Lucas gingerly approached the side of Ronnie's bed, he sucked in his breath at the sight of her bruised and bloodied face, swollen from both the attack and the needles that had worked overtime to piece her back together again. *Jeez.* Her attacker had been thorough. *The killer?* However hard he tried, Lucas couldn't picture the Eileen Muldoon that he had met, collapsed and only semi-conscious at the base of the stairs, with the scale of this attack.

'Ronnie?'

'If you think this is bad, you should see the other guy,' she quipped and he shook his head in awe, not sure whether to be impressed or saddened at how upbeat she could be at a time like this.

'I'm DI Lucas Elliott from Cliffborough Cross CID.'

'I know, we've already met.' She started to cough and Lucas reached for the jug of water on the bed-tray, poured a generous portion into the non-spill beaker and slowly offered it to her mouth.

'We have?'

'Peter Pan.'

Lucas nodded solemnly, recognition and realisation dawning all at once. Peter Pan was the nickname that he and his colleagues had given Ronnie's thick-skinned, responsibility-shirking, childlike ex who refused to get the message when their relationship had ended. *Peter.* It suddenly occurred to him. Was this why he had taken such a dislike to Lou's Peter? *Don't call her that. She belonged to you, not him! Belongs,* the voice in his head corrected him. *She's not dead, she can't be.* Another wave of acidic bile burned his chest and throat as it erupted to the surface.

'I take it you've not heard from him?' It was the obvious question. Almost twelve months after they had separated, Ronnie's ex had finally taken things a step too far and physically assaulted her in broad daylight. The courts had thankfully slapped a lifelong restraining order on the man, but the similarities to now were too close to ignore. Some people couldn't take no for an answer and Lucas was in no doubt that her ex was one such person.

'He's about.' Forgetting her injuries, Ronnie shrugged out of habit and instantly winced at the movement. 'I saw him recently but he's made no deliberate contact.'

'Good.' Lucas leaned forward and touched her hand

gently, terrified to disrupt the web of pins and wires that ran from it to the machines at the head of her bed. 'My colleagues mentioned Eileen and Malcolm Muldoon. Want to tell me about them?'

Ronnie breathed resignedly. 'A friend saw Malcolm with another woman.' She cleared her throat. 'They were very friendly, if you get my drift.' She started to cough again, pointing at the jug of water and Lucas duly obliged. 'Messenger always gets shot, I know that, but Eileen's my friend and she had a right to know.' A tear rolled down her cheek and Lucas retrieved his handkerchief from his pocket and gently dabbed at her skin. '*Was* my friend,' she continued.

'Didn't take the news lying down, I take it?'

'I've never known her so angry, but I thought, well, I assumed she was angry with him but now I'm not so sure.'

Lucas leaned forward and gently brushed a matt of sweated hair away from her temple. 'You think she's angry with you?'

'I don't know, I don't know what to think anymore,' she cried.

'Talk to me, Ronnie. I can't help if you don't talk to me.' Why assume her attacker was Eileen? It still made no sense.

'The obvious answer was Malcolm, out for revenge for telling Eileen, but...'

'But what?' Lucas still didn't get it and shook his head in confusion.

'Perfume.' Ronnie whispered the words as though revealing her most inner politically incorrect thoughts. 'Whoever attacked me wore perfume.'

47

erfume. As Lucas marched across the tarmac to his car, he couldn't dismiss the thought from his mind. If the killer was in fact female, this backed up his shoe theory but where did it leave Malcolm? The man was somehow involved, he'd be willing to bet his life on it. And what of the male victim? The connection bugged him, nagging at the back of his mind like the missing piece of a jigsaw that was never going to belong. The sooner he could get to the crime scene and speak to his colleagues, the better.

As though reading his mind, his mobile phone sounded and pulling it from his pocket, he glanced at the screen before answering. *Shit.* He should at least have kept his partner up to speed.

'Sam, I'm sorry. Got held up, but I'm on my way now.'

'Bodies are bagged up and headed for the mortuary, I'm on my way there.' Lucas stopped by the side of the car and listened to his colleague as she continued.

'Remember Lou Wilson?' Sam didn't elaborate. Whilst Lucas had never blamed the woman for her involvement in his mother's death, there was no question that her name would be etched on his brain forever.

Lucas faltered, grabbing the handle of the car door for support as his knees threatened to cave under the weight of his body at the mention of Lou's name. It could mean only one thing. Lou was dead and it was all his fault. He had failed her. He could have kept looking. He *should* have kept looking but he hadn't. So eaten up with jealousy over Peter, he hadn't been able to see what was staring him in the face. *Peter.* An image of Ronnie lying in the hospital bed flashed before his eyes. Same Peter or coincidence?

'Uniform's at her place now,' she continued.

'Get them to check...'

'Shoes, yeah they're already on it,' she interrupted. 'Which brings me to our second victim.'

'Hang on.' Lucas opened the car door and climbed in. Moving the phone away from his face so his colleague couldn't hear, he took several deep breaths in rapid succession as he tried to compose himself. *I won't fail you again, Lou, I WILL NOT fail you again!* 'Get them to look for anything appertaining to someone called Peter. Is someone speaking to work colleagues?'

'Ash and Kelly are on their way over there now.'

Lucas turned and stared at the building he had just left, the urge to march back in and demand answers immense.

'Good. Don't let them leave until they've got a full name and address for him. Works with them I think. What's that you were going to say about the second victim?'

'Well, this is where it gets interesting. I spoke to Derek. Looks like your hunch about the shoes paid off. No shoes in either property and guess what?' Sam didn't wait for him to answer before continuing. 'Our IC1 male had two sets on his person when he died.'

'Lou's corpse?' The word corpse stuck in his throat, the image of Lou's mutilated, naked torso sending a burning rush of blood to the surface that scalded his skin.

'Again no shoes.'

'ID on the male?'

'Oh he had ID alright,' Sam responded sarcastically. 'Fan of the old five-finger discount by all accounts. Now we just need to figure out which – if any – of the credit cards he had in his possession actually belonged to him.'

Lucas flinched. If their man was a known thief, the fact that he had women's shoes on his person – belonging to the victims or otherwise – was irrelevant. It could, and no doubt would, only serve to weaken any case that they had against him. And it didn't answer who had killed him. Whether they liked it or not, they still had a murderer on their hands.

'Next of kin?' He was starting to feel dizzy again, as though he were some place else watching himself from afar, and he pressed the palm of his hand on first his forehead and then one cheek at a time in an effort to regulate his body temperature. This wasn't how it was supposed to be. Meeting Lou's parents was going to be a happy occasion. One he had all worked out. The meal at the expensive restaurant, the speech he had prepared and learned verbatim, and her father smiling from ear to ear as he shook his hand rigorously and cracked open the bottle of champagne to celebrate their forthcoming marriage.

'FLO's with the parents now. They'll meet us there for the formal ID. I assume you'll be able to grace us with your presence?' The words slipped out before she could stop them. Sam had been determined not to resort to sarcasm until he'd had the chance to explain his recent absence, but when push came to shove she couldn't help it.

Lucas glanced up at the huge concrete jungle that loomed before him. Lit up like the Vegas Strip, strands of light poured into the sky from the hundred-plus minute windows. The mortuary was situated in the basement of the very building he was looking at and had exited only minutes previously.

'I'm outside. Long story, I'll fill you in later. Who've we got?'
'Erika again.'

Lucas chewed thoughtfully on his bottom lip. Erika Carter might well be the best in the business, but she was also so tight lipped, it was a wonder she didn't squeak when she did finally choose to speak.

48

D esigned in the late 1800s and utilised as an infirmary for
injured troops during both World Wars, the mortuary
had recently been renovated and updated to house state-
of-the-art equipment and integrate the various aspects of
bereavement all within the one unit. The large open hall had
been divided up into suitable areas: one tastefully furnished
with comfortable seating and low lighting to serve as a viewing
area and in another, an array of private cubicles enabled
mourners to receive counselling or simply pay their respects
to loved ones in privacy. At the far end of the room, patio
doors led to a small garden that was laid mainly to lawn and
decorated with ornamental shrubs and the occasional cluster
of tables and chairs. The views were what made this area so
special, mourners able to lose themselves for hours on end
in the unspoilt countryside that stretched over the town for
miles beyond. On a good day, when time seemed to stand still,
you could see as far as the Malvern Hills and the Cotswolds
peeping out beyond.

A direct contrast, Lucas thought ruefully, to the area that the
public weren't privy to. Namely the main autopsy room, where
he and Sam now stood, side by side and covered head to foot in
surgical attire to prevent any cross-contamination. Although
clinically immaculate, it wasn't a tidy workspace. Tables and
trolleys littered with microscopes, surgical instruments and
an assortment of sterilised containers filled the room and it

was anybody's guess how Erika could so easily locate exactly what implements she required at a moment's notice. Above the sinks and worktops, rows of embalming fluid and other chemicals lined every wall with the exception of one, which housed the large floor-to-ceiling fridges that encased trays of bodies scheduled for autopsies. Once completed, they were then taken to a further room where they lay in coffins awaiting preparation and transportation to their final send-off.

The acrid stench of chemicals and the underlying odour of death in the small space was overwhelming. As they watched Erika slowly but steadily describe the size, shape and location of each of the victim's wounds into a small hand-held Dictaphone, Lucas wiped his mouth with his fingers as he wrestled with his gag reflex. This was nothing new. He hated this part of his job the most. The reek of mortality and the inability to rid his body and mind of the smell nothing in comparison to seeing a lifeless body, slowly taken apart bit by bit to examine parts of it that no other human should ever need to see. *Not just any body,* he reminded himself as another surge of vomit rose from the pit of his belly and burned his throat as he hastily swallowed the bitter fluid.

In an effort to control the incessant urge to throw up, Lucas concentrated instead on Erika's face and wondered what possessed a person to pursue an occupation in a place like this in the first instance. She was a good-looking woman. Well educated and could presumably have had her choice of career, so why this? Why would a person who could have had her pick of any profession make a morbid fascination with death her priority? His eyes moved inadvertently to her left hand. No wedding ring, which came as little surprise. Erika Carter didn't strike him as the marrying type. She seemed so disapproving of everyone and everything, it was little wonder that her preferred choice was to work with people who couldn't talk, let alone argue back with her. Besides, Lucas wasn't sure he could curl up at night with a woman who came home with death on her hands and the stink of it on her body any more than he could wake up with one whose day started when someone else's had ended.

Eventually, Erika spoke. 'Your culprit sure was angry.'

'No shit, Sherlock.' Lucas glared at her fiercely and Sam placed a hand gently on his arm to steady him. *What the hell is up with him?* He'd been acting weird ever since she'd clapped eyes on him in the car park. Catching his eye she gave him a warning look, but he just shrugged and looked away.

Now wasn't the time to piss off the best forensic the force had, Lucas knew that, but he had kind of been hoping for something – anything – that could pass as intelligent observation instead of the kind of thing that your average kid in the school playground would notice.

'I said *your* culprit.' Unable to disguise her dislike for the impatient little man who she had always firmly believed must have engaged in something underhand to have been passed up the ranks so quickly for a person of his age, Erika glanced at Lucas patronisingly before turning her attention back to the deceased.

'Meaning what? The killer's definitely one and the same?' Despite the outward differences in the brutal attack on Lou in contrast to the others, Lucas still firmly believed that the same person was responsible. That Malcolm Muldoon was responsible, and he nodded his head encouragingly at her.

'Difficult to say definitively, *Detective*.' The sarcasm in Erika's tone as she stressed the last word wasn't lost on Lucas. 'But if you're asking me whether or not there are similarities to the other victims that simply cannot be ignored, then yes there are.'

'But how?' Sam interjected. 'The other victims were poisoned, this one was…' She stumbled over the right words to describe the beaten mess that lay on the worktop in front of them. 'Well,' she shook her finger in the direction of the body, 'how can *that* resemble a victim who the killer didn't lay a finger on except to feign strangulation?'

'And what about him?' Lucas gestured towards the body of the male on the neighbouring table. 'Where does he fit into all of this?' Wrong time, wrong place or had their culprit expanded their résumé to include men? No way did he buy into the theory that he was their killer who had then been dispatched by another. *Malcolm Muldoon.* The name bounced around his skull once more, only serving to convince him more than ever that the man was responsible.

Seemingly ignoring his question, Erika stepped forwards and leaned over Lou's body and pointed to the deep red gouge ingrained on her otherwise pale skin. 'See this?' Her finger hovered millimetres away from the wound on the side of the victim's neck. It was also alarmingly close to the bruise that Lucas had inflicted and he instantly looked away and did his best to swallow his guilt.

'Our killer is once again left-handed,' Erika continued.

Left-handed? Malcolm's left-handed, isn't he? Lucas squeezed his eyes tightly shut and pressed the tips of his index and middle fingers hard against his forehead as he tried to envisage Malcolm cleaning Eileen's blood from that stupid picture. Possibly, but not definitely. He couldn't remember. *Eileen?* Again, quite possibly but he couldn't say for sure.

'If you look closely,' Erika continued as she pointed to the laceration on Lou's neck.

Look closely? No way. It was all Lucas could do to look at all, the image of her lying peacefully in bed next to him flashing before his eyes every time that he did. If he didn't look directly at her, it was fine, he could deceive his brain into believing they were discussing someone else but his eyes refused to yield to the same trick.

'The knot in her underwear ran from here,' Erika pointed

to a section of Lou's neck, 'to here.' Her finger ran the length of the wound and as Lucas' eyes followed the course, he retched again as they settled on the bruise on her chin instead of her second point of call.

You did that, the voice in his head screamed, his eyes refusing to rip themselves away from the bruise to the gash that demanded his immediate attention.

'Ignore that, it's old.' Noticing his blatant discomfort, Erika again pointed at the two pressure points on the victim's neck. 'The knot ran that way.'

'Meaning?' Sam tilted her head sideways as she studied Lucas and his obvious struggle to look at Lou's corpse. This wasn't like him and however hard she tried, she couldn't seem to get rid of the unnerving feeling inside her that there was something he wasn't telling them. 'What?' she mouthed at him but rather than respond, his eyes shifted guiltily to the floor.

'Meaning very good news,' Erika declared emphatically as she moved away from the body towards a shelving unit at the far end of the room.

Good news? Rage boiled inside him as Lucas stepped forward and reached for the pathologist by the scruff of her neck and swung her around to face him. Lou had been brutally murdered and the bitch had the nerve to call it good news?

'Fuck you!' he spat, his face inches from hers.

'Excuse me.' Totally unfazed by his outburst, Erika picked his hands from her coat one by one and discarded them into the air as though simply retrieving pieces of fluff or dirt.

Hard as nails, Sam thought to herself as she watched the exchange, shocked into silence by Lucas' outburst.

'How is *that*,' Lucas pointed behind him to Lou's corpse, but didn't trust himself to look as he spoke, 'good news?'

'Dear boy,' Erika smiled patronisingly as she spoke, 'far be it for me to tell you your job, but whether you like it or not, the fact that a leftie killed all of the victims to date is extremely good news.'

'Ten percent of the population,' Sam nodded thoughtfully.

'Exactly.' Erika turned her attention to Sam, pleased that at least one half of the team was capable of being objective and putting the brains she was born with to good use. 'And ten percent, of ten percent, of ten percent equals?'

'A practical impossibility that the victims were killed by different people?'

'Not impossible, but unlikely.'

'And him?' Sam tilted her head in the direction of the male victim.

'Again, the killer was left-handed.' Erika smiled at her new ally before turning back to Lucas as she spoke. 'The odds that different people killed your victims don't stack up. Even *you,*' Lucas tried not to rise to the bait as she stressed the word as though he was stupid, 'must see that?'

'It's still not enough,' he shrugged, ashamed of his outburst and unable to look either of them in the eye. 'You and I both know we need a hell of a lot more than that to marry these two victims to the others. We need substantiated facts, Erika, not conjecture.'

'And facts I shall give you.' As she studied him over the rim of her glasses, she brought to mind his old school matron. The one who always seemed to take pleasure in other people's pain. Furious with her condescending manner, but also painfully aware of the filthy look that Sam was directing at him, Lucas resigned himself to the fact that they needed Erika on side.

'I'm sorry, okay, I'm sorry.' He held out his palms to her as though under arrest. 'We're all under a lot of stress here in case you hadn't noticed.'

I forgive you. I'm sorry too, the voice mimed sarcastically in his head. Had she even heard him? She didn't respond or give any indication that she had as she turned her back to him and gave the shelves behind her the benefit of her undivided attention. Reaching for a folder, she removed the contents and scattered several photographs across the table in front of her.

Lucas and Sam both approached and took up position beside her to study the pictures more carefully. The photographs were instantly recognisable as the neck wounds inflicted post mortem to both EJ Mahoney and Hannah Gregory. Without taking her eyes from the pictures, Erika then reached across to the adjoining table and retrieved the latest photographs of Lou and the male victim's injuries and placed them next to the others.

'No such thing as coincidence.' Erika spoke quietly, as though speaking to herself, and Lucas had to concede, the injuries did indeed all look identical. Nonetheless, it took everything he had to concentrate on the wounds in question and not the one that he knew first hand had been inflicted prior to this latest attack.

'No poison this time around though,' Sam shook her head thoughtfully as she spoke. 'And poison wasn't disclosed to the press.'

'Copycat killing gone wrong?' God forbid Sam was right and they had a freak out there intent on some form of notoriety. The killer to date had only killed women. The killer used poison. The strangulation had been inconsequential, but now they had two strangled corpses, no evidence of poison and a victim of the wrong gender to theoretically even interest the offender.

Lucas looked at Erika, keen to know whether or not she considered it to be a possibility. He personally didn't. He remained firm in his conviction that Malcolm Muldoon fitted the bill perfectly. It was textbook stuff. Killers always followed a protocol, but Malcolm wasn't *normal* in any way, shape or form so far as he was concerned. *Normal* killers, if there was such a thing, tended to get braver with each crime they got away with, but they didn't suddenly completely change their modus operandi without good explanation. But Malcolm? Having witnessed his feeble attempt to take his wife's life the other day, Lucas felt sure that the man was capable of pretty much anything.

Erika pulled the relevant crime scene photographs from the files and laid the corresponding photo for each strangled victim on the table with the others.

'Now what do you see?' As Lucas and Sam leaned forward to inspect the photos more closely, Erika continued without waiting for either of them to respond. 'The same person strangled them all. See that?' She pointed to each victim as found at the scene in turn. 'Your killer ties their weapon of choice very specifically. Not nautical.' She ran her fingers over the pictures as she spoke. 'In fact, it's not any specific knot at all so far as I'm aware, but in each case,' she pointed again to the photographs one by one as though to emphasise her point, 'it's an exact match. Which can only mean, since these details have never been publicised, that your copycat theory,' she paused and glanced at Lucas smugly before finishing her sentence, 'holds absolutely no weight whatsoever.'

'He's still the missing link.' Lucas turned and pointed towards the table where the male victim lay. 'If the underwear's symbolic to women, why kill him at all?' No sooner were the words out, he regretted them. No doubt she wouldn't be able to resist making a jibe that reasoning why was his department and she didn't prove him wrong.

'You're the detective, so detect!' Erika quickly carried on before he could cut in. 'Of course, there could be a perfectly simple explanation. This young man,' she jabbed a disrespectful finger in the direction of the body and Lucas could only assume that it came with dissecting them day in, day out – you stopped caring about the person within it and instead began to see them as some kind of object alone, 'stumbled across the killer at some point this morning. Inconvenienced them probably. A price he paid handsomely for by all accounts.'

'But none of this explains the beating.' Sam's voice finally broke the thoughtful silence that had followed. 'The culprit never laid a finger on the others.'

Once more, Erika looked over her glasses down the bridge of her nose at them both before responding. 'The others obviously didn't make him angry.' She shrugged. 'Who knows? But the killer's one and the same. I'd bet my life on it.'

49

'Want to tell me what all that was about?' Sam warmed her hands on the cup of coffee in front of her and locked eyes with Lucas, unflinching in her resolve not to break first.

'All what?' He glanced across the table at her, but sensing the stubbornness in her gaze he quickly looked away guiltily and focused instead on the steam rising from his drink.

'You know she could report you… I could report you.'

'But you won't.' He shrugged and slurped loudly as he took a mouthful of his drink. 'I'm sorry if I was talking while you were interrupting, young man.' Lucas spoke sarcastically in a voice heavily tinged with a German accent as he impersonated Erika, and Sam's lips twitched as a small smile escaped.

'Carry on like you did back there and you might give me no choice.' Sam studied him carefully, determined to get to the bottom of why he was behaving so erratically. 'First you go missing during your shift, then you all but attack the pathologist. Seriously, Lucas, I can't work with you unless you let me in.'

Seemingly mesmerised by the plate of pastries on the table between them, Lucas didn't speak and she tried again. 'Either you spill or I go upstairs the second I get back to the station and inform them of my concerns.'

Lucas closed his eyes and rested his head in his hands, massaging his forehead vigorously with his fingers until finally, without looking up, he spoke. 'Me and Lou. We. Well, we…'

'Oh you have to be kidding me?' she interrupted. 'You've been shagging your mother's killer?' Sam knew it was crass, but she couldn't believe he could be so stupid.

'It wasn't like that. We're in love. We *were* in love,' he instantly corrected himself.

'You can't work the case.' She pushed the plate of untouched pastries away, her appetite now well and truly depleted. 'Jesus Christ, Lucas, you haven't even explained your absence last night. You're a possible suspect. No, scrap that; you *are* a suspect!' Sam looked at him, the horror and disbelief written all over her face.

'You seriously think that little of me?' Lucas reached for her hands across the table but she ripped them out of reach as though scalded.

'So where the hell were you?' Suddenly she couldn't look at him, terrified of what she might see. Lucas had always had a short fuse. Something as simple as a traffic jam was normally all it took to trip the switch, but murder? She automatically shivered despite the warmth kicking out from the heating system above them.

Lucas pulled his hands away and rested them helplessly on his lap, looking down and concentrating on them as he spoke.

'I was looking for her, Sam. We had a row. No hear me out,' he protested as she went to butt in. 'We had a row over this guy and now I think he might have killed her. Well, maybe. Maybe not. Malcolm Muldoon's also a bloody likely contender if you ask me.'

'I wasn't asking you,' Sam snapped, finally looking into the eyes of the colleague she thought she knew so well and now quite possibly as it turned out, didn't know at all.

'I can't be kicked off the case, Sam. Not now. Not with

all these little balls up in the air. Don't you see, until I catch whoever did this I've failed her and can't put it right?'

'Bit late for all that, don't you think?' Sam knew she was being unfair, but surely he could see that his involvement was a severe conflict of interest that could seriously jeopardise the case?

'I know how it looks, Sam, but really? You've known me how long and you honestly believe I could do something like what we just witnessed back there?'

'So tell me about the older wound that Erika observed. Did that happen during this so-called row?'

Lucas jerked his eyes away from Sam's and she frowned as the meaning behind the reaction hit her head on.

'Oh my God, it did! You hit her. It's why you were being so weird in there.'

'I was being weird because I was being asked to study the corpse of the woman I love,' Lucas responded bitterly through gritted teeth. 'None of what we witnessed in there had fuck all to do with me,' he spat. Okay, so he was being slightly economical with the truth and he felt another wave of guilt wash over him as the image of the bruise he had inflicted swam through his mind. But he had to make Sam see. Questioning him and trying to apportion the blame at his door was a waste of her time. A waste of both their time. Time that could be better served trying to catch the bastard who killed her!

'I didn't kill her, you must know that,' he continued. 'One smack, that was all. I'm not proud of myself.' As Sam glared across the table at him in disgust, Lucas rubbed his fingers through his hair, his eyes pleading with her to understand. 'It was crazy, I was crazy,' he begged. 'But I'm no killer and I'm not capable of the kind of violence that she was subjected to by that... that...' He faltered over his words as he tried to find a suitable description. 'Monster,' he eventually muttered, so quietly as he stared regretfully at the table that at first Sam thought she had imagined it.

'I know.' Sam finally spoke as she studied him, all the while struggling to comprehend how he could have got himself into this mess in the first place. Someone like Lucas could surely have his pick of women, yet he chose an affair with the very woman that put his mother ten feet under? 'If this gets out, I'm not sure about the rest of them back at the station, mind.'

'Which is why you can't tell them,' he pleaded.

'Okay, so putting Malcolm Muldoon aside for a second, do we have a name for this other guy who might be able to save your ass if we can persuade him to confess to her murder?'

'Peter.' Lucas licked his lips nervously but was also pleased that she at least seemed to be thawing and coming round to his way of thinking. 'But my money's still on Malcolm.'

'Peter.' Sam shrugged nonchalantly as she spoke. 'Thank God for that. There was me thinking we'd have a job tracking him down,' she muttered sarcastically. 'Would this be the same Peter you wanted Kelly and Ash to investigate whilst they were at the hospital speaking to Lou's work colleagues? The same Peter they knew nothing about and had seemingly never even heard of? Should have him behind bars in no time.' She shook her head despairingly.

'Remember Veronica Higgins?' Sam shook her head doubtfully, the name ringing a bell but she couldn't place her.

'Peter Pan?' Lucas continued. 'Ronnie was badly attacked last night, that's how come I was already here. She's upstairs in recovery.' He gestured towards the ceiling.

'And she's put her ex in the frame?' She looked at him unconvinced. Yes the guy was a sick mother fuck, that was never up for debate, but if he was busy beating up his ex, could he really be credited with a double murder on the same night?

'Not exactly, no.' Lucas returned his attention to the plate between them, reaching for a pastry and demolishing it in two simple mouthfuls.

'Meaning what?' *Oh sod it, the diet can wait.* She picked up a chocolate éclair and bit into it with relish.

'She reckons Eileen Muldoon attacked her. I don't, but Malcolm's perfectly capable of engineering the situation to make it look as though his wife was responsible.'

'Whoah.' Sam held her hand up to Lucas to slow him down, her brain struggling to keep up. 'Two seconds ago you thought her ex did it. Didn't you?' Totally confused, she shook her head, then signalled over his shoulder to the tea lady and feigned a drinking motion to order refreshments.

Lucas shrugged. 'I don't know. Maybe. Lou *befriended,*' he stressed the word bitterly, 'some guy Peter a few days ago. Got all secretive about it. That's how come we argued. Next thing you know she leaves the house all dolled up to meet him, then bam. She's a gonna, Ronnie's in hospital with injuries that stink of Peter, and Peter's whereabouts remain unknown.'

'So where do the Muldoons fit into all of this?' Sam licked chocolate off her fingers as she spoke.

'You know Malcolm attacked Lou the other day. Out there.' Lucas gestured with his thumb towards the window. 'Denied it of course, but then told me personally that he was going to make her pay for her mistake.' He nodded his thanks to the waitress as she approached with her trolley and topped up their drinks.

'Still doesn't explain why Ronnie's claiming Eileen attacked her.' Sam took a large mouthful of coffee and tried not to look at the plate, the urge to help herself to another éclair growing by the second.

'Malcolm's spotted with another woman. Ronnie tells Eileen, who's furious, though quite why is anybody's guess. You'd think she'd be glad to be rid of him.' Lucas dared a grin at his colleague as he spoke and she couldn't resist smiling back. He had a point. How anybody could live with a man like Malcolm Muldoon was a mystery and his wife frankly deserved a medal for putting up with him the way she did.

'Next thing you know,' Lucas continued, 'Ronnie's attacked. She said she thought it was Malcolm out for revenge for dishing the dirt at first except…'

'Except what?'

'Except she swears her attacker stank of perfume, that's how come she's blaming Eileen. Reckons it's a classic case of shooting the messenger.'

'Oh… my… God!' Sam stared open mouthed at Lucas as his words sank in. 'Our killer has a penchant for women's shoes and now we have an assailant who reeks of perfume? We need to pay Eileen Muldoon a visit, and fast!' She pushed her chair away from the table and grabbing the last éclair from the plate, shovelled it into her mouth before she had time to allow her conscience to talk her out of it.

'No.' Lucas grabbed Sam's arm and pulled her back into her seat. 'We go thundering in like bulls in a china shop and we could ruin everything. There's nothing to say right now that the two cases are even connected. We need more. We speak to Ronnie again. Locate Peter. Appeal for witnesses to both attacks. Then we pay the Muldoons a visit.'

'I thought you'd have been the first to want to rush round Malcolm's and question him,' she replied sulkily, despite knowing deep down that he was right. At that very moment, she couldn't help but think she preferred *impulsive-never-quite-know-what-he's-going-to-say-or-do-next* Lucas to sensible Lucas.

As though reading her mind, Lucas rubbed his palms nervously on his trousers as he built up the courage to drop his bombshell.

'There's one other thing you should probably know.' He deliberately avoided looking her in the eye as he spoke. 'I think Malcolm Muldoon is my biological father.'

50

There was no escape. Everywhere Eileen turned, people were talking about it. Headlines screamed about the midnight murders from every newsstand and it was impossible to turn on the television without being faced with some newsreader or other appealing for possible witnesses to come forward. Even her usual weekly shop at the local supermarket had turned into a detailed exploration of the crime, the gossip-hungry assistant determined to dissect every minor detail exposed by the press with absolute minute precision.

All of this, however, paled in significance when compared to the predicament that Eileen now found herself in as she studied the photograph of the shoes displayed on the front page of every leading tabloid. Her shoes. Having stripped her dressing room bare, she was now in no doubt, although she didn't recognise the second pair. *Nice though*, and for a moment, she allowed herself to visualise her feet in them.

She turned her attention to the picture on the accompanying page, an image produced by the police of the murdered male whose identity eluded them. *Tod.* The similarities between him and the computer-generated image far too alike to be any sort of coincidence and it would certainly explain his recent disappearing act.

Did you take them, Tod? Eileen tried to think back to the time at the pool when someone had snuck into the changing room and stolen her shoes. Were they the same shoes? She couldn't remember. Only that he had been so kind, even offering to arrange for all lockers to be checked, but had it all just been a cunning ruse to disguise his own guilt? Did he have some kind of fetish that she hadn't known about? How many more had he embezzled without her knowledge?

Eileen tried to concentrate on the words in front of her but her eyes refused to obey the instruction, blurring them beyond all recognition so they just bounced from the page before her. Not that it mattered. She knew pretty much word for word what they said at any rate. Pushing the chair away from the kitchen table with the back of her knees, she walked over to the drawer where the medical supplies were kept and with shaking hands helped herself to four of the tablets from the blister pack. She knew it wasn't advisable, but with no sign of the mother of all headaches that was pounding at her temples evaporating, she also knew that two quite simply wouldn't be enough.

On the windowsill behind the sink sat a faded photograph taken of Malcolm on the beach when they were first married and she instinctively reached for it and carried it back to the table. *Weston-super-Mare.* Malcolm had promised a five-star hotel overlooking golden sand that stretched out for miles. Instead, they had found themselves in a grotty hovel with dirty sheets and flea-ridden carpets, surrounded by sinking mud that whiffed alarmingly like sewage. The very structure of the building had literally groaned and throbbed under the weight of the lowered suspension cars that thumped out bass music from their speakers as they passed, but it hadn't mattered. She had been with Malcolm, they were in love, and that was all that had been important to her back then. She smiled at the memory and dabbed at the stray tears as they escaped her eyes. She held the photograph at arm's length so she could better focus. She was doing this more and more of late and made a mental note to visit the optician as soon as time would allow.

As she studied her husband's face, she couldn't help but notice how handsome, how utterly relaxed and carefree he looked as his eyes smiled into the lens. Not at all like the murdering monster who had sat opposite her at this very table, crunching his cereal loudly and slurping the milk from his spoon only hours previously. She'd had a lot of time to think over the past few hours and she had never been so sure of anything in all her life.

Malcolm killed EJ. And he killed that other woman, although she had yet to figure out why. And then he killed this Loopy Lou woman, the details of whose death currently littered every last inch of the kitchen table. He had been lying all along, as she had always known he had. That woman never attacked him. Truth was, her husband was a bad sport. Always had been. He didn't like losing and rather than do the right thing and accept defeat gracefully – apologise even for his irrational behaviour in the car park – he had clearly decided to punish her for daring to challenge his word.

And then he had killed Tod. The papers were wrong about that part. His death was no accident, she'd be willing to bet her life on it. How could she have been so blind? Malcolm had found out about the affair and chucked his dummy out of his pram and into the dirt just like he always did when he heard something he didn't like.

Only once he had finished his little killing spree had he released her from the car boot, behaving all the while as though butter wouldn't melt and he had done no wrong. So disturbed by his irrational behaviour and exhausted from the ordeal, she hadn't had the energy, nor the inclination, for a fight and so had simply gone upstairs for a hot bath to relax her aching muscles and mind. Besides which, she hadn't trusted herself to speak. She had wanted to kill him not talk to him and it was only now, hours later as the news had leaked, that it occurred to her exactly what her husband had been up to whilst she was trapped in the boot of her own car.

Her mind wandered to Ronnie. She'd had a lucky escape by all accounts. She was a good friend. It took real courage to do what she had done and Eileen felt dreadful now that she'd thrown it all back in her face. Yelling down the phone and accusing her of making up stories about her husband when in fact she had already known the truth, but how could she admit to her oldest friend that she had been right about her husband all along? Had Malcolm overheard the exchange? Decided to punish her too for stepping on his toes and telling tales?

The only real surprise to Eileen was that the police hadn't already come knocking to arrest him. She would have to speak to them of course. The fear of them finding out of their own accord and concluding that she was somehow implicated didn't bear thinking about. But what exactly would she tell them? And would they be duty bound to be discreet or would the fact that she had cheated on her husband with the dead man be splattered across tomorrow morning's headlines? How would she ever face the neighbours again?

Never in all her years had Eileen felt as alone as she did right now. She needed to talk to someone, but who? Once upon a time she would have turned to Malcolm for advice, but not now, she thought regretfully. Sensing her distress, Buddy nudged her knee under the table.

'I know,' she said as she stroked his ears tenderly, but it wasn't the same. Buddy might be the best listener she had ever met but right now, she needed more. *Ronnie?* She idly played with the idea in her mind but soon dismissed it. Even if her friend was ready to forgive and forget, if the papers were to be believed she was in no fit state to help.

Lucas. The image of the kind detective's concerned face when he had called round the house and witnessed the unfortunate incident the other day took her by surprise.

She didn't know why she hadn't thought of speaking to him before. He would almost certainly know what she should do. Reaching into her bag, her fingers eventually settled on the small business card that he had passed her discreetly before leaving her with the paramedics.

51

Only when he was sure that there was nothing left inside him, did Malcolm dare step back from the toilet. His guts ached with the exertion and he grabbed at the loo roll, unravelling an overly generous portion in his hand before wiping at the stray vomit surrounding his mouth and the pan.

Having digested the contents of every newspaper he could get his hands on, he knew pretty much all the sordid details off by heart and try as he might, he couldn't see how he wouldn't be incriminated. What the hell would he tell them? That he was only at the scene of the crime because he just happened to be trying to kill his wife at the same time? *Well, that's alright then,* he thought to himself. *You're free to go. Glad you popped in to clear that one up.* He could literally hear the sarcasm oozing from every corner of the police station.

Gently dropping the lid of the toilet, he sat down. Eileen was downstairs, in the kitchen right below where he sat. He could hear her moving about but he wasn't ready to face the Spanish Inquisition just yet. He needed time to think. Time to figure out whether or not he even needed to come clean with the police at all. Surely, if the only person likely to have seen him at the scene was this Cross Killer they were hunting, then he was in the clear? After all, it wasn't as though the culprit was likely to rush to the police station to give their version of events anytime soon.

Eileen. As per usual, his wife was giving him problems.

Should have got rid of her when you had the chance. She hadn't spoken a single word over breakfast. She hadn't needed to; the look on her face had told him all that he needed to know. Eileen believed he was guilty of these murders and unless he came up with a plausible excuse for locking her in the boot in the first place, she was sure to create merry hell.

He pulled out the newspaper cutting he had secretly stashed earlier in his trouser pocket from Eileen's collection and studied it for the umpteenth time. The man in the computer-generated image was without doubt his wife's lover. He'd recognise the cocky smirk and mocking eyes anywhere. *Well, good.* Malcolm was glad he was dead. It served him right for dipping his nib in somebody else's ink. He could picture him now, all muscles and God knows what else bulging from his skimpy briefs as he strutted his wares back and forth across the edge of the pool and eyed up his next target. He gave a little tremor of pleasure as he read the details once more of his final moments. Karma really was the most remarkable thing ever invented.

The female victim worried him. He didn't care two hoots that the mad bag lady had got her just desserts, only that the interfering detective was sure to come knocking and try to pin the blame on him yet again. Ordinarily it wouldn't have bothered him. With no proof the man would be wasting his time, but with his wife lurking in the background, eager to blab about his whereabouts during the time in question, it would be nothing short of a miracle if he wasn't arrested for the crimes.

The unmistakable crunch of gravel underfoot and muffled voices filled the air and caught his attention. Eileen on the move? *Not likely.* There was more than one person talking out there, so unless Buddy had finally found his voice it wasn't Eileen he could hear. Gripping the shower cubicle door for support, Malcolm slowly climbed on top of the toilet cistern and balanced precariously on one foot as best he could as he leaned forward and tilted his head at an awkward angle so he could peer out of the tiny hopper window.

It was no good. However hard he tried, he couldn't get his head far enough out of the small gap to see anything. Whoever was out there was determined, however, and he shook his head in irritation as they banged a clenched fist against the door and pressed their finger firmly against the doorbell as though it had somehow got stuck.

'Eileen,' he hissed. 'Eileen? Answer the bloody door, woman!' At this rate they would break it and he'd only just had it repaired. Unable to see anything and about to give up, the shadow stepped back from the door and looked up at the house – directly into Malcolm's line of vision. *Detective Inspector Lucas Elliott.* What the hell did he want now? As if he couldn't guess. Bloody woman was a liability and the sooner he got rid of her once and for all, the better.

Malcolm staggered backwards in his haste not to be seen, almost losing his balance as he clambered down from the cistern as fast as he dared. *Easy tiger.* One wrong step could easily mean the difference between falling flat on his back or getting his feet firmly back on the floor. The banging on the door started up again, rattling against the hinges and reverberating up the stairs towards where he now stood, stock still as though afraid to move for fear of giving himself away.

'Police. Open up,' the voice yelled towards the window. Malcolm cowered by the bathroom door, his fingers hovering over the lock as though deliberating what to do for the best. *What would Rita do?* Right now, he craved her calming influence and assurance that everything would be okay. Retrieving his secret mobile phone that Eileen knew nothing about from the bag in the cistern, he jabbed hastily at the buttons as he dialled her number. *Voicemail. Again.* Why wouldn't she speak to him? Did she know more about all of this than she was letting on? Or worse still, did she also suspect him of the murders?

The paranoia was devouring him now, like a starving animal that refused to let go of its prey as it shredded every last inch of flesh from the bone. *Pick up the bloody phone!* He dialled again, and again, and again, determined to hound her until she picked up, but still there was nothing. Just silence. Except for the automated voice on the answering machine, and the dull crunch of splitting wood downstairs as his newly repaired front door caved in once more, followed by heavy footsteps as they pounded up the stairs.

52

'So people are finally talking.' DCI Steven Smith eyeballed each member of the team assembled in the incident room one by one.

You can say that again. Lucas fidgeted in his seat and raised his eyes to the ceiling. He didn't want to be unsympathetic. Everyone was entitled to excel at something or at least feel as though they did, but he was sick to the back teeth of every wannabe murderer from across the city who had come forward to confess to a crime they clearly hadn't committed in exchange for their five minutes of fame.

'Any more on the unidentified male?' The DCI addressed Lucas specifically and all eyes now focused on him as they awaited his response.

Lucas cleared his throat and ran his tongue absently across his gums. *Over vigorous brushing,* according to his dentist who had chastised him like a naughty child during his last visit. Having been plagued with problems from an early age, it beggared belief that a person could actually manage to cruise through life without ever visiting one.

'Dental records drew a blank, Sir. Not a single match for any of the names on the cards in his possession. The response from the public's been something else, however,' he continued. 'Jennie and Rob are still wading through the images now.' Lucas was still reeling at how many people had attended the station in the past twenty-four hours armed with photographs of missing loved ones, their desperation to locate them even if they were dead tangible as they clamoured for answers.

'What do we know about him?' The DCI eyed his audience carefully and Sam grabbed the reins firmly with both hands.

'Approx. 35, possible vagrant…'

'Possible?' Smith interrupted.

'With no positive ID, it's difficult to say for sure, but it would seem that way yes, Sir. Our male was clearly sleeping rough and had a number of stolen possessions on him at the time of death.'

'The shoes.' The DCI nodded knowingly.

'Yes, but also the credit cards and other items, Sir. To include a pay-as-you-go mobile phone with texts of a threatening nature to our first victim EJ Mahoney.' An audible intake of breath filled the incident room. This was the first exciting lead that they had to connect this victim to the crimes.

'The man was a thief. The phone may not even belong to him,' Lucas interjected, shaking his head in frustration at the numerous brick walls that seemed to erect themselves in front of them every time they finally appeared to be getting somewhere.

'What do we know about the shoes?' the DCI asked.

'Well, this is where it gets interesting,' Sam continued. 'So our latest victim, Lou Wilson's shoes were removed, whereabouts currently unknown. Results are in from the lab and the one set found at the scene definitely belonged to our first known victim, EJ Mahoney.'

'And we now know that our male cadaver was connected to Mahoney.' Smith nodded, pleased to at last witness some progress.

'Exactly. But Erika is adamant that Mahoney and our IC1 male were both killed by the same individual and so how the shoes came to be in his possession in the first place remains a mystery. The other shoes at the scene don't appear to belong to any of our victims, which is why it was decided to disclose the pictures to the press. If there's any possibility of a further fatality we don't yet know about, we need to enlist the help of the public at large.' Sam glanced at her notes to check that there was nothing important she had forgotten.

'As yet, there's been nothing, Sir,' Lucas chipped in, concerned that Sam was refusing to look him in the eye. Smith had requested his presence in his office after the briefing to explain his whereabouts on Wednesday night and he was starting to question how much of his recent situation she had divulged.

'Actually, that's not strictly true, Sir,' Sam interrupted. 'We have a possible claim on the shoes but I'll return to that in a moment if I may?' Lucas looked quizzically at Sam but yet again, she completely blanked him and turned her attention back to her notes as the DCI nodded his agreement.

'Any suspects?' he asked. 'Need I remind you that the AGM's fixed for Monday week?'

Lucas squirmed in his seat and now deliberately avoided eye contact with Sam for a change. She was definitely still being weird with him after his shock confession and he could kick himself for trusting her with such delicate information.

Sam, meanwhile, feeling severely compromised thanks to Lucas, had already anticipated the question. Not trusting herself to disclose the relevant information objectively without blurting out the sordid details of Lucas' recent revelations, she had briefed the new recruit who had recently relocated from London and she now nodded at DC Kelly Watkins to continue.

'Three suspects, Sir.' Kelly licked her lips nervously and looked down at her notes as though trying to recall the names. In truth, they were ingrained on her mind. Kelly was, and always had been, terrified of public speaking and had been building up to this moment ever since Sam had appointed her the duty.

'We have a Peter Wainwright, whereabouts currently unknown. May be using an alternative alias, also unknown.'

'Peter Wainwright? As in, Peter Pan?' Saliva pooled around the DCI's lips as he spoke, a bizarre trait that Lucas had noticed happened whenever the man got excitable. How his wife tolerated something so gross was anybody's guess.

'The one and the same, Sir.' Sam smiled awkwardly at Kelly as she intervened. During his previous stalking stint on his ex, Peter Wainwright had become something of a local celebrity so far as Cliffborough Police Station was concerned.

'Ronnie Higgins is currently in Cliffborough Community Hospital,' Sam continued. 'Viciously attacked by person unknown on the night in question. Making a good recovery by all accounts. Remarkable similarities to Wainwright's previous assault on Higgins, but also the latest attack on Wilson. According to her work colleagues,' aware of Lucas' blatant discomfort, Sam deliberately concentrated on her notes as she lied about the source of the information she was about to disclose, 'prior to her death, Lou Wilson had befriended a man by the name of Peter. Given the aforementioned similarities, Wainwright must automatically be considered a suspect, Sir.'

'Which leads me to our next suspect.' Feeling a little like a puppet, Kelly acknowledged the nod from Sam to continue. 'According to Ronnie Higgins,' she looked down at her notes as she spoke, aware that most people in the room were familiar with the characters who she was speaking about, but had yet to have the pleasure of familiarising herself with first hand, 'her friend's husband was seen with another woman. She told the friend, an Eileen Muldoon, who was apparently furious.' As Kelly looked up and caught Sam's eye, Sam signalled her encouragement to carry on. 'Ronnie is adamant that Eileen Muldoon attacked her.'

Perfume. Whoever attacked me reeked of perfume. The words rang in Lucas' ears, but however hard he tried, he couldn't envisage the Cross Killer as a woman. Less so Eileen Muldoon who had seemed anything but when he had last encountered her unconscious at the base of the stairs. The nagging gut instinct that he and his colleagues were always warned to ignore at all costs threatened to take over, continually reminding him that their culprit didn't display any female characteristics. Except perhaps the obvious obsession with the shoes – that fact, he could no longer deny. And perhaps now also the fact that the only potential surviving victim also seemed to believe that her attacker was female.

'Can this Ronnie Higgins substantiate her claim?' The DCI licked his lips in anticipation of finally having a valid suspect behind bars.

'Not really. Only to say that her attacker wore perfume.' Kelly shrugged apologetically as though it was her fault that they didn't have more to go on.

'And the Muldoon woman? Is she in custody?' An unintentional spray of saliva left the DCI's mouth as he spoke and Lucas flinched.

'Lucas and myself went around personally this morning to bring both of them in for questioning.' Still Sam refused to make eye contact with Lucas as she spoke. 'You might remember Malcolm Muldoon: gagged and bound a district councillor to a chair in his basement a few months back until he agreed to approve the planning application for his new conservatory? A district councillor who just happened to be the father of our second victim, Hannah Gregory. Time and time again, the man has proven himself to behave erratically until he gets what he wants. According to Ronnie Higgins, Malcolm has never liked her. Having disclosed the details of his affair to his wife, we consider him to also be capable of such a crime.'

'Go on,' the DCI urged as Sam paused to allow him to catch up. He might be approaching retirement, but there was nothing wrong with his memory, thank you very much.

'Lou Wilson attended the station recently and claimed that Malcolm Muldoon attacked her in broad daylight. Now she's dead. Muldoon's downstairs awaiting interview. Lucas has managed to obtain his DNA, so we do at least now have that on record.'

'Eileen Muldoon?' the DCI asked. More saliva, Lucas noted as he looked up at him before casting another glance in Sam's direction. *I owe you one,* he mouthed gratefully as he finally managed to grab her attention.

'Absconded from the house, Sir, but...' she continued rapidly before he had the chance to interrupt, 'she's since phoned the station. Doesn't know why she did it, just panicked she said. She has, however, agreed to come in this afternoon of her own accord for an informal chat.'

News to me, Lucas stiffened in his chair as Sam revealed this latest bit of news, more uncomfortable than ever with his relative closeness to not only one of the victims, but also the main suspects in the case.

'Is she a serious contender for the crime?' the DCI asked thoughtfully.

Not very, Lucas scoffed to himself, but chose not to answer the question out loud. *Malcolm: my father,* he felt sick at the prospect. *He's your man.*

'I want a DNA sample for her as well.' The DCI turned his attention to Lucas as he spoke.

'Shouldn't be a problem, she's keen to help by all accounts. Bit too keen if you ask me.' Sam nodded knowingly at the room as a whole, well aware that each and every one of them would be thinking the same thing. A helpful suspect usually equalled a guilty suspect.

'Which brings me back to the shoes,' she continued.

'Muldoon believes they're hers – we'll get a swab this afternoon. And she's given us a name for our male victim. A Tod Anderson who she believes stole them.'

'Could she be creating excuses for why they were at the scene of the crime?' This wasn't a question the DCI expected an answer to, more a thought spoken aloud. There was nothing rare or unusual in a killer befriending the police and giving the impression of trying to help them with their enquiry with the sole purpose of pushing suspicion away from themselves.

'What do we know about this Tod Anderson?' he continued.

'Anderson was Eileen's swimming instructor. Allegedly lived in a bedsit on Archway Drive, but according to Eileen Muldoon, he's since moved on. Officers are trying to make contact with the landlord now. Muldoon and Anderson were apparently having some kind of affair. Seemed to think the husband had found out about it but was still very concerned that no reference be made to it.' Sam lowered her voice a notch before continuing. 'I got the impression she was more worried about what the neighbours would think than her husband to be honest.'

'Of course.' The DCI was thoughtful as he spoke. 'If she was having an affair with the victim, we have ourselves another good reason to make interviewing Malcolm Muldoon a priority.'

'I knew it!' DC Ash Campbell, who hadn't uttered a word throughout the proceedings exploded and everyone turned and stared at him in surprise at his untimely and totally uncharacteristic outburst.

'Muldoon! I knew I'd heard the name before.' He waved the piece of paper about in his hand enthusiastically as though any of them could read the contents from that distance.

'Everyone's heard the name before,' the DCI scoffed and much as he was loathe to admit it even to himself, Lucas couldn't deny that the man was right. His biological father, for those results had come back as a positive in that regard, seemed to be making a habit of cropping up at the police station of late.

Ash pressed on, talking overly fast in his excitement. 'A witness saw a vehicle hanging around the old boat yard on the night in question. Couldn't tell us much, but reckoned the driver was male and had been loitering around the vegetation that separates the yard from the towpath. I ran the reg through the PNC and the car belongs to an Eileen Muldoon. Lives on the border between Cliffborough Cross and Adderley. Checks came back clear and it's not been reported stolen. Uniform's on their way over there now.'

The driver was male. Car registered to Eileen Muldoon. Sam's head snapped up at this latest snippet of information. *Could the Muldoons be in on it together?* 'Any chance our driver could be Malcolm Muldoon?' Sam looked at each of her colleagues in turn as she inwardly gauged their reaction to this latest news.

'Or this Tod Anderson?' the DCI responded. 'Make tracking down the landlord a priority, see what he can tell us about the man. And Ash,' he continued, looking across at the DC, 'rein uniform back. Last thing we want is to alert Eileen Muldoon to any kind of problem until we're good and ready. Let her come in of her own accord and we'll see what she has to say for herself first.' Ash immediately gathered his papers together and rushed from the room.

Lucas sat stock still, painfully aware of the newly formed beads of sweat trickling down his sides and soaking his shirt. His father and his wife were both at the scene of the crime on the night in question? The thought chilled him to the bone and he shivered involuntarily as he tried to drown out the background chatter and concentrate on what this latest evidence could mean.

Or had this Tod Anderson driven Eileen's car to the yard, and if so why? Because Eileen was his next intended victim or had Eileen killed him? And where did Lou fit into that scenario?

Did this have anything to do with Malcolm's recent attack on her in the car park? Did Eileen plant the shoes to implicate Tod and free herself of any suspicion? Lucas swallowed, the acidic bile burning the back of his throat and making his eyes water as the blood pumped from his heart and pounded in his ears.

They were both at the scene of the crime on the night in question. This latest probability reverberated in his mind, determined to haunt his every thought. How was it possible to want something so badly, yet not want it at all? Lucas wanted nothing more than to catch the Cross Killer. Except perhaps, the pleasure of witnessing Malcolm Muldoon behind bars for years to come. But at the expense of his own reputation if it ever got out that he was inadvertently associated with a killer?

53

The interview room was small and poorly ventilated and Eileen's clothes clung awkwardly to the sweat building up on her skin beneath them. The lack of windows was starting to make her feel uncomfortable and she idly wondered if the design was somehow a ploy to prevent offenders having their last glimpse of the outside world. Or worse still, a last minute opportunity to escape the confines of prison.

You're here of your own volition, she reminded herself as she smiled nervously at the two officers sat opposite her. Neither returned the gesture. Apparently Malcolm was also in here somewhere. Was he scared or was being questioned by the police second nature to him these days?

What if they didn't let either of them go? The thought hadn't even crossed her mind until now. She had promised Mrs Deville from Clock Cottage to pick up Buddy by five o'clock latest. Fridays were bridge night. Poor woman hadn't missed a single one in over forty years and would never forgive her if she were late. Nor would Buddy come to that; he was very punctual when it came to mealtimes.

On the table in front of her sat a sheet of paper listing her legal rights, which she had been invited to read, but since they had already been read out to her it seemed a little pointless. Much the same as the invitation she had received to attend the station when she had called them earlier. It all seemed a little contradictory since had she refused the request, she had been left in little doubt from their bombastic attack on the front door earlier that they would have arrested her anyway.

Eileen had hoped to see the one from before, that Lucas what's-his-name who had attended the house when Malcolm had pushed her down the stairs, but there had been no sign of him this time around. *Why did he turn up at the house that day?* He still hadn't explained his presence and as the paranoia of her predicament kicked in, she found herself wondering whether Malcolm had somehow set all of this up to make her look like something she wasn't.

Instead of the friendly detective, she now found herself confronted by these two women, neither of whom looked remotely approachable. The younger of the two, a DC Kelly somebody or other, was pretty she supposed – if you liked that sort of thing. She attempted another smile, but rather than reciprocate, the officer gave her a sucking-lemons-grimace that didn't compliment her features at all. She averted her gaze and allowed it to settle on the older woman instead. Samantha was it? The expression on the woman's face, however, terrified her and she quickly turned away and reverted her attention to the paperwork on the table in front of her, absently fingering the edges as she waited for the taped introductions to conclude so they could get to the point of why she was here. She didn't have to wait long.

'I just need you to sign this.' The younger woman pushed a piece of paper across the table towards Eileen and she eyed it suspiciously. Was this a trick? In the movies, suspects signed at the end of the interview, not the beginning. *You aren't a suspect,* she reminded herself. At least she hoped she wasn't although they were starting to make her feel as though she was. They hadn't even explained properly the need to record their little chat and she wished now that she had contacted the family solicitor before agreeing to it.

'It's just a list of the items you had to leave behind the

desk.' Noticing Eileen's discomfort, Sam handed her a pen and smiled encouragingly at her. 'Custody sergeant should have done it downstairs but we've been a little over-run today.' She waved the pen again, gesturing at Eileen to sign within the box marked with a large cross at the bottom of the sheet of paper. Eileen took the pen, careful to scan the page for anything that could incriminate her before signing her name at the bottom. It wasn't her usual signature and she didn't doubt that they would find a way around it to prove otherwise if they needed to, but she still felt better about not putting her proper signature to anything formal.

Right handed? Sam made a note on the pad in front of her. *Accepted pen with left, signed with right.*

'Nice perfume.' The comment took Eileen by surprise and she looked up at the older woman as she spoke, pleased to dispense with the formalities for a second but also unsure as to why she was suddenly trying to be nice.

'It's my mother's birthday next week, I might get her some. What is it?' Sam continued.

The mother jibe stung and Eileen studied the woman a moment before responding. She couldn't be a day shy of forty at best, so what was she trying to imply? That she smelt like an old woman, was that it? *How dare you!* Perhaps her chosen fragrance was a little dated by modern day standards, but it also happened that it had always suited her skin. It was a split-second decision, one that Eileen had no idea could be crucial to her freedom as she looked the woman in the eye and blatantly lied to save face.

'Dolce and Gabbana.' She watched the two women exchange knowing glances and seemingly satisfied, the officer who had posed the question made a note on her pad. *Looks like Mum's getting perfume for her birthday,* Eileen thought to herself.

Kelly glanced over Sam's shoulder at her notes. *Suspect and perpetrator both wear D&G.*

'Tell us about Ronnie Higgins.'

'Ronnie?' The mention of her friend was unexpected. Surely, they didn't think she had anything to do with her attack? 'Ronnie's my friend.' Eileen spoke quietly as she tried to decipher the fleeting look that the two women had given one another a moment ago.

'But you argued recently, is that correct?'

They do. They're going to try and blame you for Ronnie's ordeal. 'More a little disagreement,' Eileen mumbled, so quietly that Kelly asked her to repeat herself for the benefit of the tape.

'A little disagreement,' she said again, anger starting to build within her at their attitude. She had come here to help, not to somehow be set up for the despicable assault on her dearest friend.

'A little disagreement that resulted in Ronnie being ferociously attacked, isn't that right, Eileen?'

'What? No!' Sam indicated to Eileen to sit back down as she rose from her chair indignantly. 'Why? I wouldn't, I couldn't. I'm not capable,' she muttered as she slowly sat back down. 'Surely Ronnie doesn't believe I had anything to do with it?' Eileen looked pleadingly at the women in turn, desperate for reassurance.

'Where were you during the early hours of yesterday, Thursday, January 15th, Eileen?' Eileen's pre-prepared excuses tumbled to the forefront of her mind, but suddenly she found herself unable to voice any of them out loud. *Tell the truth,* the voice nagged inside her. She knew it was the right thing to do – necessary, even, if she was going to protect herself – but somehow exposing her husband and his irrational behaviour went against everything she believed in and had promised all those years ago. *Oh my God. Malcolm attacked Ronnie.* Suddenly, it all made sense.

'I don't remember.' Two sets of unemotional eyes fixed on her, their penetrating glares burning deep into her flesh and

Eileen hurriedly looked away. Rooted to her seat, an ominous shiver rippled down the length of her spine and she stared awkwardly at the floor as she tried to decide what on earth she was going to do.

'Let us help nudge your memory, Eileen.' She didn't look up, but she knew it was the younger of the two women. 'We have a witness who can place your car at Taylor's Boat Yard between the hours of one and two on the morning in question.'

'It's not what you think.' Eileen fidgeted in her seat, still unable to look either of her captors in the eye.

'So what is it?'

The air caught in Eileen's chest, suffocating her breath and much as she wanted to, she found herself unable to express the words she so badly needed. It was all so embarrassing and degrading to have to admit that her husband was mentally deranged and she didn't think she could do it. And what if she did? What then? Would they drag all that stuff up about Tod? She couldn't tell them what her husband had done. Not until she knew herself what he had done. *He attacked Ronnie. Killed Tod. And the others.* The words rumbled in her ears and she reached for the glass of water that had been placed in front of her at the beginning of the interview and downed the contents greedily.

Drinks with left hand, Sam noted.

'Do you want to tell us about the man who was seen driving your vehicle, Eileen?' Sam looked up slowly from her notepad and focused her attention on Eileen as she studied her reaction and body language for any sign of guilt, but the woman was a closed book.

They know. They already bloody well know! Eileen's eyes shifted to the table in front of her once more as she tried to figure out what the hell to do. *If they know, you have to tell them. They'll think you helped him if you don't.* Still Eileen didn't look up at them, afraid that they would put her off as she tried to concentrate and compose what she was going to say next, but before she had the chance, the older of the two spoke again and completely threw her off balance.

'We believe the driver of your vehicle to be Tod Anderson. You were having an affair with Mr Anderson, is that right?' It was a stupid question, irrelevant to have even asked it. She had already told them as much and that aside, the woman didn't even come up for air long enough to allow her to answer it before she ploughed on.

'Mr Anderson was mercilessly killed at some point between the hours of one and two on the morning of January 15th.' Even though Eileen had been in no doubt from the pictures in the paper, she still reeled at the confirmation.

'We have your car – and by your own admission, certain personal belongings – at the scene at the time the crime was committed,' the younger interrogator chipped in. 'So, let us ask you again. For the purposes of the tape, where were you, Eileen Muldoon, between the hours of one and two o'clock on the morning of Thursday, January 15th of this year?'

They think you did it. You have no choice. Eileen took a deep breath, painfully aware that she could no longer protect her husband. By revealing her whereabouts on the night in question, not only would she be a laughing stock but her husband would undoubtedly become the number one suspect. It took a while to pluck up the courage but eventually, when she felt as ready as she would ever be, Eileen lifted her eyes from the table and fixed them firmly on the younger officer who had posed the last question. Steeling herself, she spoke loud and clear for the tape to be sure she wouldn't be made to repeat herself.

'I was locked in the boot of my car… it's my husband you're looking for.'

54

'She said what?' Lucas looked back and forth between Sam and Kelly, an uncomfortable smile twitching at the corners of his mouth. First the fiasco with the district councillor and now the man had allegedly locked his wife in the boot of her own car?

They were huddled around the only remaining table in the staff canteen and Kelly studied Lucas sympathetically. Sam had filled her in briefly on the situation and she couldn't even start to imagine how it must feel for a man in his position to discover that one of the suspects in a murder investigation was his biological father.

'Bloody fool, stuffed up his only alibi.' Kelly didn't particularly believe that Malcolm was innocent, but suddenly, the urge to give Lucas hope took precedence.

'Except spouses don't make good alibis at the best of times,' Sam shrugged, still sceptical and unconvinced of Eileen's claims.

'Where is he now?' Lucas frowned at them both suspiciously. Did Kelly know more about his situation than she was letting on?

'Downstairs in custody. We'll interview him in a bit once he's had chance to stew.' Catching the look of delight on Lucas' face, Sam hastily continued before he got carried away. '*Me and Kelly* will interview him.'

'But...'

'But nothing, Lucas,' she interrupted. 'You've compromised the case, not to mention your job, enough already.'

His eyes darted to Kelly and she hurriedly looked away. 'Bloody hell, Sam, who else have you told?' Lucas brushed his hands irritably through his hair, gripping the strands between his fingers and tugging hard at them as he tried to think and blank out the issues of paternity by a killer from his brain.

'I had no choice, Lucas, and you won't say anything will you, Kel?'

Kel? Best friends now are they? 'You'd bloody better not.' He directed his gaze on the new recruit, unable to disguise the bitterness from his expression as a wave of nausea swam through his gut at the prospect of everyone finding out. But Sam was right. He couldn't interview Malcolm, or at least he certainly shouldn't, but he was so knackered he could no longer think straight, his imagination continually running wild and suffocating any sense of the madness from his mind.

'Cheer up, Lucas.' Sam steeled herself. He wasn't going to like what she was about to say. 'You're not off the case. That would take too much explaining upstairs.' She pointed a finger at the ceiling towards the superintendent's office. 'So you get to contact the relatives and let them know that the victim didn't belong to them.'

Lucas visibly cringed, suddenly feeling as though he was destined to do nothing in life except deliver disappointment. As strange as it might seem, this would be exactly what the job he had been assigned would entail. So desperate would relatives be for answers, even the murder of a loved one would bring relief and comfort for many in place of simply not knowing what had happened to them.

'He attacked Lou in the retail park, for crying out loud.' Lucas glared angrily at Sam. He had been determined to have it out with him, smack him into submission if needs be, and now he was being excluded from going anywhere near their chief suspect through no fault of his own?

'We know she claimed that he did.' Sam placed a comforting hand on Lucas' as she spoke. 'We have to keep an open mind. Let's just say that Malcolm had a reason to attack her, something other than murder in mind.'

'What?' Lucas ripped his hand from under hers as though he had been burned and glared angrily at his colleague, furious that she was even considering that Malcolm might have had any kind of valid reason to attack her. The idea was ludicrous. 'What possible reason could there be to excuse his behaviour?'

'Whoa, let me finish.' Sam held the palm of her hand up at him. 'I'm not saying it's excusable, just that it might be explainable. Did Malcolm love your mother do you know?' She watched Lucas carefully as he digested the question, recognition slowly dawning on his face.

Finally he spoke. 'If you think he attacked her because she killed my mum, you couldn't be further from the truth. That man doesn't love anyone… except himself,' he spat angrily.

'But *she* must have thought something of *him*,' Sam persisted. 'She left a heap of money to him on her deathbed.'

'To do the right thing via me,' he growled. 'Didn't though, did he? Acts like he doesn't even know but I've seen the evidence for myself. He knows exactly who I am – and where to find me. He just chooses not to. He stole her money – *my* money – and I for one won't rest 'til he's been made to pay!'

Sam and Kelly sat in silence, both thoughtful as they studied their colleague. *Did you deliberately set out to make Malcolm look guilty?* Kelly thought to herself. *Just how involved in all of this are you?* Sam wondered. Both of them knew only too well how tempting it was to abuse the position of power from time to time. Sam, who had misused her warrant card on more occasions than she cared to mention, and Kelly, whose violent scumbag of an ex-husband was only behind bars because she knew the system and how to use it to her own advantage. Kelly suddenly felt very sorry for Lucas. She had been lucky and had got away with her situation without any questions or anyone pointing the finger of blame.

'I don't suppose anyone at the hospital had an address for Peter?' Kelly already knew the answer to the question, but found herself wanting to change the subject before he dug himself a grave so deep he would never be able to escape.

Lucas glanced up from the table, tears of frustration welling in his eyes. 'Nope,' he shook his head. 'Just used to hang around outside and befriended her by all accounts.'

'Wainwright?'

Lucas shook his head ruefully. 'Negative.'

'He can't have just disappeared off the face of the earth?' Kelly felt his irritation tugging at her own insides.

'Did a runner months ago according to the landlord. Asked us to remind him about the rent arrears if we do catch up with him, and before you ask,' he continued, 'his last known place of work don't know his whereabouts either.'

'Someone must have seen him.'

'Ronnie reckoned she did at the surgery, but…'

'But what?' Sam interrupted.

'They've got no record of his visit. It's like she got it wrong.'

'Oh come on!' Sam scoffed. 'Hardly an easy mistake to make.'

They all sat in an awkward silence that felt like an eternity but was in reality only a few minutes until finally, Lucas spoke once more.

'You know Malcolm's left-handed.'

'Eileen isn't.' Kelly looked at Sam for confirmation. 'Or at best, she's partially ambidextrous.'

'You said in the briefing that Eileen had ID'd the male victim as her lover. Has that been confirmed?' He looked at

Sam as he spoke, so convinced of his convictions he couldn't let them go and she nodded her confirmation.

'In which case, it makes perfect sense that Malcolm's our man. Truth's staring us in the face if you ask me.'

'More sense than Erika's *wrong-time-wrong-place* scenario, I'll give you that. And for what it's worth, I think there's more chance that Ronnie's assailant was Malcolm than his wife,' Sam conceded. 'But we still need to locate Wainwright, if only to rule him out.'

'Of course, none of this explains how Anderson came to have the victim's shoes in his possession does it?' Kelly interjected.

'Malcolm tried to set him up, how can you not see that?' Lucas fidgeted in his seat, totally narked that she could be so short-sighted.

Sam nodded in agreement once more. His theory certainly made more sense than Erika's and she certainly didn't intend to discard the possibility, but it wasn't enough. If the murderer's trophy of choice was shoes, any profiler worth his weight would confirm that it would be the last thing they would then choose to leave behind at the scene of a crime. And why take Eileen to the murder scene at all? Surely by doing so he was just making life ten times more difficult for himself?

'Assuming the two definitely are connected, it also doesn't explain why Ronnie's attacker wore perfume,' Kelly added.

Lucas kicked the table leg in frustration. 'Malcolm was setting the scene. Wouldn't exactly be difficult for him to get hold of some of his wife's perfume, now would it? Quick splash of the old panache and what do you know? Suspicion from him averted.' He shook his head despairingly. How could she not see Malcolm for what he was?

'The murdered male still had a set of shoes belonging to one of the victims and a mobile phone containing threatening messages in his possession, Lucas. Kelly's right, we can't just rule that out.' Sam rubbed her head wearily with her fingers. Maybe Lucas was right? Maybe Malcolm was their perpetrator, but with no firm facts to back it up, it was little more than a happy convenience that he seemed to be the most obvious contender of their suspects to date.

'Disregarding the fact it's hardly brain surgery to plant incriminating items on a dead body,' he muttered sarcastically, 'someone still killed him in case you forgot. Besides which, Erika maintains the person that killed him killed the others. She might wander around the lab with a face like a slapped bum, but you and I both know she's never wrong.'

'First time for everything and all that.' Retrieving a nail file from her bag, Sam commenced her ritualistic manicure and Lucas swiftly pulled the plate of food closer towards him. Having finished his food ages ago it was a knee-jerk reaction, her lack of hygiene in that respect never failing to repulse him. A thousand times or more he must have asked her not to do it, but it was like a nervous habit that she wasn't able to break and he sometimes doubted she was even aware that she was doing it at all.

'Malcolm Muldoon was inadvertently connected to each of the victims.' Lucas spoke through gritted teeth. If he was to be excluded from Malcolm's interview, he needed to open their eyes and make them see. 'Our killer also knew all of his victims.'

'Tut tut, Lucas, you know the rules. *Their* victims until gender is established,' Sam quipped. 'But go on,' she continued. 'Enlighten us.' Lucas couldn't help the tiny flutter of pleasure in his chest as she dropped the nail file back into her bag and placed her elbows on the table, resting her chin on her knuckles as she seemingly gave him the benefit of her undivided attention.

'The strangling of EJ and Hannah wasn't about confusing the cause of death. Think about it,' he added, imploring them each in turn with his eyes. 'Any old idiot would know that the proper cause would be established soon enough. No. The killer wanted to move the goalposts. To revert attention away from the fact that he knew his victims.'

'Or *her* victims.' Kelly had no wish to be pedantic, but Lucas needed to get his head around the fact that their culprit was quite possibly not only not Malcolm Muldoon, but also not male at all.

Ignoring her sarcasm, Lucas pressed on. 'Persuading a random stranger to consume a lethal concoction of poisonous cleaning fluids would be near on impossible. A friend on the other hand, or a colleague, acquaintance or lover... Now that would potentially be a walk in the park.'

'But neither of the last two victims were poisoned at all, which surely weakens your argument?'

'Weakens it how?' He glowered across the table at her. 'According to Erika, our killer is one and the same. On that basis, our culprit knew all of the victims. And what would you know? Malcolm Muldoon also knew all of the victims!'

55

Malcolm's interview wasn't going well and within minutes, both Sam and Kelly were rapidly losing patience, neither of them confident that their suspect was the same man that was now sat opposite them in interview room number two. The person they were looking for was calculated, cunning and methodical. A monster who was clearly capable of carrying out the most heinous of crimes with neither remorse nor detection. Malcolm Muldoon, on the other hand, was none of these things. Instead, he was a man who was almost childlike in his defence of his recent behaviour and seemed to be more concerned with tit for tat with his wife than the charges laid before him.

'Tell us about Ronnie Higgins.' Sam studied Malcolm as he picked at the skin around his fingernails so vigorously one finger started to bleed. The similarities in mannerisms between him and Lucas were frankly alarming now that she'd had the relationship pointed out to her.

'What about her? Interfering cow.' He didn't look up from the job in hand but it was interesting that he made no secret of the fact that he disliked her so intensely. More often than not, offenders would lay on a pretence of liking the person they were supposed to have wronged but that certainly wasn't looking to be the case with Malcolm.

'You know she was attacked?'

'I do read the papers, you know,' Malcolm grumbled in response like a petulant teenager.

'Ronnie believes her attack was a direct result of her telling Eileen about your lady friend.' As Sam spoke, she watched his face intently for the slightest reaction that might indicate that Ronnie was right in her assumptions. *Poker face.* Either the man was a bloody good liar, or he truly wasn't bothered by the news.

'Ronnie's a troublemaker,' he muttered. 'Always telling tales. There's probably a list as long as this table of people wanting to punish her for stirring up problems.'

'And did you want to punish her?' Kelly pounced on the statement.

'Too right I did,' Malcolm exclaimed. 'Looks like someone beat me to it though, doesn't it?'

'Eileen?' Sam was keen to move the conversation on to his wife. It was a toss up right now as to whether she considered Malcolm or Eileen to be more capable of the crimes, and if there was any possibility that he would substantiate her claims and provide her with the alibi she so badly needed, Sam wanted to be the first to know.

'Eileen and Ronnie are like that.' Malcolm held his hand up, index and middle fingers clearly crossed. 'There's no way my wife would harm a hair on her head.'

Sam raised her eyebrows in surprise. According to Lucas, Malcolm had recently pushed his wife down the stairs in what he believed to be an attempt on her life and now he was defending and protecting her?

'Why was your wife in the boot of the car on the night in question, Malcolm?' Kelly couldn't lie, she was literally itching to hear what he had to say for himself on that count.

'She was trying to kill me... I had to do something.' *Bloody woman. Killing me not enough, you've got to frame me with the pigs as well?*

'She said you were trying to kill her,' Sam stated, all the while trying to maintain eye contact as she spoke but the man's eyes flitted between her and Kelly and the wall behind them. 'She said,' she paused for effect and to make sure she had his undivided attention before continuing, 'that you were angry about her affair with her swimming instructor.'

'Affair? Swimming instructor?' Malcolm hoped that his attempt at surprise did him justice. Inside, however, he didn't feel so calm. *Bitch!* Was it not enough she was cheating on him, but now the whole world knew about it?

'You knew all about the affair didn't you, Malcolm?' Sam pushed on, determined to make him break. 'You were angry weren't you, Malcolm? And so you killed him!'

'Of course I didn't. I had no idea,' he responded indignantly, the shock and disbelief on his face palpable, so real that both Sam and Kelly were inclined to believe him. *Oh, you'll pay for this, my love. You'll pay!* Despite his best endeavours not to, he released a little chuckle as a thought occurred to him. *Little taste of her own medicine.* He grinned aimlessly at them as though they were privy to his private little joke. *Or poison to be precise.* Yes, that's what he would do. Administer a nice, big, fat dose of whatever it was she was sprinkling on his meals and swap the plates. The idea was genius. Why had he not thought of it before? Finally, he could be rid of her once and for all.

Snapping out of his reverie, he gave both women the most innocent expression he could muster under the circumstances. 'Killed, you say? And who was this lucky man who was engaging in extra marital activities with my wife?' He smiled, but the question was directed through gritted teeth as Malcolm did his best to disguise his real feelings. 'Of course he's not so lucky now, is he?' he giggled. Unsure which one was in charge, Malcolm was careful to give both officers the benefit of his undivided attention in equal measures. Best to humour them both and make them feel equally important given the circumstances.

'Is that what happened, Malcolm?' Sam tried again,

curious as to why he was suddenly behaving so erratically. 'By the canal? You saw him sleeping there and you were angry about the affair, weren't you? Maybe you didn't actually mean to kill him. Tell us, Malcolm, tell us what really happened that night so we can understand.'

'My wife was shagging a tramp?' Malcolm's face, a mixture of disgust and disbelief mirrored his tone. Despite recognising the dead man in the paper as being his wife's lover, it was only now that the full implications dawned on him.

'When you were arrested there was a list in your jacket pocket. Do you want to tell us about it?' Kelly decided to change tack, distract him awhile, and they could return to the issue of Tod Anderson's murder when he was least expecting it.

'That was for my wife,' Malcolm sniggered. Kelly didn't. That much, from the title, 'Ways to kill my wife', was quite apparent.

'Not exactly a shopping list though was it, Malcolm?' Kelly snapped sarcastically.

'She's trying to kill me.'

Kelly and Sam exchanged a look that agreed Malcolm Muldoon was clearly deranged. But their killer? They both somehow doubted it. He couldn't even push his wife down the stairs without making a mess of things by all accounts.

'The list detailed ways to kill your wife, Malcolm, not the other way around,' Kelly persisted.

'Self-defence wasn't a crime last time I checked,' he responded sulkily. 'Besides, I was just angry, that's all. Sometimes it helps writing stuff down to get it off my chest.'

'And Lou Wilson? Was attacking her in the retail park a way to get things off your chest?'

'How many times?' Malcolm slammed his fist down on the table making the contents and both women jump. *Like father, like son,* Sam thought to herself as she scribbled the words *short fuse* and *left-handed* on the pad in front of her. 'She attacked me! Ask Rita,' he continued.

'Rita?' Both Sam and Kelly spoke in unison.

'She was there. I already told all this to the other detective – she saw the whole thing.' Malcolm was animated now, pleased that they finally seemed to be listening and for the opportunity to clear his name. 'Rita will tell you, I didn't lay a finger on her.'

'Does this Rita have a second name?' Sam pushed.

'No. I mean yes. Well, obviously she does but I don't know it.'

'An address?'

Malcolm shrugged as it dawned on him for the first time that he didn't even know where she lived. Kelly dropped the pen, which had been poised over her notepad to scribble down the address and let out a deep sigh. They were getting nowhere. Instead, just going round and round and round like an overloaded washing machine stuck on spin.

'If we can't locate this Rita, we can't collaborate your version of events.'

'She works at the Beds 'R' Us store on the park.'

Rita? Hannah Gregory worked at Beds 'R' Us. Suddenly it dawned on Sam why the name rang a bell.

'Would this be the same Rita who alibied you over the Gregory murder?'

'Yes,' Malcolm declared excitedly. 'That's her... I don't suppose you happen to have an address for her, do you?' It was a long shot, but it would be great if they did. He could pay her a visit once they were done and dusted here. She still wasn't picking up his calls, but if he could just see her face to face and explain everything, not to mention ask her about the little thing that was bothering him, he felt confident everything would be okay between them.

Ignoring the question, Kelly ploughed on, determined to make a friend of him and bring him around that way.

'If your wife is trying to kill you, Malcolm, we can protect you.' She smiled amiably at him as she spoke.

'She's trying to poison me.' The accusation was like a slap in the face and Kelly inadvertently jerked at the comment. The Cross Killer used poison, a fact that they had deliberately withheld from the press.

Sam nudged Kelly's leg under the table and pushed a hastily scribbled note in front of her. *Witness places Eileen's car at scene of crime. Eileen herself concedes that her own shoes were left at scene. Her only alibi is her husband and an inconceivable claim that'll never stand up in court. And now, even her own husband seems convinced she's capable of using poison to commit the unlawful death of another.*

'Do you have any evidence to substantiate that claim, Malcolm?' Sam enquired in a voice she hoped came across as concerned as opposed to desperate. Eileen had currently been released without charge pending further enquiries. If she was their killer, which was looking more likely by the second, they needed to move – and fast – before she did any more irreparable damage.

'Very particular is my wife. This is my plate of food and this is your plate, that kind of thing. If she hadn't tampered with it, why would it matter who had what plate? Gets really angry she does when I won't eat what she's prepared. What other possible explanation could there be?'

Sam could think of one, but since the man clearly wasn't in possession of all of his faculties, now probably wasn't the time to enlighten him. She shook her head in despair. Even if he could tell them anything useful, she somehow doubted he would ever prove to be a reliable witness at any rate. *Or alibi for Eileen,* the thought thundered through her brain once more.

'Okay. Let's go back to the night at the boatyard when Eileen was in the boot. What did you see, Malcolm?' *That's it, he saw something. It's written all over his face!* A flutter of excitement threatened to explode in Sam's chest.

'Malcolm?' They both sat and watched the man who was blatantly nervous all of a sudden as he fiddled with the papers on the table in front of him and refused to look either of them in the eye.

'The sooner you tell us what you saw, the sooner you can go home.' *Always promise the child a treat for being good.* It seemed to work and Malcolm finally looked up from the table and focused his attention on them both.

'I thought,' he paused before continuing, 'I thought there was something, but I was wrong.'

Malcolm had both of their undivided attention now.

'What did you see, Malcolm?' Sam pressed on, determined to make the man talk.

'The car.' He paused and pressed his fingers over his lips like a child who was trying to stop himself from disclosing something he shouldn't. 'There was something about the car.'

56

Upon his release, Malcolm had taken the liberty of visiting Rita's place of work. He was worried that the police may have beaten him to it but so far so good, the coast was clear. To his dismay however, Rita's supervisor had informed him that she hadn't turned up, nor had she called to explain her absence although it was so out of character that he suspected she was unwell. This would at least explain her lack of contact, but did little to settle the dissension that was currently rattling around inside him. Was she okay? If he could just speak to her, everything would be fine, he felt sure of it. Except that he still had no idea where she lived and the police, not to mention her colleagues, refused to budge and share the information he so badly needed.

The drive home was a long one and what should have taken a matter of minutes took almost an hour as Malcolm manoeuvred the car down the winding country lanes, taking his time as he tried to get matters straight in his head. Five years of migraines, tiredness or some other feeble manufactured trick to avoid her duties. *Hadn't thought twice about dropping her knickers for the tramp though, had she?* Malcolm was furious. He had rights. Legal, marital binding rights and she had reneged on every single one!

As for blabbing to the police, did she have any idea of the problems that her needless gossip had caused? He somehow doubted it. Thanks to her, his reputation was now in shreds, he was the prime suspect in a murder investigation, and he'd had to tell them about what he'd seen at the boatyard – a situation that still bothered him immensely. If he was right, then why? Had she been checking up on him? Spying on him even to make sure he carried out his threats to Eileen?

His mobile phone vibrated in his pocket then and pulling over to the side of the verge, he wiggled awkwardly in his seat as he tried to lever it out of his pocket. *Eileen.* His heart sank. *Rita, where are you?* He quickly scanned Eileen's message, all but demanding his presence at home so that they could talk before sending another hasty message to Rita. Eileen could wait.

THE LAST SUPPER IS IMMINENT XXXX

He didn't usually bother using smilies, but this was a momentous occasion. One that signalled the start of their future together, so adding a couple of laughing faces, he hit the send button. And then he added some extra kisses and sent them as well. Just for the avoidance of doubt.

As he pulled back onto the main road in the direction of home, he had a change of heart at the last minute and swung the vehicle around and headed in the opposite direction. Another couple of hours wouldn't hurt and there were one or two matters he needed to address sooner rather than later.

Traffic was heavy and as he concentrated on the road ahead, try as he might not to think about the dratted woman, his mind still wondered back to Eileen. She was a complete liability. A total nuisance and his body literally itched with the prospect of being rid of her once and for all.

57

The figure paced back and forth across the tiny sitting room waiting for some of the unspent energy that threatened to explode from within him to subside. He badly needed a little something to help him relax and lighten the mood. Anything that would stop this feeling in his guts that the walls were about to cave in, but lying low was of the utmost importance right now.

The recent press coverage wasn't helping, making him edgy as fuck as day and night, newsreaders and journalists bleated on about the same old stuff and created an unrivalled and frenzied public furore. *Why can't they all just mind their own bloody business?* Nonetheless, to zone out now would be crazy. Far too big a risk. He needed to be one of the first to be made aware of any new developments and unable to resist, he reached for the remote and increased the volume to high so he could better hear what was being said.

'Detectives involved in the hunt for the Cross Killer this morning revealed that the suspect may be female,' the newsreader smugly announced as though she were disclosing a crucial piece of evidence. 'Over to our reporter, James Eggins, who is currently outside Cliffborough Cross Police Station and who recently had the opportunity to speak to detectives working the case.'

'*May* be female. Ha,' he chuckled loudly. 'Is that the best you can do?' DI Lucas Elliott, the tenacious little prick who was now making his life an utter misery, had appeared on the screen and he addressed him personally.

'Well,' he persisted, 'is it?' The detective looked him in the eye but refused to answer the question. As he had known he would. 'Why not just admit you don't have a clue? Flick a coin even and let that decide the gender.' He shook his head in awe of the man's stupidity and satisfied that there was no need for concern at this stage, he moved to the far end of the room and glanced fondly at the display cabinet attached to the wall. To move them would be sacrilege, but displaying the shoes so brazenly now was too big a risk.

Determined to save the best until last, he opened the glass-panelled door, reached in and selected the newest additions. Admittedly they were more delicately crafted than the others, but they were also bringing more than their fair share of misfortune and the time had come to bundle up and bury the bad luck once and for all.

Carrying them over to the kitchen table where the necessary materials had been laid out to enable the task that lay ahead, the Cross Killer worked slowly and methodically, the rich scent of cool leather caressing the air, and he kept pausing momentarily to inhale deeply and savour the aroma whilst it was still possible. He cleaned each shoe carefully with the special fluid before gently packing them with acid-free paper. Finally, he wrapped them in the muslin cloth to protect them from any moisture or dramatic changes in temperature and placed them in the appropriate container.

Only once they were all boxed and ready was the sofa pushed away from the wall and using a flat-bladed screwdriver, he gently prised out and removed the specially prepared floorboard. One by one, he then placed the boxes in a tidy little row beneath the floor: favourites closest to the hatch, least favourites furthest away.

Once the task was complete, he turned his attention back

to the display case and carefully positioned the assortment of cheap trinkets and knick-knacks he had specifically selected for the purpose from the charity shop on the high street earlier that day. Standing back to admire his handiwork, the end result was better than he had envisaged, the blatant mishmash of junk still smattered with a light film of dust, complementing each other perfectly and giving the appearance of having been there forever.

Placing the kettle on the hob, he finally rewarded himself by sitting down on the ancient sofa to catch up properly with the latest developments on the case as they evolved on the television screen. But it was no use. However hard he tried to concentrate and tune into what the newsreader was saying, the words just seemed to blend together and merge into an incomprehensible mess.

The shoes were the problem and it was hard not to feel despondent. His cherished possessions were now buried beneath the boards underneath where he sat but he consoled himself that it wouldn't be forever. Just until the dust had settled and then they could be returned to their rightful, proper place.

His mobile phone vibrated on the coffee table and picking it up irritably, he viewed the screen, the anger instantly rearing its ugly head to the surface once more.

'Leave me alone,' he growled, despite the fact he hadn't connected the call. 'Why can't you just leave me alone?'

58

The fact that the incident room was so small only went to exaggerate how busy it was. That aside, there was no question that this morning the place was bustling with activity, each and every dedicated enquiry team focused on their allocated roles.

As Lucas entered the room, he strode purposefully towards the charts that lined the far wall and made it his business, as he always did, to quickly scan the updates before him and bring himself up to speed on any new developments. His eyes paused briefly over each of the victim's faces in turn, before finally landing on Lou's. His eyes instantly jerked away as though stung and he concentrated once more on the others. Innocent, fresh expressions smiling out from the pictures that had been provided by loved ones pinned next to the more macabre crime scene photographs that served as a poignant reminder of how each of their lives had been brought to untimely conclusions by the Cross Killer.

Only when he trusted himself not to crumble and collapse did Lucas dare look again at the picture of Lou, a solitary tear rebelling against his demands and escaping down his cheek as he did so. He brushed at it irritably with the back of his hand before gently stroking her cheek with his thumb as he promised yet again to catch her killer if it was the last thing that he ever did.

Turning his attention to the room behind him, he spotted

Ash and Kelly poring over reams of paper at the nearest table. Neither of them were scheduled to work this weekend, but he was pleased to see that they had their priorities in order. Grabbing three coffees from the vending machine and cradling them as best he could in his hands without spilling the contents, he moved as fast as he could in their direction. His father, although he was still in two minds as to whether or not he was prepared to disclose that bit of information, had eventually come up trumps and described a vehicle that had caught his attention parked up in the boat yard during the early hours of the date in question. Unfortunately, with only a partial index it was going to be a long slog, a drawn-out affair that in truth they didn't really have time for, but it was by far the best lead that they'd had so far.

Lucas still felt sure that Malcolm knew more than he was letting on, was quite possibly more involved than he was letting on, but the man had clammed up and the clock had been ticking. The time to charge or discharge had come and with very little to go on except gut instinct, there had been no choice but to release him pending further enquiries. For now, the only option remaining was for the team to concentrate their attention on the suspect vehicle.

'What we got?' Neither Ash nor Kelly looked up as Lucas approached the table, but both gratefully accepted their coffee and instantly slurped at it as though their mouths were made of asbestos. Lucas couldn't resist a smile. It went with the territory and he doubted either of them had visited the canteen or the restrooms since they had been allocated their latest task.

'A hell of a lot of Volvos with the letters KS in the plate,' Kelly answered, wearily rubbing her face with her hands before rearranging her hair in a ponytail.

This was nothing they didn't know before the decision had been made to delve deeper, since the letters Malcolm had observed simply provided an indication of where the vehicle had originated. It was, however, all that they had to go on, so it was simply going to have to do.

'If it had been yellow it might have helped.' Ash had a point, but somewhat typical of this case, they weren't going to be granted a break in that department either and the Volvo they were looking for was a far more common metallic grey.

'What we talking?' Lucas asked, concerned by their obvious lack of enthusiasm, which could only mean there were too many to carry out house to house enquiries before the Cross Killer had the opportunity to strike again.

'Hundreds,' Kelly replied, shuffling the thick pile of papers that detailed every metallic grey Volvo and their registered keeper details with the initials KS in the plate throughout Cliffborough Cross.

Lucas had an idea. It was far from fool-proof and he would need to get the thumbs up from his superiors, but for now they would run with it.

'Narrow down the search area.'

'But we were told…'

'Just do it, Ash,' Lucas interrupted. He pointed to the map on the table. 'What do you see?' Lucas didn't wait for either of them to enlighten him, the excitement of the hidden possibilities that hadn't occurred to any of them previously gripping at his insides.

'Look,' Lucas reached for a pen to use as a rule. 'See?' he asked as he carefully measured the approximate distances with the pen. 'Let's assume for now that our killer doesn't like to travel far from home. Narrow it down to a ten-mile radius and see what it brings back.'

'But…'

'Just do it,' Lucas interrupted again. 'I'll sort it up above, but for now we focus on a more concentrated area.'

'I've got it,' Kelly blurted excitedly and for one moment, Lucas allowed himself to believe that she had found the very car that they were looking for, but then he realised that was ridiculous. Until they had waded through all the spreadsheets again, this time narrowing down the search area to the suggested ten miles, there wasn't a hope in hell.

'We're looking for a woman, right?' Kelly continued. 'So how about we reduce the search further to just those vehicles registered to women?'

'No.' Lucas still wasn't convinced that the Cross Killer was female and was furious that one of his own had taken it upon themselves to disclose such sensitive, possibly completely inaccurate, assumptions to the press before time. Hopefully he had made his position clear on that count during his earlier interview. Besides which, to weed out the results so severely based simply on a hunch about shoes and a whiff of perfume would be madness, but they didn't have time to get into the whole gender argument again right now.

'Too risky, Kel,' he continued. *Kel. Sam's got you at it now,* he grinned to himself. 'Plenty of wives drive their husband's car and vice versa.'

'Malcolm Muldoon being the perfect example,' Ash added. He didn't agree with Lucas about reducing the search area so drastically, but he couldn't agree more that to place the onus on Volvos only registered to women would be complete madness.

'I still think keeping the car secret from the press is crazy,' Ash continued. 'We tell them the killer might be female, when let's face it, we have nothing to substantiate that claim, but then we go and hide something crucial from them?'

'We can't afford to alarm the offender, you know that.' Lucas could see Ash's point of view and was in two minds himself if the truth be known. A member of the public could almost certainly recognise the vehicle and lead them to the killer's door, but alerting the Cross Killer about it before they were able to at least narrow down their identity and whereabouts carried far more risk than reward. Lucas just hoped that they would find the information required and fast. Before they – whoever *they* were – had the chance to kill again.

'Yes!' Kelly, who had been busy entering the appropriate new details into the system suddenly punched the air, interrupting the mass of thoughts and doubts that Ash and Lucas were currently battling with in their respective minds. Kelly had their undivided attention now and they both turned towards her and waited for her to elaborate on her excited gesture.

'If you're right, Lucas, we'll have our culprit in no time.' She pulled a sheet of paper from the printer and placed it on the table in front of them, her fingers moving frantically across the printed words as she spoke.

'Nineteen in total. Four pensioners so we can pretty much write them off, especially to start with. Leaves us with twelve males and three females, so I say we start with them and work our way backwards.'

Squeezing her shoulder by way of appreciation, Lucas grabbed the sheet of paper from the table and made for the superintendent's office, all the while studying the names on the list as he walked. One in particular, which bounced from the page before his eyes. Could it be the same person? It was crazy. A stab in the dark. Smith didn't like hunches, never had done, and before he had even reached his office, Lucas could hear the lecture ringing in his ears about gut instinct having no place in modern policing.

Worth a look though, surely? Lucas didn't have the authority to make such a monumental decision without Smith's approval and so, like it or not, one way or another he had no choice but to talk the man around. And if the answer was still no, he had already made up his mind. He was going to check out the place anyway. With or without permission from the higher powers that be.

59

The immaculately tended gardens that separated the extravagant houses from the electrically operated wrought iron gates on Rothwell Street exuded wealth and prosperity, and it was any wonder that the local residents hadn't got together and formed a petition to rid the eyesore that was number 22 from their otherwise perfect existence.

Wanting to familiarise himself with the building, but keen not to draw attention to himself at this stage, Lucas stood on the opposite side of the street and studied the rotten wooden sash windows and moss and lichen that plagued the old slate roof. A planning application had been clumsily pinned to the gate and flapped in the wind, but he didn't need to get any closer to know what it said. The property oozed its lack of love from every single brick that held it together, testimony that the landlord didn't wish to spend a penny on the place in preference to demolishing and rebuilding it. Possibly even less surprising was the fact that the tenant was also clearly unprepared to invest in the upkeep since she could presumably be given notice to quit at any time.

The house was registered to a David Miller, although it was clear from the preliminary investigations that the property was the result of an inheritance from his late father. David Miller wasn't local to the area. Nevertheless, despite not being able to disclose the reasons for his interest, the man had seemed keen to help if possible when Lucas had spoken with him earlier on the phone.

'This Rita Tate is the sole tenant, yes?' Lucas had asked, hoping to get to the bottom of why the Volvo was registered to a different person at the same address. And not just any person if his hunch was right but a man who Lucas had always known deep down equalled trouble. A man who was clearly a danger and a liability to those he came into contact with. A man who belonged behind bars, out of harm's way for a very long time.

'No sub-letting. It's in the contract,' Miller had responded. 'Although she may have a partner, I suppose,' he added as an afterthought.

'But you never met him?' Lucas persisted, needing as much information as possible on the man whose name the Volvo was registered to and who could quite possibly be this Cross Killer who had outwitted them at every turn.

'Never met her either. All done over the internet on one of those Rooms to Rent sites,' he answered.

Interesting, Lucas thought. *So the tenant could be anyone he or she wanted to be.*

'So the tenancy agreement and the rent were...'

'Electronically processed,' he interrupted. 'Keys posted on completion by Special Delivery.'

They both fell silent for a moment, but when David spoke again, he seemed nervous all of a sudden about the nature of the call in relation to his tenant.

'Should I be concerned, Officer? It's just you hear about these things don't you and I don't want no trouble at the place. I'm trying to sell it see, hence the planning application.' He paused, before continuing. 'I don't suppose you could give me an idea what she's supposed to have done?'

Lucas couldn't help but feel sorry for the guy. Mud had a tendency to stick and if the owner of the Volvo was their killer and living under his roof, selling the place was going to get a whole lot harder than it had proved to be already. But he couldn't tell him anything. To do so would be more than his job was worth, but more than that, it could risk compromising the case. Instead, smothered in guilt about the blatant lie, Lucas had assured him that he had nothing to worry about and that he would be the first to know of anything that could alter or affect his circumstances in that regard.

Lucas turned his attention back to the house. Was anybody home? It was hard to tell, since despite the early hour of the day every single curtain throughout the property that he could see was firmly drawn. He should probably give up and leave. Going over the heads of his superiors and coming here without any back-up or knowledge back at the station about his whereabouts was stupid, but the urge to clap eyes on the occupant had been too great. He needed to see the man for himself. See what they were up against. And then – and only then – would he pass on the information to his colleagues. Not all of it though. If his suspicions turned out to be right, there was no way on earth he would be discussing his association to the suspect.

60

Coming here had seemed like a good idea at the time – to his own special place that nobody knew about – but now that he was here, he was starting to feel like a caged animal and he didn't like the feeling one little bit. He paced back and forth across the small room as he tried to think, pausing every now and then to sit down on the sofa before standing once more to re-enact the ritual.

Evil? They were calling him evil now. He wasn't evil. These recent urges to kill weren't even in his nature, but what was he supposed to do? Extracting himself from temptation clearly didn't work. If anything, hiding away was only making the cravings more intense and he wasn't sure how much longer he could resist the desire to relieve some of this tension that was building inside him and threatening to explode.

He had hoped that the shoes would help. That having them close by, where he could see and touch them, would be enough to rid his mind of the terrible yearning for more, but if anything they were making him feel more anxious and he realised now that the sooner he put them back in their hiding place, the better. He picked up his favourites once more, studying the intricate webbed design and delicate little buckles. *Soon.* He'd replace them soon. *Just five more minutes.* Sitting down on the sofa once more, he positioned them carefully on his lap, holding them gently in his hands as he rocked back and forth as though nursing a weaning child.

His eyes moved to the mobile phone on the coffee table in front of him. Despite trying to call umpteen times, he still hadn't been able to get hold of her and it was starting to make him angry. He just wanted to explain. The opportunity to make her see that she had given him no choice. She'd had a choice though. If she had behaved differently, none of this would have been necessary.

Was she deliberately avoiding him? He had no way of knowing and no way of finding out. *Unless...* He shuffled forwards on the seat and contemplated his next move. Turning up when she least expected it could be a lot of fun.

'Think if you ignore me I'll just go away? Over *your* dead body.' He chuckled uncontrollably at his little joke.

He glanced at the clock on the mantelpiece. He should have been in work hours ago. Would they be understanding of his predicament, or would he face a disciplinary when he did finally return to work? He had no idea, only that he couldn't skive off forever. If he didn't show his face soon, they were sure to start asking awkward questions. Besides, burying himself in his work might take his mind off things and he could certainly do with the distraction. Anything to divert his attention from the increasing itch that was becoming more persistent by the minute.

His leg started to jig involuntarily and despite leaning hard on his thighs with his elbows, the action did nothing to prevent the sensation. Who was he trying to kid? He couldn't go to work. Not yet. He wouldn't be able to concentrate at a time like this however hard he tried. Maybe if he just popped in to see everyone and explained his absence to his supervisor? But with the heavy police presence outdoors and the even more oppressive media coverage indoors, leaving this place was too big a risk. Or was it?

Hastily replacing the shoes back under the boards, he quickly checked his appearance in the mirror before grabbing his coat and belongings. As he unbolted the deadlocks on the front door, he paused briefly and checked over his shoulder one last time that nothing had been left out of place. Satisfied that all was in order, he stepped out and pulled the door firmly closed behind him, careful to check, check and check again that it was firmly secured in his absence.

61

When Malcolm arrived home, he was pleased to note that his wife seemed to be in a more subservient mood than she had been of late. Perhaps her recent stint under police interrogation had done her more good than he had anticipated? Yesterday, expecting a confrontation as opposed to a sensible discussion, he had decided not to bother coming home at all.

Fully dressed, yet wrapped in a dressing gown and those silly fluffy slippers of hers covering her feet, she now sat huddled on the sofa, cuddling Buddy. Neither of them seemed prepared to look him in the eye, which so far as he was concerned only served to confirm the guilt she was feeling over her recent betrayal. *Soon, Buddy. Soon you're going to have to give me some of that attention. If you want feeding, that is. I'll be all that you have.* He grinned conspiratorially at the dog as though they were sharing their own private little secret, before glancing once more at his wife who gazed vacantly at nothing on the wall behind him and seemed to be in a world of her own.

Daring to hope that this was going to be easier than he had envisaged, he decided to play along and walking over to the drinks cabinet, he poured two overly generous measures of brandy into the special cut glass goblets that he normally reserved for best. It was ridiculously early to be partaking in the hard stuff and he wrestled with his conscience momentarily before raising one of the glasses to his lips and downing the contents in one. After the week he'd had, he not only needed it, he had damn well earned it, he thought to himself as he topped up his glass.

The heat emanating from the fireplace was so hot it smarted Eileen's skin, but as she watched her husband busy himself preparing the drinks, she barely noticed. Chilled to the very core, she somehow doubted she could get warm even if she were to climb right inside it. Accepting her glass gratefully, she in turn dared to hope that she had seen the last of her husband's recent bizarre and erratic behaviour. Finally, she spoke.

'Are you mad?'

Malcolm sat down on the other end of the sofa and smiled. It wasn't a pleasant smile and Eileen shuddered instinctively.

'Not at all, dear, I completely forgive you.' Malcolm knew that to enact his plan, he first needed to get his wife back on side.

'You... forgive... me?' Eileen could barely believe her ears and felt all the pent-up anger and resentment starting to resurface from within her. *As if trying to kill me wasn't enough, you implicated me in not one, but several murders, yet you forgive me?* Despite telling the police everything she knew, she was in no doubt that they still considered her to be a suspect; they'd warned her as much by forbidding her to leave the area, and the news on every channel only served to confirm her paranoia since it was quite clear that they still believed a woman was responsible for the murders.

She studied her husband over the top of her glass, the nagging feeling reappearing in her gut and gripping her insides as the slideshow of images being played out on all the news channels whizzed around her mind like a frantic Wurlitzer at the fairground.

Did you murder EJ? The Gregory woman? Tod? The woman from the retail park? However hard she tried, she couldn't eradicate the thoughts from her mind. According to the papers, the police still suspected that Tod's death could be a wrong-place-wrong-time killing but she knew her husband better than anyone. Malcolm had found out about the affair. That's why he had killed Tod and if the poor girl from the retail park had witnessed the episode, it would almost certainly explain the vicious beating that she had received.

Murdered the neighbour's cat in cold blood. Malcolm's mother's words pounded in her ears. *Peeling the potatoes at the kitchen sink, I was. Grabbed it unceremoniously by its tail, he did. Swung it round in the air whilst it squealed all the while to be released. Said later it was because it scratched him. Like that made it all okay.* Eileen had read an article once about serial killers. Allegedly torturing animals as a child was a classic warning sign. She glanced nervously at Buddy. Who knew what her husband got up to when she wasn't there? *Course, I banged hard on the window;* his mother's words increased in volume at the memory. *Determined to make him stop, I was, but it was like I didn't exist. It didn't stand a chance. Caved the poor creature's head in with an ornamental rock from beside the pond.* Eileen shivered again. Maybe a hot bath would help?

'We all do silly things in the heat of the moment.' Malcolm's voice broke into her thoughts and brought her back to the present. He was trying his best to look relaxed, but inside he was livid. He had known about the affair for a while, but to have it confirmed by a random stranger? It was embarrassing. Humiliating. Degrading even! His wife was greedy, end of. What other possible explanation could there be for choosing to sample cheap rump when prime Aberdeen Angus was on offer at home?

Silly things? Getting madder by the minute, Eileen was struggling to contain her anger. Her husband had killed four people and almost added her to his rapidly growing list, yet he had the nerve to sit there and act holier than thou? Why the hell had they released him at all? Were the police really so blind in their convictions that they couldn't see the truth that was staring them in the face? She couldn't go on like this. *They* couldn't go on like this. At this rate he would end up killing them both.

She needed space and time to think, neither of which were available to her whilst he sat invading her space, and so excusing herself as politely as she could for fear of antagonising him further, she went upstairs to run herself a bath.

As she left the room, Malcolm quickly leapt up from his seat and closed the door firmly behind her so Buddy couldn't follow. He knew it was childish, vindictive even, but it was fun watching the dog squirm. Returning to the comfort of his armchair, he then leaned back and took another sip of the brandy, relishing the burning sensation as it spread through his chest. Retrieving his mobile phone from his pocket, he pressed the home button to awaken the screen and check for messages. Nothing. It still worried him that Rita hadn't returned any of his calls, but he felt confident that once it was all over she would soon get in touch. He quickly typed out another text and hit send.

TONIGHT'S THE NIGHT DARLING XXXX

Excitement galloped in his belly at the prospect. *Oh yes. Tonight is definitely the night!*

62

When the door finally clicked open and the occupant stepped onto the path and walked confidently towards the Volvo, Lucas wrestled with his inner emotions, the excitement of finally clapping eyes on his prey soon suffocated by the heavy disappointment that he could have got it all so wrong.

It wasn't their man and the realisation that he had been chasing a wild goose hung oppressively in the air as he watched the Volvo crawl gently out of the gates and accelerate onto the main road. Nonetheless, he wanted every last inch of the property searched at the first available opportunity and so following the car at a safe distance, he called Sam to fill her in on his movements and request an application for a search warrant to be fast tracked into the system. He'd explain to Smith later why he had chosen to ignore his instructions in preference of nothing more than a bad vibe.

None of it made any sense and as Lucas followed the vehicle down the dual carriageway towards the town centre, he glanced sideways at the pile of files brimming with notes that littered the passenger seat awaiting a miracle. He didn't think they held the solution and as he tried to assemble the jigsaw in his brain, the nagging feeling in the back of his mind started up again. The answer was staring them all in the face, he was sure of it – so glaringly obvious that they had all missed its prominence.

Miller had been adamant that his tenant was a Rita Tate,

yet the registered keeper of the vehicle at the same address was a man by the name of Peter Tate. *AKA Peter Wainwright.* Ronnie's ex, and the man who had befriended Lou only to subsequently kill her, he had been sure of it. The fact that Miller had never actually met his tenant had only served to convince Lucas more that Peter had tricked his landlord in order to protect his identity, but now, the fact that a woman did clearly live at the premises after all totally kiboshed this theory.

So if the woman he was currently tailing down the A38 was this Rita Tate woman, where did she fit into all of this? *Spouse? Sibling?* Another concealed connection also nibbled away in the back of his mind, but however hard he tried, the pieces just wouldn't fit. *Rita.* What was it about her that was bugging him? He racked his brains, pleading with the answer to appear, but despite being certain of something, he still couldn't place what it was.

Until, that was, the Volvo pulled off the main road and entered the retail park. Lucas held back, determined not to take his eyes from the woman for a single second as she made her way across the tarmac into a very specific building.

And then the penny dropped with one God Almighty thud.

63

Malcolm's voice drowned out Freddie's as he sang along and tapped his foot in time with 'Another One Bites The Dust,' whilst preparing his special meal for Eileen. She was still upstairs in the bath, just where he wanted her, out of harm's way until he was good and ready. He glanced at the clock on the wall. She'd been up there for hours and would dissolve at this rate. Not that it mattered. *All good things come to those that wait.*

A quick taste of the bolognese simmering on the stove was enough to confirm that it was absolutely delicious if he did say so himself, which just left his special little marinade to prepare. Grabbing a suitable dish from the cupboard, he reached under the sink and pulled out the various cleaning products, only briefly pausing what he was doing to creep into the hall and listen silently at the bottom of the stairs for any relevant sound of movement upstairs.

Satisfied that she was still splashing away in the tub, he rushed back to the kitchen, determined to prepare his concoction as quickly as possible. It was unfortunate he couldn't sample it for obvious reasons, so he was just going to have to trust his judgement on this one. *Buddy?* He frantically eyed the dog who was watching his every move. *No.* He dismissed the thought no sooner than it had entered his head. Unlike his wife, the dog didn't deserve to die.

Having blended together what he considered to be an

ample portion of washing up liquid, stain remover, bleach, dishwasher detergent and glass cleaner, he squeezed the juice of half a lemon into the mixture and finished it off with a good measure of salt to hopefully disguise the taste. Oh God, the urge to taste it was immense, but no, he mustn't. Even just one tiny little drop could make him feel very poorly indeed. Carefully pouring his creation into a jug and then into the miniature hip flask that he had bought specifically for the occasion, he screwed the lid on tightly and popped the flask back into his trouser pocket.

Turning his attention back to the lemon on the chopping board, he cut two generous slices. Then he poured out two strong portions of gin and added a dash of tonic, three cubes of ice and a slice of the lemon to each. About to return the gin to the cupboard, he changed his mind. If this evening was going to go smoothly, the last thing he needed was his nerves getting the better of him, and so taking a large gulp from his glass, he promptly topped it back up before picking up both drinks and wandering through to the lounge.

He could hear the sound of the hairdryer upstairs now, which was promising. Eileen wouldn't be long now. *It* wouldn't be long now. Turning off the main lights, he switched on a couple of table lamps instead to provide what he hoped was a more relaxing ambience and awaited his wife's imminent arrival. *Not to mention departure,* he chuckled to himself.

64

A s the sky darkened into an evening bathed in the ominous shadow of a forthcoming storm, Lucas pulled his vehicle into the nearest available space to 22 Rothwell Street and walked up the road towards the house. Within seconds, the first smattering of raindrops bounced on the pavement around him and he sped up his pace, running the last few yards for cover before the heavens opened.

Standing on the stone steps beneath the flimsy plastic sheeting that covered the front porch, the rain ricocheted above their heads and Lucas suppressed a smile as Sam stubbed her cigarette and discreetly discarded it over the wall of the adjoining garden. Old habits died hard, the risk of contaminating a possible crime scene clearly at the forefront of her mind.

'Please tell me you have some good news.' He looked at her as he desperately tried to read the expression in her eyes and hoped above all else that he wasn't misreading the excited glint in her pupils.

'They found a loose floorboard in the lounge.' Sam grinned at him, enjoying teasing him by delaying the result he so badly craved.

'And?'

'And you were right. Our woman does have a penchant for quality shoes... Assuming she doesn't make a habit of preserving her own footwear under the floorboards, I'd say we've found ourselves a proper little treasure trove. They're bagging up the evidence now.'

'YES!' Lucas punched his fist in the air by way of a victory gesture.

'Loads in the wardrobe too but they,' she gestured over her shoulder with her thumb at the forensic team working the other side of the window as she spoke, 'reckon the shoes under the boards were removed from the dead women. Seven pairs in total.' Sam shuddered as an ice-cold chill crawled down the back of her neck. 'Meaning there's every likelihood she's killed others we don't yet know about.'

'He,' Lucas interjected, sickened at the prospect that there may be more victims but also desperate to fill in his colleague about his recent discovery.

'Huh?' Having turned to make her way back into the house as she spoke, Sam only caught the tail end of what he had said.

'There's every likelihood *HE's* killed others,' Lucas stated, unable to hide the amusement from his face as he recalled the feast that his eyes had hungrily devoured earlier.

'I don't follow.' Sam tilted her head to one side as she looked at him, her curiosity now well and truly peaked.

'*She* is a *he*, Sam. There is no Rita Tate, there never was.'

'But the landlord said... Didn't we meet her?' At completely crossed purposes, Sam was struggling to keep up.

'Rita is an alias. Although,' Lucas continued, 'there would, as you say, seem to be a Rita Tate of sorts. He's good, I'll give him that – had all of us fooled.'

'The Volvo...'

'Is registered to a bloke called Peter Tate – exactly!' Lucas interrupted. 'Otherwise known as Peter Wainwright.' He paused a moment to allow her brain to catch up. 'I spoke to Ronnie – Tate was apparently his stepfather's name. No wonder we couldn't trace him. Clever little bastard obviously decided to make it official.'

'The woman from the bed shop was Peter Pan all along?' Sam released a nervous giggle, suddenly uncomfortable with the bizarre image that had started to weave its way into her brain.

'I'd say we've now definitely got more than enough to make an arrest, wouldn't you?'

65

Eileen sat at the kitchen table sipping from the glass of wine that Malcolm had gleefully poured for her. Had he put some kind of drug in it to liven up the evening? She wouldn't put it past him and tried to subtly sniff it when he wasn't looking. She'd never been able to prove it of course, but she had always suspected he had done something similar all those years ago on their first date.

As she sat and watched him, a bolt of suspicion shot through her. She couldn't help but notice that he seemed to be in a particularly good mood this evening, something more rare these days than rocking horse excrement. She put her wine back down on the table and decided to take it slowly. The gin and tonic already seemed to have gone to her head and for all she knew, he'd probably drugged that as well.

'More music, dear?' Malcolm turned from the stove and smiled at her, the very action unnerving her and making her even more edgy.

Did she want more music? She wasn't sure that she did since his choice of songs lately all seemed to be decidedly odd, but there seemed little point antagonising him when he was clearly making an effort for a change.

'Yes… yes, I think that would be rather nice, dear. A little classical do you think?' Something soothing to take her mind off his peculiar behaviour would be perfect.

Crossing the room to the hall where the tablet was plugged

into the speakers, Malcolm grinned inanely to himself. *Something classical.* Oh yes, he had the perfect song in mind and selecting a variation of classics that he knew his wife liked, he deliberately selected his special song within the playlist in excess of ten times to ensure that she would hear it.

While Malcolm fiddled with the music in the hall, Eileen stood up and approached the stove. She wasn't used to being waited on hand and foot and wasn't sure she liked it. Not one little bit. It made her feel rather useless and so she carefully piled a large heap of spaghetti on Malcolm's plate and a much more reserved portion onto her own. He was so lucky in this respect, seemingly able to eat whatever he liked whereas she only had to so much as look at food before the weight started to pile on.

'Scales are for fish,' Malcolm used to joke when they were dating, but that was easy for him to say; he wasn't the one who only had to think fat to achieve it. Reaching for the bolognese, she piled both plates high. She couldn't live off air alone after all and it was the carbs that caused her problems, she was sure of it. Placing the plates on the table, she turned her attention to the sink and started to stack the pots and pans to soak in the hot, soapy water.

Taking advantage of her back being turned, Malcolm seized the moment. First, he swapped the plates as per usual. *Must think I was born yesterday.* Then, he liberally added some of his own special little delicacy to Eileen's plate and quickly gave it a small stir with his finger.

Since Eileen was still busy at the kitchen sink, Malcolm entered the adjoining utility and stuffed the empty flask firmly under the pile of rubbish already spilling from the waste bin. He would deal with it later – play safe and pop it in the neighbours' bin in case there were any repercussions after her death. Then he scrubbed his hands with hot soapy water to rid any of the dreadful poison from his skin.

Drying her hands, Eileen turned to the table and shook her head in confusion. She was sure that she had placed the larger portion in front of Malcolm and couldn't help but think it was so typical of him. Trying to fatten her up so no one would find her desirable. Hearing his footsteps approaching behind her, she quickly switched the plates once more and they both took their respective seats.

Almost five minutes had passed since they had sat down to eat and Malcolm studied his wife carefully, searching for any obvious signs that she might be about to croak it, but as yet it didn't look too promising. *Did I add enough to the recipe?* Chewing his own food vigorously, he was slightly concerned to note that she seemed to be picking and pushing the food around her plate. *Come on, woman, we haven't got all night.*

Shovelling another large spoonful of bolognese into his mouth, he fidgeted excitedly in his seat as the next song started to play. Oh yes, it was definitely time to say goodbye. *Wouldn't it just be so perfect if she were to drop dead now during this particular song? A little something I could keep with me as a fond memory for the rest of my days.*

As Andrea Bocelli broke into the chorus of 'Time To Say Goodbye,' Malcolm joined in with gusto, but then his throat seemed to tighten and he coughed in an attempt to clear whatever it was that had got stuck. He tried again, coughing harder this time but it still wouldn't budge and trying to clear the problem only seemed to exacerbate it. He reached for his drink hoping that the moisture would shift it, or at the very least soothe the swelling sensation in his mouth and throat, but it just burned all the more, making him choke and hack so hard that his back and ribs ached in rebellious protest.

I feel sick. Or, maybe the other end? Oh God, please no!

'Help me,' he cried but he didn't think any words had come out, so he tried again. Except that he could no longer move his lips to form the words he so badly needed. *Am I drooling?* He had a horrible suspicion he might be. *What the hell have you done to me?* He glared through glazed pupils at his wife, begging her with his eyes to help him but she didn't even seem that fazed, which only served to convince him all the more that this was all something to do with her.

Eileen meanwhile stared in horror at her husband, watching as though in slow motion as the sweat poured from his green, bloated face and pooled onto the table beneath him.

'Malcolm? Are you all right, love? What's that you're saying?' She cocked an ear towards him, terrified to take her eyes from him for fear she might miss the words, but except for an exaggerated gurgle, he made no sound as he grabbed the tablecloth between his fingers and started to convulse. Rooted to the spot in shock, Eileen watched as his limbs jerked erratically as though he were having some kind of fit. Suddenly snapping to attention, she clambered from her chair and rushed into the hall to dial the emergency services, a loud crash reverberating behind her as Malcolm and the entire contents of the table collapsed to the floor.

66

Convincing herself that the distraction from her colleagues and customers might help, Rita had agreed with her supervisor yesterday that she would return to work. *Big mistake.* Rather than keep her mind occupied with other matters, they all just served as a constant reminder of her predicament, each and every one of them seeming to want nothing more than to dissect and discuss every last little remnant of detail disclosed by the press. The strain of keeping up appearances was starting to take its toll.

'I heard it's a woman,' Rita's colleague Claudia told the lady at the counter.

'Well, I've a friend who has a friend and her friend works at the local nick. She said a witness saw a car at the scene of the crime.' Rita's ears pricked up as she pretended to study an information sheet in front of one of the displays whilst she eavesdropped on the conversation behind her.

'No?'

'Yeah, but they aren't telling the public so they can catch the mother fucker.' The customer nodded emphatically. 'I also heard that weirdo Muldoon, the one who locked the district councillor in the cellar a while back, was arrested.'

'Wasn't he one of the victims' dad? The district councillor, I mean.'

'And he's apparently in hospital. Muldoon, that is. Suspected poisoning.' Rita held her breath as the customer spoke. The woman certainly seemed to be well informed and she was determined not to miss the slightest snippet. *Hospital? Cliffborough Community Hospital?*

'Hey, Rita, you know that Muldoon guy, don't you?' Claudia shouted across the floor.

On and on and on like a CD jammed on repeat and unsure how much more she could take, Rita rushed out the back of the shop and stepped into the dimly lit basement that served as the storeroom. Mobile signal was always null and void down here but she could usually link up to the WI-FI in the supervisor's office above if she hovered close enough to the small window at the far end of the room.

So Malcolm had stuffed up again? She didn't even know why the news had surprised her. The man clearly couldn't be trusted to do anything right. Retrieving her mobile phone from her bag, she jabbed her finger at the screen in frustration. Ronnie still hadn't opened her messages despite the fact that she'd sent them hours ago. Logging into Facebook, she then checked on the message she had finally sent to Malcolm earlier, frustration and anger mingling in her belly at the sight of the undelivered icon.

What the hell are you playing at, Malcolm? And what was Facebook playing at, come to that? Up until now, the ability to pinpoint the exact second that he opened and read his messages had worked perfectly. Yet now, when she needed the instant messaging service the most, their stupid little blip in the system was thwarting her and letting her down beyond all recognition.

A wave of fury washed over her at the injustice of the situation and she chucked the phone against the far wall as though the action would somehow help or make her feel better. It didn't, and the fact that it survived the attack without so much as cracking the screen only served to make her angrier still about the technological conspiracy that seemed to be ganging up against her.

Was it Malcolm who had told the police about the car? 'Did you?' She glowered fiercely at his profile picture as though it could provide the answers. 'Well? I'm talking to you. Did you?' she spat angrily at the screen.

'Tonight's the night,' she scoffed at the phone. 'Last supper for whom exactly?' She laughed then, and as the tsunami of emotions increased in their pace, Rita embraced both the hysteria and the rage that surged through her veins like long lost friends.

'If a job's worth doing, it's worth doing properly.' She giggled. 'Oh yes. Time to welcome the organ grinder. The monkey has definitely left the building!' She cackled loudly and stuffed the phone back into her bag just as the stern voice of her supervisor over the internal tannoy system reverberated around the room.

'Rita to customer service… Rita to customer service.'

She glanced at her watch, suspicion suddenly clenching at her chest. Ten more minutes until her break officially ended – her colleagues knew that, so why would they interrupt it? Pressing her face up against the small window, she peered through the glass for a better look. Sure enough, the brightly lit blues and yellows of the patrol car parked directly outside the store glared smugly at her, daring her to reveal herself as they reflected in the sunlight. Grabbing her belongings as quickly as she could, she moved fast, not even stopping to look back or consider what reaction her sudden disappearance would create as she sneaked out of the rear entrance of the store.

67

The manager of the bed shop looked nervous as he shuffled the papers on his desk and answered the questions being fired at him. Feeling guilty for being pushy, yet too focused to worry about polite formalities, Lucas gave him what he hoped was an encouraging smile.

'It's what's expected of 'em... and us. Left work on the Friday as Peter, only to turn in on Monday as Rita and there weren't nothing we could do about it except turn the other cheek.'

Lucas raised his eyebrows in mock shock at Sam and mouthed 'I told you so' in her direction before glancing nervously at his watch, painfully aware that time was no longer on their side. 22 Rothwell Street had been under police surveillance overnight, but so far, despite distributing both descriptions, there had been no sign of either Peter or Rita. Why the hell hadn't they covered the rear exit before entering the store? It was a schoolboy error – one he would pay handsomely for if they didn't catch the man before he had the chance to kill again.

Lucas turned his attention back to the man in front of him. 'Did Peter... Rita,' he corrected himself, 'have any particular friends that you are aware of? Anyone that he... *she* might turn to in times of trouble?'

The manager shook his head thoughtfully before responding. 'Always kept himself to himself... herself to herself.' He raised his eyebrows to the ceiling and slapped the back of his hand jokingly with his other hand as though telling himself off. 'I rather liked it if the truth be known. Less I had to do with him – *her* – the better.'

In some respects, his attitude could be construed as extremely narrow-minded but nonetheless, Lucas couldn't help nodding sympathetically. The world had gone PC mad and having to spend every minute of every working day treading on eggshells for fear of causing offence was bound to take its toll.

'I've got to ask,' he continued. 'I'm sorry, I know it's a matter you'd rather put to bed.' He cringed at the non-deliberate pun. 'Did Rita and Hannah Gregory have much to do with one another?'

'Not at all. Hannah didn't like her as it happened, but we just put that down to prejudice. Dare I say it, but Hannah was a little like that if you know what I mean? Always ready to judge another before taking a good, hard look at herself.'

Interesting he didn't mention his dislike for his employee previously, Lucas thought to himself, instantly dismissing the observation. It was only too easy to become paranoid and suspect anyone and everyone at times such as this.

'So there was no one?' He pushed on.

'I don't think so,' he stated. 'Although… well, there was Malcolm, but no, that was nothing.' He waved his hand to dismiss the idea. 'Forget I said anything.'

Lucas had been waiting for Malcolm's name to crop up and he looked up from his notepad and studied the man behind the desk, inwardly urging him to continue. The fact that Rita and Malcolm had already provided alibis for one another over Hannah Gregory's murder wasn't lost on him. *How deep in all of this are you, Malcolm?* he wondered. Of course, having been admitted to the A&E department last night with suspected poisoning, it was too late now to question Malcolm on his version of events. The man wasn't talking, nor was he expected to anytime soon, and a lurch of relief fluttered in his belly. Lucas wasn't proud of himself. Being pleased that the man might not live to tell any tales did nothing for his self-esteem, but he couldn't deny that it felt good – safe even – to know that Malcolm couldn't disclose the details of their relationship and compromise his position at such a crucial stage of the investigation even if he wanted to.

'Malcolm Muldoon?' Lucas suggested. He was keen to get the man talking without any risk further down the line of accusations about leading a witness.

'Yeah, that's the one.' The man seemed lost in thought as though considering the man's presence in his employee's life for the first time. 'Suddenly started hanging around. More than's healthy if you get my drift? Peter... Rita,' he looked up and grinned sheepishly, 'reckoned he was a pest. Found him a nuisance she said, yet they were always huddled up together, whispering in draughty corners and sneaking off on her breaks together.'

Were you partners in crime, Malcolm? Lucas tried to dismiss his concerns, but his brain refused to play ball. Lou had claimed all along that someone had stolen her boots when Malcolm attacked her – accusations that Malcolm had denied. Under interview, he had then later claimed that Rita could confirm that Lou attacked him in the retail park that day and not the other way around – a claim that Rita subsequently denied. But if they were in on it together, why would she lie? *Because she stole the boots? Yes, that's it,* he thought to himself. Rita needed an alibi for the Gregory murder. For Lou's, she needed an alternate suspect to keep suspicion away from her front door.

And what about Eileen Muldoon? The woman absolutely convinced that her husband must have poisoned his own food, but why? It made no sense. Unless the plan had been another attempt on his wife's life, no doubt spurred on by a man who Malcolm believed to be a woman. Was his father in love with him? What a mess! Lucas had tried so hard for so long to make sense of the puzzle but now, as the pieces all slotted into place, the truth was enough to make him want to run and hide like a child.

Malcolm must have known that the Volvo belonged to Rita; that was why he had clammed up about it under interrogation. What else had he done to protect her? Did he know that she was a killer? *Please God, no.* The supervisor gave a small cough, as though to remind him of his existence, and snapping out of his reverie Lucas turned his attention back to the man sat opposite him.

'We'll need time-sheets appertaining to him… *her,*' he corrected himself yet again as he continued, 'for the past month.'

'And what if she comes back here?'

'You act normal, but call me immediately.' Lucas passed him a business card with his private phone number on and retrieving his jacket from the back of the chair, he signalled to Sam that it was time they made a move. He had a damned good idea where Peter might turn up next and he didn't like the concept. Not one little bit.

68

The idea of death itself didn't scare Malcolm, but as he lay in the hospital bed slipping in and out of consciousness, the realisation that he could cease to exist at any moment haunted his every waking second. Saying goodbye to Rita would be the hardest part and in his darker moments, when the pain kicked in and prevented sleep, he would lie awake and practise what he would say.

And then there was Eileen. He had plenty he wanted to say to her as well, such as asking her why the hell she wasn't dead. And why she had to go and ruin absolutely everything that he tried to do. At first when she had visited, he had convinced himself it was all part of the nightmare that had become his very existence, but as the hours turned into days it soon became clear that she was going nowhere. Eileen intended to finish what she had started.

As he slipped out of consciousness once more, he asked himself what people would say about him when he was gone. Was he a good person? Had he been the person he wanted them to think that he was? Had he lived up to their expectations? Rita wouldn't think so and the thought of what she would be thinking right now ate away at him, just like the poison that seemed so determined to debilitate each and every organ that currently kept him alive.

He could just about make out the written words on his obituary now. *Malcolm was a... what was I?* The words suddenly faded and blurred and he could no longer read them.

'You can run but you can't hide, Malcolm.' Death spoke to him often, making sure that he knew there was nothing he could do to escape its greedy clutches. Knowledge wasn't power. Knowledge spelled grief and the more he became aware that his life was pretty much over, the more he happened to want to prolong it.

When Eileen had first come calling disguised as the grim reaper, he had been terrified. She was here with him now. Her aura hung heavily in the air as she slipped through the darkness, her every movement as fluid as the muscles that supported them as she moved stealthily and with absolute precision towards his bedside. They didn't discuss his imminent death, but as he looked deep into her eyes, he knew that it was time as the image of defeat stared back at him from the opposing side of the bed.

He tried to move, but his limbs, somehow disjointed from his body, refused to obey the instruction. Painfully aware of the surreal cloud of activity going on just the other side of the closed door, he then tried to call out but no sound escaped his lips. Nurses, doctors, visitors – all of them moving back and forth, oblivious to his very existence as though it were already just a distant memory. However hard he seemed to try, Malcolm's body rebelled against him at every turn, refusing to yield to his demands under the stiff cotton sheet. Defeated, he lay motionless and resigned himself to his fate.

Death had arrived. Death was calling his name and he no longer had the strength, nor the energy to fight it. Finally, he was at peace and he said the word over and over out loud, hoping that those who cared enough would understand.

69

Rita visited Malcolm's bedside often. Watching, waiting, willing him to beg for mercy. She wouldn't show him any of course, but neither would it do to put him out of his misery too soon. Ronnie would have to wait of course. *Shame.* The plan to finish her off right under the pigs' nose had felt rather poetic, but sadly it would also have been to her own detriment. Only once the police presence relaxed could she reach Malcolm.

Deciding how to approach him for the very last time had been the hardest part and it had taken Peter longer to get ready than the trip across town to the hospital. Dressing up as the grim reaper had been fun. A nice touch, and witnessing the fear as it glistened in Malcolm's pupils had been incredible. Indescribable. Nonetheless, all good things had to come to an end, including Malcolm's existence, and to permit him to die without the knowledge of who he really was would be sacrilege.

To just be himself this one last time, booted and suited, held a lot of appeal – especially if the police were still concentrating their search on Rita, but in the end, he settled on Rita. He could have more fun with Malcolm before revealing his true self this way.

And so it was just them now: Rita, Malcolm and Fate. The latter had stepped in and handed him to her and in return she must express her sincere gratitude for the opportunity. It was just that watching him like this, so dependent and reliant on her, was kind of nice. Nobody had ever needed her like he did right now and she wasn't sure she was ready to relinquish that kind of power just yet.

Closing the door quietly behind her, Rita stepped forward to study the man more carefully. Surrounded by tubes and wires attached to machines designed to keep him alive at any cost, he was barely recognisable from his former arrogant self. It was hard not to feel pity for him despite the lack of justification.

'You were supposed to kill her,' she spat through gritted teeth. 'And carry the can for the others. I was going to be happy. Whilst you were banged up, I was going to have everything I ever wanted but now thanks to you, I've got nothing. NOTHING!' she hissed. He didn't respond.

Glancing over her shoulder to make sure they were still alone, she prodded him gently in the arm with her finger. His eyes were squeezed tightly shut, but she was pleased to note him wince. And so she jabbed him again, harder this time, and once again, he flinched. *Good.* Now things were getting exciting. She didn't want him to miss the best bit. Her eyes travelled from the clear tube fed through his nose to the machine closest to the bed and on to the socket behind it that was feeding it, an automatic shudder of excitement hurtling through her veins at the mere prospect of what was about to come.

'In due time their feet will slip,' Rita whispered as she leaned over the bed. She was so close, her breath tickled Malcolm's skin and he tried in vain to move away. 'Their day of disaster will arrive and their destiny will overtake them.' She smiled as the image of her father came to mind. His favourite proverb and she had remembered it as though it were yesterday. He would be so proud. All she had ever wanted was to make him proud.

She placed her lips against Malcolm's, the sensation of his

skin against hers disgusting her but also having the desired effect, and he finally opened his eyes. As she had always known that he would.

'Hello, my darling.' Rita grinned as she spoke, her lips forming a tight barrier across her teeth as she ripped the wig from her head and placed it on Malcolm's chest. She didn't bother to disguise her voice any longer. That would be pointless and only serve to spoil her fun. Neither did she take her eyes from his for so much as a second for fear she might miss something crucial.

Malcolm didn't move, nor did he speak, which suited her just fine. It was enough, more than enough, that he was aware of her presence and of that, she was in no doubt. The thin layer of petrified perspiration that had formed and glistened on his skin and the fear that screamed out from within his eyeballs as he had opened them ample indication of his lucidity in that regard.

Rita chose not to speak to him either for now, although part of her desperately wanted to. She wanted to scream and yell and shout and make him finally understand once and for all the result of his stupidity, but what would it achieve? Words were pointless now. Words couldn't save him. Nothing could save him from his destiny.

'In due time their feet will slip,' she chanted as she paced back and forth across the room. 'Their day of disaster – *your* day of disaster – will arrive.'

Malcolm started to wriggle, desperate to move, and she stifled a laugh. Even in death, the man was a hopeless, hapless imbecile. A useless creature placed on this earth solely for the amusement of others, and she watched awhile with delight as he tried in vain to retaliate, before finally speaking once more.

'Cat got your tongue?' she sneered, enjoying the fact that despite his obvious efforts, Malcolm was clearly unable to speak. Laughter gurgled in the pit of her stomach like a simmering pan on the stove before finally erupting to the surface like a bolt of magma.

'One simple task, Malcolm, and you couldn't even get it right.'

Clickety-clack, clickety-clack, click clack. Rita closed her eyes, determined to better appreciate the sweet melody of approaching heels on the tiled floor. The chorus of clicks and clacks intensifying in volume as they drew nearer demanded her undivided attention now. *Eileen.* She couldn't have timed things better if she tried and Rita trembled with excitement and licked her lips in anticipation.

'Looks like I'll just have to finish the job for you,' she snarled menacingly in Malcolm's ear as she grabbed the wig from the bed and ducked into the concealed alcove behind the door.

70

There were certain events in life, such as the death of Princess Diana and 9/11 that would be cemented in a person's memory forever: what they wore, what they were doing, even how the air smelled on the day in question. *Today is definitely such a day,* Eileen thought to herself as she shuffled in the rickety old plastic chair that was more suited to a school assembly hall than a place where loved ones wished to pay their last respects.

A solitary tear escaped down her cheek as she studied her husband's pale, weathered face and she brushed it away irritably with the back of her hand. *How can he be so cruel, even in death?* When she had entered his room a moment ago, he had looked horrified. So distressed – disgusted even – to see her at all, that she had considered turning about heel and fleeing the scene as fast as her shoes would allow.

But something had made her stay: an unknown force that refused to allow this complete stranger that had taken over her husband's body and mind to relegate her to the back lines. *'Til death do us part.* Words spoken all those years ago, but it was only now, when faced with the inevitable, that she truly realised that she had meant every single one of them.

As Malcolm shifted uncomfortably once more in the bed, she in turn did the same in her chair. This was happening a lot now, as though re-enacting his actions could help ease his pain or better still, make it go away altogether. Watching him try to speak was a grind. She wanted to complete the sentences for him but she couldn't find the right words. Despite everything, including his inability to talk, his eyes told her everything she needed to know. Malcolm didn't want her. It was written all over his face. He wanted *HER* – Rita – and the pain of such knowledge ripped at her insides and shredded them beyond all recognition.

'Rita.' Eventually, after much choking and a huge struggle, the words finally came out. A hushed whisper, barely audible over the sound of the vacuum in the corridor, but Eileen knew that she wasn't mistaken in what she had heard. Even now, in his last moments on earth, her husband wanted that woman over her and being faced with such an unbearable truth hurt more than she could ever have thought possible.

'Sssh,' she responded, stroking his forehead and urging him to be quiet, as though she could somehow delete the memory of Rita with her hands. She couldn't lose him now, not after everything. If only she could somehow get through to him, but it was no good. He wasn't listening, seemingly obsessed with the vacant space behind her as his defeated eyes glared right through her. Despite knowing that there was nothing there, Eileen found that she couldn't resist a quick peek over her shoulder any longer.

Rita?

'Hello, Eileen,' Peter sneered as he stepped out from the shadows behind the door and grinned at her menacingly before slowly and deliberately focusing his attention on her feet. He licked his lips, biting down hard on them with his teeth as he stared animatedly at the exquisite pair of shoes that he was about to claim for his own.

71

How had it all gone so wrong? Both Eileen and Malcolm Muldoon brutally murdered in the very place that was supposed to keep them alive at all cost and the killer still at large, presumably currently plotting his next kleptomaniac splurge.

And how had *he* got it all so wrong? Had Peter been there all along? Hanging around in the shadows, waiting for the opportunity to pounce and claim his prey? Lucas shook his head bitterly. None of it made any sense. Convinced that Peter would turn up there next, every last inch of the hospital had been searched but to no avail. Only when the minutes had turned to hours, and the hours to days, had Lucas made the decision to call off his officers. The fateful decision as it transpired, but it wasn't as though he could keep up the surveillance forever.

Ronnie had since filled in some of the blanks. Coming home early one day to find Peter wearing her favourite outfit had apparently been the major factor to signal the end of their relationship. Despite witnessing him recently in public disguised as his other persona – and despite being accused of stealing a woman's shoes before they had even moved to Cliffborough Cross – she had remained oblivious to the scale of his addiction.

Lucas walked over to the draining board and started to swill the pile of dishes ready to load the dishwasher, the gruesome scene of that fateful day galloping through his mind on replay with the same velocity that he had sped through the streets to the hospital when he had received the call… The abandoned vacuum cleaner carelessly discarded outside the door and the stifling smell of death permeating into the corridor from beneath it. The plastic bag strategically placed over his father's head, his bloodshot eyes depicting pinholes in his pale, bloated face. And Eileen. Legs buckled awkwardly beneath her body as she lay sprawled in a crumpled heap on the floor, her eyes gouged out with the heel of one of her own stilettoes.

Lucas let out a sob, a huge wail that reverberated around the walls and brought Buddy running to his side. The dog collapsed at his feet and rolled onto his back, his tail thudding so hard on the ground it should hurt. Lucas knew he should seek solace from him, but he couldn't. Turning his back to the sink, he eyeballed him and pointed to the small basket in the corner of the kitchen.

'In your bed,' he instructed, instantly impressed at how well trained the dog was as he duly padded over and curled up in the small space that didn't look capable of holding a dog even half his size. As Buddy rested his chin on his paws and studied him, Lucas in turn took a moment to assess his surroundings. A pile of washing sat on the worktop in the far corner of the room waiting to be ironed. Paint flaked and peeled from every wall that he could see. Dog hairs collected in lumps around the edges of the skirtings, and the occasional dead fly sat amongst the thin film of dust that coated the window sills. The list was endless. Whilst neither of the Muldoons had struck him as the kind of people to be middle-aged and mundane, he had always assumed that they were the type of individuals who would make it their business to keep on top of the housework – or at the very least employ someone who was. *Malcolm soon put paid to that though, didn't he?* Lucas thought to himself ruefully. Albeit thankfully as it turned out: Malcolm hadn't been responsible for getting rid of his cleaner by the despicable methods that Lucas had at first suspected.

Reaching for the bottle of wine that sat beside the draining board, he poured himself a healthy measure and sat down at the table with a heavy thud. And heart. He had failed them all: EJ, Hannah, Lou, Tod, Eileen, his colleagues, but worst of all Malcolm. And even worse still, he had failed himself. He pulled out the crumpled piece of paper from his pocket once more, pressing down the folds with his fingers on the table as though to iron out the creases.

This WILL dated the 13th day of May two thousand and fourteen is made by me MALCOLM EDWARD MULDOON of The Old Spinney, Adderley, Cliffborough Cross VE32 9LR. I hereby revoke all former Wills and testamentary dispositions made by me and declare this to be my last Will.

Lucas knew the contents off by heart now and his eyes scrolled further down the page and landed on the sentence he was still struggling to believe even though he now knew it beyond all doubt to be true.

In the event that my wife, EILEEN MARGARET MULDOON of The Old Spinney, Adderley aforesaid should precede me in death, I hereby bequeath my estate and all of my property, both real and personal to my said son, LUCAS EDWARD ELLIOTT.

Malcolm had never intended to deny him as his son after all and a solitary tear escaped and fell on the sheet of paper. Lucas wiped it away and reached for his wine, downing the contents in one swig before hastily refilling the glass. All this time, his father had known, yet said nothing and like the idiot he was, Lucas had avoided confronting him for fear it would somehow compromise him and his job. And now it was too late. The man was dead and he no longer had a job to worry about at any rate. Sam had tried to talk him out of handing in the resignation letter, but what would have been the point? He wasn't fit to call himself a detective and the time had come for a fresh start. For the first occasion in months, Lucas had actually felt good. Better than good in fact as he had strategically placed the letter on DCI Smith's desk for him to find in the morning, and casually walked out of the automatic doors of Cliffborough Cross Police Station for the very last time.

'Here, boy.' As though finally awaking from a nightmare and suddenly seeing the light, Lucas patted the back of his thigh and reached for his coat and Buddy's lead from the hook behind the door. The Old Rec would be busy this time of night but Buddy seemed to like it there. So did he, if the truth be known. Making idle chitchat with random strangers enabled him to forget his problems awhile and that suited him just fine.

EPILOGUE

SIX MONTHS LATER

As was so often the case, the estate agents hadn't done the small town of Heel any justice whatsoever in their blurb and Rita was glad that she had taken the gamble and decided to rely solely on her gut instinct.

Quintessentially English, the cobbled streets were lined with an eclectic mix of ancient and modern higgledy-piggledy buildings, all seemingly thrust together as though to boast the creative prowess of the men who had built them.

Tucked away down one of the many side streets, Rita had found the small coffee shop by chance as she browsed the fanciful window displays of the vast collection of fashionable boutiques and mentally spent her first wage packet. The small table in the window was perfect. It enabled her to sample the various delicacies that they had to offer whilst providing an excellent view out onto the street – and more importantly, the comings and goings of the wealthy clientele that visited the many emporiums that filled every last nook and cranny.

In front of her sat a book, opened midway, which she had purchased from the old-fashioned bookshop located in the adjoining alley. She hadn't read a single page, the many architectural merits of Heel holding no appeal whatsoever, but this time she was determined that things would be different. This time, Rita would be welcomed into the community and she knew better than most, appearances could be deceptive.

As she sipped her cappuccino (a little strong for her taste if she were entirely honest), she pretended to study the text but her interest went a little further. To the window and beyond to be precise, where she could assess those visiting the various architectural assets detailed within the book from her chosen vantage point.

As though reading her mind, Sophie appeared in her line of vision. Of course, Sophie wasn't her real name. Rita had no idea what that was but Sophie seemed to suit her somehow and being able to put a name to the face made life so much easier.

Clickety-clack, clickety-clack, click-clack, click-clack. Rita leaned forward to study the shoes more closely, the melodic synchronised harmony as Sophie made her way into the cobbled street playing out in her head like Beethoven's 5th Symphony. Or was it the 9th? Rita couldn't remember. Not that it mattered. Either way, the sound was music to her ears. *Although…*

As though becoming truly aware of her purpose for the first time, Rita pushed her chair away from her table and thanking her hosts, she rapidly made her way towards the exit as fast as her own shoes would allow. The cobbled surface wasn't to everyone's tastes and Sophie was clearly struggling.

Luckily, Rita knew just the person to help her with that particular predicament.

ACKNOWLEDGEMENTS

Well obviously, I'd like to thank my mum and dad – both of whom truly have been the best parents a person could wish for. Without them, none of this would have been possible.

I'd also like to thank everyone who has taken the time to read this. *Cross Killer* wasn't the novel that I intended to write but when writer's block kicked in, it soon became my literary laxative. Nonetheless, I've loved the journey and sincerely hope that you do too. (If not, hopefully you read the above and now realise that it's my parents you need to blame, not me.)

Particular thanks must also go to my very dear friend and fellow author, Stevenson-Olds. Firstly, for reading this novel more times than is perhaps natural, but most of all for his words of wisdom and calming influence, not to mention his relentless enthusiasm and support.

Also to BJ Sheppard (further friend and fellow author)… I miss our brainstorming (also known as drinking) sessions already!

Thanks also to Miguel – the man who pretends he knows nothing, but who actually knows a great deal. Pon and Von, for a friendship that knows no boundaries. Ms Muldoon… well, just for being you, and of course Boost and Scoobs for tolerating me (and the erratic mealtimes) on a day-to-day basis.

And lastly, the team at Troubador: you have all been absolutely amazing and I can't thank you enough.